GENERATION OF RUST

GENERATION OF RUST

a novel by ENDRE FEJES

Translated from the Hungarian by
SANFORD J. GREENBURGER with TERANECE BRASHEAR

McGRAW-HILL BOOK COMPANY
New York   St. Louis   San Francisco
London   Sydney   Toronto   Mexico   Panama

Library of Congress
Catalog Card Number: 70-107287
FIRST EDITION   20376

First published in Hungarian
under the title ROZSDATEMETŐ
by Magvető Kiadó, Budapest, © Fejes Endre, 1965.

TRANSLATORS' NOTE

In his probe of the effect of a new society on a Hungarian peasant, the author has chosen writing techniques not usually found in fiction of universal impact. These are:

a) narration as well as dialogue in the informal language used by residents of a specific working-class district of Budapest;

b) a virtually cinematographic succession of happenings without transitions to connect them.

Consequently our translation had to preserve an apparent poverty of style which deliberately tries to reproduce illiteracy. Frequently the English is awkward; the scenes are disconnected in a kind of loosely chronological montage.

There are also gaps in the frame of reference that may be disturbing to the reader of this translation:

Queen Borbella: the peasants' escape from abject poverty into an imagined world of fairy-tale existence combined with superstition;

Private sector: in all of the Communist states of eastern Europe, minuscule undertakings may be licensed to operate as free enterprise; all employers and establishments mentioned after the dawn exodus to Brügecs (end of the Second World War) are state–owned and managed;

Streets, espressos, and sweet shops: use of these proper names offers Hungarian readers instantaneous recognition of their location relative to the quarter in which the

Habetlers live. This quarter (the Jozsef City) remains the hub of the Habetler universe throughout the forty years of the story.

Sanford J. Greenburger
Teranece Brashear

THE CEMETERY OF RUST is a yard enclosed by a stone wall behind the warehouse of the Metal Finishing Plant. A railroad track comes in through a high iron gate, and ends at the loading platform. On either side of the spur discarded machines, huge boilers, unidentifiable monsters haphazardly push into the black mud and cinders. Rusty arms point to the sky, waiting for a fiery reincarnation.

It was in the Cemetery of Rust, in the spring of 1962, that Janos Habetler Jr. killed a man.

The police took pictures of the victim, filled in a report, questioned several workers and Bela Klein, the boss of the stockroom, but they could find no eyewitnesses. I watched them lead the handcuffed lathe-operator out of the yard and shove him into a car. Gnashing his teeth and locking his knees, he resisted with all his might.

Then the body was carted away. The uproar in the yard subsided as the gray hearse disappeared into the street. Finally, the clerks vanished from the upstairs windows, and the workmen, still arguing about the incident, returned to their benches.

I spoke to the shop foreman and to a few other men who had worked in the same shop with Jani Habetler for years. We smoked a cigarette beside his lathe, and looked at the pieces he had finished that morning, the aluminum shavings on the floor still damp with oil. We wondered what could have happened between the two men out there in the Cemetery of Rust, and what punishment might await the one who survived.

I said that if intent to kill were proved, Jani Habetler's yellow eyes would not see sunlight for a long time.

A fellow named Grof, a redhead, was surprised:

"Yellow? Where do you get that? He has light blue eyes —or green. Whenever he got a splinter in his eye, I took it out for him. I've seen his eyes up close many times."

The shop foreman shrugged:

"The law doesn't care what color eyes a murderer has, cornflower blue, violet, or pitch black or sea green. The dead man doesn't give a damn, either."

"Jani isn't a murderer," Grof said. "He hollers and shouts sometimes, and insults you, but afterwards he's always sorry."

The foreman smirked: "Oh, sure! The fellow they just took away bashed in his own head, I suppose. So it was suicide. You'd better go and tell the police, so they won't get the wrong idea!"

The redhead was silent. He took a drag on his cigarette, and crushed it on the concrete floor.

"I don't know what happened—let Jani tell them."

Jani Habetler did not tell them anything. He was stubbornly silent. The police warned him that he was playing a dangerous game which could cost him many years, but he answered that he had killed the man, he had signed the statement, and the rest was not up to him.

I wanted to know his secret. I was given permission to talk to him in the Central Jail. I told him that his behavior made no sense and that he ought not to make things harder for himself; he had a family waiting for him at home. He listened attentively, his cold eyes never leaving my face. Then he stood up and asked to be taken back to his cell.

I studied the data gathered during the investigation. When I learned that the man he had killed was his brother-in-law, I decided to dig into the history of the Habetler family. I talked to many people; names filled my notebook—Bela Sapadt, the house painter; Sandor Seres, an employee in the

Ministry of Foreign Affairs; a building superintendent in Nagyfuvaros Street; Juli Csele, a factory worker; Istvan Küvecses, an electrical engineer; Lajos Küvecses, an Air Force colonel. They and many, many others supplied important details.

Many a long night I sat at my desk, trying to fit the pieces together. Finally one Sunday afternoon I felt my material was ready. Two days later, with the permission of the Prosecuting Attorney, I visited Jani Habetler, now awaiting trial in the Marko Street Jail.

I knew his life and his secret, so I blackmailed him. It was a cruel game. I demanded that he tell me the last act, what had happened in the Cemetery of Rust. He was silent. Finally, he asked what I planned to do with my notes. I answered that I would publish them.

"And if I talk?" he asked.

"Then I'll burn them. I'll forget everything."

He glared at me out of his yellowish eyes.

"Do what you want!" he snorted. "Write it! Shout it from the rooftops! What do you know? You know nothing!" He gritted his teeth. "Nothing!" he roared. "Drop dead! You don't know a thing! Not a goddamn thing!" For a long moment he was quiet. He stared at his hands, then at the barred window. "Goddamn this fucking life!" he said.

Then he talked.

At the trial it will be my duty to tell the whole truth. But this story begins during the First World War, before my hero was even born. For this reason I have uncompromisingly recorded everything. If you feel that I am partial to Jani Habetler, I won't deny it. I admit I like him. He is raw and outspoken. One police official even called him an anarchist, but I don't agree—only at times he rebelled, and then one feared his eyes. Was he a coward? I believe there were things in this world he didn't understand—and that is why he was helpless.

His punishment will be determined by qualified judges. They will be just.

Only two experiences from that long, drawn-out war stuck in the elder Janos Habetler's memory. Sometimes he related them over a glass of wine.

On the Italian front, a blue-faced corpse with a hole in its forehead began to move. First his groin rose, then his back arched, finally his head bobbed. A mole was burrowing in the earth underneath the dead soldier, and the living laughed hollowly. About his other memory Janos spoke more solemnly, and with a touch of shame.

One late fall afternoon they had shot an enemy biplane out of the sky. It crashed not far from them and its two pilots rolled out of the cockpit. Habetler and his buddy ran to the flaming wreck; and as they were unbuttoning the pilots' leather vests, his buddy went to sleep forever. He lay back and joined the pilots staring wide-eyed at the dirty gray clouds.

Moving like a caterpillar under the hail of bullets, Habetler managed to reach the forest. He prayed, and took an oath to live an honest life forever after.

He never broke that vow.

In the spring his regiment was transferred to Budapest. By that time Habetler was a corporal, decorated with the Károly Cross, the Franz Joseph Silver Medal, the Bronze Medal, the Casualty Cross, and the War Memorial Medal. He was particularly fond of the Memorial Medal. Above the Hungarian coat of arms *Pro Deo et Patria* was embossed. When he was told that it meant "For God and Country" he was thrilled.

They were billeted in Buda in a requisitioned schoolhouse. The soldiers sat around playing cards and eating. Janos Habetler gained weight. He weighed more than 165 pounds, but he was not fat. Rather, his muscles, his chest, filled out and the deep folds disappeared from his face.

Professor Doctor Vilmos Matyas, his Captain, ordered him on sentry duty at the Southern Railway Station. From five o'clock in the morning until ten at night Janos paced back

—4—

and forth along the tracks, listening to the clanking of the freight cars, never taking his rifle from his shoulder. He set his own duty hours. Since no one arrived to relieve him by ten o'clock in the evening the first day, nor had anyone said anything, he marched back to the school, came to attention at Captain Matyas' desk, and reported that he had been forgotten.

Captain Matyas himself was surprised. He said he was very sorry and offered Janos a drink. Someone would be assigned to night duty immediately. But he forgot his promise, for Corporal Habetler was not relieved the next night, or any other night.

Janos never mentioned it again. With the heavy rifle on his shoulder, he tramped up and down the platforms, watching the travelers and the swaying hips of passing women. At ten o'clock every night he strolled back to the schoolhouse. He ate his supper, got his next day's rations, proceeded to the classroom, lay down on the straw pallet under a topographical map of Europe, said his prayers, and fell asleep.

Janos Habetler did not like noise. He was a sensitive, religious man whose quiet, biting humor often surprised people. Whenever his fellow soldiers asked him to sing, he obliged with old psalms and folk songs in a deep, clear voice. Healthy and robust, he wanted a woman and by the end of July, after much torment, he decided to take action. Another corporal suggested that there was an abundant choice at the Green Hunter Restaurant on Arena Avenue. There in its spacious garden soldiers and girls danced and sang lustily: "My mother bakes, the baker bakes, my mother bakes three pans of muffins." A military band blared under a red-and-white awning hung from the chestnut trees.

The corporal, a man of experience, offered more advice:

"Pick a girl, dance with her until she's dizzy, buy her half a pint of wine and tell her she's pretty. Then find a bench in the park far away from a lamp post."

Habetler washed in cold water, trimmed his mustache,

pinned his medals on his chest and strode toward the promising garden of the Green Hunter Restaurant.

He chose a girl named Maria Pek. He saluted, summarily put his hands on her shoulders, and danced with her all through the blistering afternoon. A row of paper lanterns already illuminated the garden when they finally sat down at a plank table under one of the chestnut trees. Corporal Habetler wiped the sweat from his face.

Maria Pek laughed. She was a thin creature, short, cold-eyed, with a big bosom. She alone among the girls in the garden of the Green Hunter wore a black satin dress with white collar and cuffs. She asked for a pint of sour white wine and said:

"I never sweat; that's why I get spots on my skin every summer."

Tilting her head to one side, she showed Habetler the tiny blotches on her short neck.

Above their heads bugs smacked into the lanterns. In the center of the packed-earth dance floor a bed of flowers, impervious to the dancers, waited for rain.

Habetler picked a carnation and brought it to the girl. He sat down and spoke quiet compliments to her, a slight tremor in his voice. Maria Pek lifted her bony face. Her eyes widened and slowly began to sparkle.

That night Janos Habetler did not say his evening prayers. He lay down under the topographical map of Europe and fell asleep immediately.

They met again in the garden of the Green Hunter on a Sunday in August. It was sweltering. Sweating soldiers wooed the girls and sang at the top of their lungs.

Maria Pek again wore the black satin dress. Her hands fiddled with the tablecloth; her short legs swung back and forth like the clapper of a bell; the wooden chair groaned irritably beneath her; the carnation trembled in her hair. She asked for a pint of the same sour white wine, blushed, and said she was pregnant.

"It doesn't matter," Habetler replied. He stared at the brass band, then at his hands, and grinned like an idiot.

The next morning he knocked at Doctor Matyas' door. The Captain's voice was faint and distant: "Come in, whoever you are."

Corporal Habetler straightened his tunic, opened the door, and stopped in the doorway. The windows were covered with heavy curtains; it took a moment for his eyes to get used to the gloom.

The Captain was crouched on the floor in the darkest and most distant corner of the school's physics laboratory, gazing at a rusty pharmacist's scale on a crude shelf. A gentle smile sat on his face.

"Come over here and listen!" he said. "I want you to hear my last will and testament."

Next to his feet a pair of silver candlesticks stood watch over some scattered sheets of music, a dirty handkerchief, and a shepherd's flute.

Janos Habetler crossed the dim room, sat down near the stump of a candle, put his hands on his knees, and waited.

The Captain had a handsome, manly face. The skin over the strong bones was still smooth; only his croaking voice and slow-moving eyes betrayed his delirium, his nearing dissolution. He was almost at the end of the line. He wiped his moist nose and burped loudly. But the wine he had been drinking still held him in a soft rapture. It erased the grin from his chapped lips and led him gently toward the beckoning shadows. But he could still laugh as if from a distance and hold forth on lofty subjects in melancholy tones.

Now as he gathered his thoughts, his eyes glowed again. His emaciated hands reached for the flute. In a quivering voice laced with rather unpleasant pathos he said: "The time will come when people will no longer remember this war. Shrewd hawkers will peddle bananas in the streets, and glamorous women will ride horseback along the Fasor Allee. No one will talk about the senseless deaths and the oceans of blood any more."

Unfortunately the Professor Doctor was so moved that he had to interrupt his speech. He began to cry, the torrent of tears flowing from his torpid eyes. He covered his face with bony hands. He said that he was a miserable, contemptible wretch, swept up the scattered sheets of music, and pleaded that his symphony must not be lost. It must be carefully preserved, because he would not be able to do so himself—before long he would stand before his Maker, but the symphony would forever engrave in the memory of all Hungarians the senseless deaths and the oceans of blood.

Habetler felt great pity for his Captain. His heart softened and he vowed that he would gladly preserve those notes—after all, they didn't have to be fed. He would take them with him to Brügecs. He was going to be married and would like to visit his family. For this reason he respectfully requests a ten-day pass.

Captain Matyas groped for his dirty handkerchief, slowly pulled himself together and asked the Corporal to be indulgent. He couldn't imagine how he could have let himself go so completely—it must be the crisis, his days were irrevocably numbered.

Respectfully Habetler declared that the Professor Doctor still had a long life in store. He wished permission to remark that Doctor Captain ought to try to avoid wine and spirits.

Captain Matyas did not answer. He turned his head away because his eyes filled with tears. Two days later, Habetler left for Brügecs, taking with him the Captain's symphony and his new wife, Maria Pek.

The newlyweds' train stopped at Felsö Akác early in the morning. They had to walk twelve kilometers in the ground-fog, past the village to the hamlet of Brügecs at the edge of a poplar wood where Janos Habetler's foster parents lived.

The hovels of Brügecs were inhabited by simple, deeply religious Catholic people. They were hardworking and so laughably pious that they gave no one any trouble. Weekdays they slaved, and Sunday afternoon they plucked at their zithers. When their time came, they simply left the poplar wood and moved to the cemetery under the yellow sand.

The honest and devout peasants of Brügecs seemed to have been forsaken by the Great Protector or, perhaps, He was just as perplexed at the corpse in Paul Forro's yard in the sultry heat under the swarm of flies as were the barefooted people. It was indeed a difficult and very complicated situation.

Wednesday night one of Paul Forro's nine children, year-and-a-half-old Adam, after a brief spell of screaming, had departed this earth to serve the Lord as an angel. That had been four days ago, and Adam was still lying in the yard, in a wooden drawer. It was a completely impossible situation; even the slow-witted peasants saw that.

These good people were filled with pity, and a deep desire to help, but no one had any money. Finally Master Paul Nyari had sent a light-blue casket, five crowns for its sanctification, and fifteen pennies for the tolling of the death knell. But then Mrs. Mascal, the coroner, stopped at the fence and brought the news that the little boy could not be taken to the graveyard because there were smoke-blowing devils around, all the way from the roots of the wild grape hedge to the water ditch.

The people crossed themselves; they understood that evil times were upon them, and in their despair they began to moan, to howl, to shriek and wail. They stared at each other and sniffled, wondering how they could have come to such a predicament.

Such was the heartrending, misbegotten scene that

greeted Janos Habetler and his wife as they came through the cornfield. They stopped and stared at the biblical confusion in Paul Forro's yard. Maria Pek sized up the situation. She spoke harshly to the tattered crowd, her tone commanding respect; she pushed them around; pounded their backs with her bony fists, then bent over the tiny corpse, and, looking like an undertaker from another world in her black dress and her high-heeled black shoes, she demanded silence. She said that the boy was beginning to rot; he had to be taken away immediately. Bury him somewhere, anywhere. And the black hearts of the smoke-blowing devils be damned . . .

But as the wailing continued she realized that talk was of no use. Because Mrs. Mascal, the coroner, had never been wrong, and also because no earth could be broken within the wild grape hedge of the cemetery for less than fifty crowns, more money than was to be found in all of the hovels of the hamlet. And besides, little Adam would not be at peace among the headstones where the dead sleep with their shoes on, in silk shrouds.

There seemed to be no hope left, when Habetler's foster mother cried out:

"My God! The garlic! Everyone! Run to the cemetery, everyone! Queen Borballa Pereces must make the sign of the cross over the ditch along the graveyard with the garlic."

The people remained silent, shifting from foot to foot. The Queen Borballa Pereces said nothing, nor did she make a move. They all looked at Paul Forro, but Paul Forro was silent too. Nor did his wife say anything to encourage the people; she didn't move, she merely looked up at the blinding sky, sweat pouring down her face.

Maria Pek angrily punched the air with her arm. She asked for a clove of garlic and demanded that she be shown the way to the cemetery. She would go and make so many signs of the cross that even the skunks would flee from this mad hamlet.

The women, fingering their beads, huddled around Borballa Pereces, but even she could not say whether at this season, before the grapes are ripe, garlic is effective for devil-chasing. So it was decided to send a fleet-footed little girl to Mrs. Mascal's hut. Her reply was, "Garlicking is effective only on the thirteenth of December, on St. Luca's Day; on all other days of the year, it is worthless."

This distressing news pleased only Janos Habetler's foster mother. Because of her daughter-in-law, whose name she didn't even know and whose audacious behavior would bring disaster upon the Habetler family. What did the hussy think she was doing? Adam Forro would be buried sooner or later. Providence would help get him into the earth, that was obvious! There could be no doubt that he could not lie there until the maggots got at him; that was as true as the Good Book. Why tempt the smoke-blowers? More than one house had been devoured by the yellow-tongued unquenchable flames. Was there anyone who didn't remember Istvan Csokos, the drunk, who urinated over the barbed-wire fence of the cemetery on All Saints Day, desecrating the helpless dead? That very night his wagon burned to ashes in the pouring rain at the station of the cross where he had never removed his hat.

And Janos Habetler's foster mother was right. That same day, Adam Forro was buried in the yellow sand of the cemetery. The priest blessed the light-blue casket in Latin and the death knell was sounded. Yet the bell tolled timidly, as if embarrassed, even though it had not arranged the strange funeral, and was not to share the fifteen pennies. Nor would it be the cause of the sleepless night to come.

The weighty problem was lifted from the souls of the people of Brügecs otherwise.

After hearing the depressing news, the honest and pious villagers of Brügecs finally realized that only prayer could help them. The women kneeled on the hot sand, fingering their beads, and prayed. They beseeched the King of the Heavens and the Prince Jesus not to forsake the heavily laden, to lead His flock from the valley of sorrow to quiet, peaceful pastures, and to charge the angel Gabriel to banish all devils from the vicinity.

The sun stared down at the yard and in its blaze two gendarmes strolled up and brought so much silence to Paul Forro's yard that everyone could hear the plop of mulberries falling off the tree in the corner.

The two troopers were friendly; there was nothing threatening about their brownish-pink faces. They stopped at the gate, slipped the carbines off their shoulders, and surveyed the frightened company good-naturedly. But they did not mount the long bayonets; evidently, they did not intend to stab anyone in the belly or touch the little boy's coffin either. They merely stood there with the butts of their guns resting next to their boots.

As could be expected, it was the women with the beads who started the senseless, hysterical protest. Wailing and flapping their arms, they ran to the casket and surrounded it protectively to show that they would not let Adam Forro's body be handed over to the Devil.

They behaved like lunatics. The Queen, Borballa Pereces, rolled her eyes and emitted such weird sounds through her toothless mouth that the chickens screeched and beat up the dust in the yard like epileptics.

Goose pimples ran down the men's backs. In their fright, they outshouted each other and began to threaten the gendarmes. Some shouted the name of the great landlord, His Excellency Krajcsovics. Others used Paul Nyari as a threat, and still others the long-dead Populist Prime Minister Wekerle. Only a few mentioned Mihaly Gaal, the local landlord—these protested somewhat less loudly and less vehemently, as if they were ashamed that their protector was master of only three hundred hectares. It was not hope but terror that fired them.

A gendarme must not hesitate. The sergeant, an experienced trooper, thoughtfully scanned the faces of the men of Brügecs. His eye shifted from one to the other and came to rest on Gyuri Vargha, the welldigger, because he had such a villainous glint in his eye. The sergeant walked up to Vargha and slapped his face.

Silence followed. Borballa Pereces opened her cavernous mouth. The women stopped wailing and stood still.

The sergeant's face remained impassive. Flexing his hand, he watched the slapped man with expectant curiosity. The other gendarme, a young man, fiddled with the strap of his carbine.

At Felsö Akác the church bell summoned the Catholics to Sunday Mass, the distant tolling of the bell could be heard from across the poplar wood. The welldigger crossed himself, wiped his bleeding mouth with the back of his hand, and walked out of the yard.

The huts of Brügecs were inhabited by laughably docile people. When the sergeant shouted at them to stop their nonsense and get the hell home, they did not protest. They nodded complacently and admitted that the sergeant was right. Wordlessly they began to file out of the yard.

There was no need for further blows. But the younger gendarme could not control himself. It may have been a desire to prove his manhood that spurred on the tall, rangy, wide-browed fellow. Perhaps he wanted to show his strength or flaunt his power. Perhaps it was cowardice that drove him wild, or the sight of the welldigger's crooked, pitiful smile. Possibly he was scared of the ragged, taciturn, troubled crowd. Nobody in this now-silent yard could know, nor could he. In an inexplicable rage he began to slap, to strike; he pulled Borballa Pereces' hair and kicked Paul Forro in the knee.

That kick made no sense. In fact, it was stupid, for when at last Paul Forro pushed the wretched wheelbarrow to the graveyard, he limped so badly that the sergeant almost had a fit. Every time the sergeant yelled and the poor beggar tried to hurry, the casket slipped off into the sand. That is how they walked the three kilometers to the graveyard in the sweltering heat.

As a consequence of Maria Pek's outrageous behavior, the young couple spent only three days in Brügecs. But even those were three miserable days, filled with incessant quarreling. It was only Janos Habetler's exceptional patience that spared the black-clothed little woman her first beating, though at times the Corporal's hand itched unbearably.

The night of their third day the sky clouded over; the moon and stars disappeared. By morning a strong wind had risen. Fear gripped the countryside. The trees groaned and the cornfield rasped. Beads of copper sulphate glistened on the leaves of grapevines planted in endless rows. In the distance the poplar wood protested angrily.

Her mouth wide open, Maria Pek gasped for air. She began to run, to escape, straining against the wind, stumbling in the yellow sand in her modish shoes.

But just before she reached the railroad track, she stopped and turned back toward Brügecs. With a mad look in her eye, she shook her fist at the storming countryside and shouted curses. Then she began to sob.

Janos Habetler took pity on her. He wrapped his coat around her and took her claw-fingered, ugly hand. They continued along the lonely road wordless in the wind that beat at their faces.

Their ill-fated wedding trip was followed by a strange surprise. Corporal Habetler could not find a single man at the school in Buda. Captain Vilmos Matyas and his entire company had disappeared. Janos Habetler considered the situation, then made his way to number 14 Bajza Street, where Lawyer Kolisch lived. Maybe Maria Pek could tell Janos what he ought to do next.

Maria Pek kept him in the kitchen all morning. She set some roast and a bottle of wine before him.

"Well, I still have a couple of kilos of sheet music," Habetler said to her. "I could always buy a flute and play them."

Maria Pek said that this was nothing to joke about. It was a matter of life and death they had to discuss with Lawyer Kolisch.

Lawyer Kolisch was a friendly man. He offered the soldier a seat and listened attentively, but said nothing. He went to the window, drew the fawn-colored curtain, and looked out onto the street. Then he sat down at his massive coffin-shaped desk decorated with lions and propped his head in his hands.

Habetler thought the lawyer had fallen asleep; he did not know what to do with himself. He scrutinized the furniture, the books, the silver bowls.

When Maria Pek, in her black dress with the white collar and cuffs, brought in the coffee tray, the lawyer raised his head. He wiped his glasses with a chamois cloth, dropped some sugar into his gold-rimmed cup. Sipping the fragrant coffee, he assured Habetler that there was no reason to worry: mass desertion was already commonplace all over Hungary.

"Do you have a trade?"

"Yes," said Habetler. "I am a building carpenter."

"*Bravo, citoyen!*" the lawyer nodded. "Then we'll meet on the Place de Grève."

He unfolded the light-green monogrammed napkin and shrugged his shoulders.

"You may stay here with your wife until you take over." And he laughed bitterly.

That day Janos Habetler moved into Kolisch's big, six-room apartment. But it soon became clear that he would be of very little use to Maria Pek. He was clumsy-handed and slow-moving. His wife did everything there was to be done. All that Janos Habetler could be used for was lugging firewood from the cellar and cooking glue for Ilona Kolisch, the daughter of the house, who spent her time binding books. Most of the time he just hung around, feeling terribly ashamed of his idleness.

No wonder he was overjoyed when Lawyer Kolisch sent

for him one rainy, sleepy day and firmly advised him to enlist in the Home Guard, adding a few words about the chaotic situation, the international constellation and the Russian threat.

"The command post of the Mixed Brigade is practically around the corner," he said. "Maybe you will even be able to come home to your wife every night."

Maria Pek had no objection to military service. So Janos Habetler was in an excellent mood when he presented himself at the Command Post of the Mixed Brigade Command, which indeed was not far from Lawyer Kolisch's home. By a quirk of fate, that same afternoon he was assigned to another railway station, this time the Western Depot.

It was a pleasant job: he welcomed transient soldiers and supplied them with food and cigarettes. When the Red Army came into being, the red-white-and-green rosette on Janos' kepi was replaced by the five-pointed star. At peace with himself, he performed his duties faultlessly.

It was stupid, the way they left Lawyer Kolisch's. One morning the entire month's milk-ration coupon could not be found. The lawyer's wife claimed that Maria Pek had lost it. Maria Pek burst into tears and turned the place upside down searching for it. When the coupons were finally found in a drawer, she was in such a state of nerves that the air around her vibrated. She would not be appeased. When Mrs. Kolisch tried to apologize, Maria Pek shouted obscenities at her.

Lawyer Kolisch lost his patience. He took back the black dress with the white collar and cuffs, and threw Maria Pek out without her workbook.* After she had changed into her own things, she told Lawyer Kolisch what he could do with her workbook and left. She went to see her cousin, Jozsi Stadinger, a journeyman stonecutter who held high rank in the Red Army. But the time had passed when a Red Army rank could help.

* A kind of passport into which successive employers had to enter details of employment. It was illegal to hire any domestic who did not have one.

The Habetlers' first child was born on January 20, 1920, in the Zita Hospital. She was baptized Gizella in a Calvinist service.

Jozsi Stadinger's employer, stonecutter Paul Beleznay, let them live in the basement among unfinished headstones. In return, Maria Pek cleaned house for the Beleznays. The house was on Fiume Avenue but the six windows of the basement opened onto the cobbled sidewalk of Legszesz Street. Every night, after they had blown out the candles, Janos and Maria Pek quarreled because they were scared and saw no way out of their misery.

Jozsi Stadinger sided with one, then with the other, and eventually said that everyone was right, even Lawyer Kolisch. In the end Maria Pek always screamed at him: once she even threw a wooden mallet. Finally, she would take the crying Gizike in her lap and croon for hours:

Hopla, Hopla, Hopapa
Here we go with a Hopseessa!

Jozsi Stadinger was a nervewrecking fellow. Every night he wrapped himself in a horse blanket, climbed into the lap of a fifteen-foot-high stone angel with sadly folded wings, made odd gestures with his arms, and prayed in a quaking voice. He was a frightening sight in the yellowish-green gaslight which seeped in from the street. One night Janos Habetler politely asked him to stop posturing because God would not look kindly on it; besides it scared the baby. Jozsi Stadinger froze in confusion and began to explain: he was cold, he said, they should move the baby's basket behind a tombstone. But frantically and softly, he continued to pray.

Around ten o'clock one morning a squad of crane-feathered White Guards marched through the wrought-iron gate of Stonecarver Beleznay's yard. Maria Pek was sweeping the steps on the office. The blood drained from her face.

Paul Beleznay came to the door and asked the Lieutenant what he could do for him, then he led the officer to Jozsi

Stadinger, who was working on a narrow black slab. Jozsi flinched when the Lieutenant addressed him by name. He put down his mallet and chisel, stood up from his low stool, and faced the Lieutenant.

The Lieutenant read questions from a notebook.

Jozsi Stadinger answered softly and clearly. He said that he was born in Nagykeszi, September 10, 1891; his mother's name was Zsofia Pek; he had served in the Red Army; he had fought at Salgotarjan—nowhere else.

Suddenly his face reddened. "Lieutenant, Sir," he spoke up excitedly. "Sir, I'm a God-fearing Magyar. I can prove it! Anybody can tell you—Reverend Patay can. . . . I'm a hardworking man—my carvings are everywhere in Nagykeszi, in the church, in the cemetery, on Miller Missak's house; my work is praised and admired everywhere. Ask anybody!"

The Lieutenant ordered his soldiers to tie him up. Jozsi meekly held out his hands. While the officer talked to Paul Beleznay, they made Jozsi Stadinger face the fence with his back to the yard. One soldier watched him to see that he kept quiet, but the journeyman stonecutter only beat the fine dust from his smock and wagged his head. A few minutes later he was marched away.

He gave them no trouble along the way either; he made no attempt to escape. Head bowed, he walked quietly among the soldiers. It was not until they reached the forbidding portals of the Maria Theresia Barracks on Üllöi Avenue that he balked. He turned his head and squinted into the winter sunshine, but all he could have seen were a few shivering people hurrying by along the avenue lined with bare trees, and a dung cart bumping down the street. He didn't have time to look at anything else. The officer told him to keep moving and shoved him. Stadinger lost his balance and fell on his belly just in front of the portal. The unexpected fall infuriated him. He began to bellow, rolling around in the horse manure under the boots of the soldiers.

"Let me go!" he cried. "I have work to do!"

At the Lieutenant's command, the red-white-and-green barrier which closed off the vaulted entrance from the court-yard was raised. The soldiers dragged Stadinger inside, and beat him to death behind a woodpile.

All this happened at noon on Julianna's Day, February 16, 1920. Maria Pek stood on Üllöi Avenue, leaning against a tree; Jozsi Stadinger's blanket was at her feet. She folded her claw-fingered hands over her belly and sobbed. The bells of the Church of the Adoration were still tolling noon when the crane-feathered soldiers chased her away.

Barely two hours later Janos Habetler took his little girl to Brügecs.

Maria Pek refused to go with them. She would not cross her mother-in-law's door until that shrew apologized, she declared.

Habetler made no comment. He was going through his personal documents. He set fire to a few of them behind a headstone, but he did not know what he ought to do with Captain Matyas' music. He turned the pages, gazed at the fading musical notes, shrugged his shoulders, and stuffed the sheets back into the pocket of his velvet-lapelled overcoat, which Lawyer Kolisch had given him.

Maria Pek lifted Gizike out of the laundry basket, bundled her up warmly and pinned the shawl with a safety pin. The child was not pretty—she had her father's long face. Awakened from a deep sleep, her toothless, purple mouth trembled and she began to scream with all her might. Maria swore and shook her.

Habetler took the baby and said: "Lawyer Kolisch was right, you're not fit to live among human beings."

Janos headed for the street. He stepped over the marble urns and the stone crosses laid out on the earthen floor, gave the fifteen-foot angel a wide berth, and hurried up the wooden stairs.

Maria Pek followed him to the wrought-iron gate, where she stopped to shout curses into the afternoon sunshine. Across the street at the yellow fence of the gasworks the seedy inhabitants of the quarter gathered to enjoy the free show. Noisily they encouraged the tiny young woman who was angrily shaking her fist at her husband.

Habetler broke into a run. On Berzsenyi Street he stopped beside a mailbox and switched the baby to his other arm, then continued toward the railway station with long strides and slightly bent back.

Maria Pek went back to her work. She swept the yard, tidied up the office, then went across to Paul Beleznay's three-room apartment. She beat the rugs, dusted the furniture, waxed the floors, and scrubbed the kitchen, toilet, and bathroom with lye water. When she had finished, Paul Beleznay's wife told her that she was unwilling to employ her any longer without her work permit.

For two days Maria Pek slept on a straw pallet in the jam-packed cellar of the Salvation Army. There she was advised to go to the St. Marta's Women's Auxiliary. If she were lucky, they would find her a job even without a work permit. She should tell the ladies that she was a Catholic, that she went to Mass regularly, that she went to confession, that she took Holy Communion: in short, she was to say what a Catholic organization would have every right to expect.

So Maria Pek went to the apartment house at number 6 Realtanoda Street in the Inner City, where the Women's Auxiliary had its two-room office on the second floor. She was asked many questions and her data recorded. Then she was sent into the waiting room. She sat down on a bench among chattering peasant girls and joined in their conversation. Whenever someone shopping for a servant came into the room the girls stopped talking. After one of them was picked, the others all sighed and started to chatter again.

A thin-eared, tubercular physician chose Maria Pek. He

was a bachelor, a taciturn man who never smiled. His apartment on the Wesselenyi Street had two balconies. The walls were covered with religious oil paintings, except in the bedroom where his own photograph looked down from the wall onto the silk-covered bed.

In Maria Pek's capable hands the apartment began to gleam. The meals she served were tasty and varied. In the afternoon she opened the door for the Doctor's patients, helped them off with their coats, and offered them a seat in the waiting room. The only thing she would not do was to dust the skull on the Doctor's white desk—she wouldn't touch it for anything in the world.

After Maria Pek had worked for the Doctor two weeks—it was a Sunday, and he had just returned from hearing the Mozart Coronation Mass in the Church of the Inner City, he gave Maria Pek permission to have her husband move into the servant's room. Her husband could live there for three months, but only during sleeping hours, from nine o'clock in the evening until seven o'clock in the morning.

Habetler went out to look for work every day. Some days he unloaded sacks of potatoes, others he delivered vegetables and fruit on a flat, two-wheeled cart from the market place to greengrocers around the city. On the days he found work he was in a good mood and cheerfully handed his entire day's earnings to Maria Pek. Every Saturday they went to the post office to send money to Brügecs. It was always much more than was needed for Gizike's keep—Maria Pek insisted it be so.

The end of the third month was drawing close and the Habetlers were more and more restless in the tiny servant's room. The only solution that Habetler could think of was to move to Brügecs. There would be shelter in his foster parents' attic, and he could work either for Mihaly Gaal or on Master Paul Nyari's land. But Maria Pek closed her ears to the suggestion.

Among the Doctor's patients was a dyspeptic architect. Maria Pek hoped this short, round man would solve their problem. One afternoon, after she had taken his coat and bamboo cane, she approached him. She waited until he had made himself comfortable on the settee, fastened her ice-blue eyes on the dumpy man's glasses; she begged his pardon and briefly told him their troubles.

The architect smiled at the tiny, full-breasted woman. He said that he would try everything; he hoped that they could work something out. She and Janos were to see him at his office on Tükor Street.

Next day Habetler went to see the architect. He bowed respectfully and told him that he had been apprenticed to Imre Némöth, a master carpenter in Nagykörös, for four years, and had earned his journeyman's certificate. Then he was called up to the artillery. Modestly, he listed his medals.

The architect sent him to a construction site on Vasut Street. This lucky day was the seventeenth of August 1920. Janos hurried to Vasut Street and handed the architect's note to a red-faced Burgenlander dressed in lemon-yellow corduroy trousers, who was hollering in front of a shack. The man read the note, glanced at Janos' journeyman's certificate, nodded, and told him to report for work at five o'clock the next morning. But Janos Habetler did not report for work the next day, nor did he ever handle a carpenters' adze again.

On his return to the Doctor's apartment he found a summons ordering him to report to Department IV of the Main Political Division of the Defense Ministry, 7 Szinház Street, on August 18 at 10 *A.M.* Under the St. Stephen's Royal Seal the signature was clearly legible: Capt. Vilmos Matyas, Deputy Commandant.

The Habetlers did not sleep that night. They drank a lot of wine and worried about the summons and argued about what it could mean. Maria Pek sat on the bed, her hair in disorder. She insisted that Habetler deny everything. The hysteria in her voice and the terror in her eyes finally affected Janos too. His mind addled by the wine, he talked in circles and scattered the sheets of music. He slammed the table with the flat of his hand and declared that he was not worried, because any man who had made his last will and testament knew he would soon stand in the presence of God, and whoever is about to stand before God cannot have evil intentions.

This reasoning soothed him. Praising his own intelligence, he wiped his sweaty brow, picked up the scattered symphony and crawled into the iron bed next to Maria. Then he showed his wife how the drunken Captain Matyas would talk; making a stupid face he imitated the Captain's sickly, whining voice:

"The time will come when people will no longer remember this war. Shrewd hawkers will peddle bananas on the streets, and elegant women will ride horseback along the Fasor Allee. No one will talk about the senseless deaths and the oceans of blood any more."

Maria Pek giggled. Habetler began to laugh too—they could hardly stop. But what happened the next day was very different from what had set them off.

The Political Division of the Defense Ministry was on Royal Castle Hill. House No. 7 was a freshly stuccoed three-story building halfway up a short, steep street. There were gray iron bars on the windows. Janos Habetler walked through an oak portal into a quiet, whitewashed hall. At the foot of the staircase a young officer asked to see his papers and demanded to know whether Habetler was carrying a weapon. When Habetler said no, the officer frisked him from head to foot.

A soldier escorted him to the second floor. They proceeded up the stairs, down a long corridor, past identical doors. The soldier stopped at one of them and waved Janos Habetler into a room. Two officers sat there, Captain Imre Tasnády and Major Antal Borbás, whose brown collar patch with the tiny ivory cross identified him as a Lutheran chaplain. A few minutes later he was ushered to the desk of the Deputy Commandant, Captain Doctor Vilmos Matyas.

This time Captain Matyas was pale but sober. His brown eyes were alert and reserved. Despite his rigid bearing and frozen look he seemed restless in the cheerless office with its barred window and big safe. His thin, well-groomed hand trembled slightly; a precious stone set in platinum changed colors on his finger.

Habetler gave him the score. Captain Matyas thanked Janos with a smile, visibly moved. Resting his forehead in his hands he bent over the sheets of music and slowly turned the yellowing pages. Eyes flaming, he searched the ink-written notes. One could see that he was hearing the music in his mind.

Finally he locked the packet into a drawer and began to talk; his eyes still burning, the words spilled out of him in torrents. Plans and dreams glittered in his impassioned speech. He quoted complete verses from the letters of the Apostle Paul and explained that he wanted to create a divine symphony, like the voice of God, and a hymn to the Holy Trinity and a pagan Magyar work for kettledrums and tárogató.

Suddenly he declared that it was hot as hell. He peeled off his shirt. His torso shone with sweat. He went into an adjoining washroom, where he could be heard snorting and splashing.

He came back to his desk drying his neck and chest with a towel. The water dripped from his black, gypsylike hair. He stepped to the window. His expression became grave. He motioned to Janos Habetler, who obediently joined him.

Below in the tiled courtyard, several officers sat at a long green baize table. A Judge Advocate Captain was reading the sentence. The condemned man, a short fellow about twenty-five years old, listened to the long list of articles of the military code and to the complicated reasoning of the verdict. Even from the window one could see that the prisoner's knees were trembling. He scratched his nose and turned his head. A civilian was watching somberly and a major was already opening the Bible.

The blood rushed to the prisoner's face. His eyes bulged, he spat at the Judge Advocate Captain and hurled vulgar words, streams of vulgar words, at the officer. The Captain paled and retreated a few paces. He read faster. The prisoner laughed and shouted:

"In farewell, I piss on you all, gentlemen!"

And he began feverishly to unbutton his pants. An officer signaled a command and a few seconds later the short man hung from the gibbet, a black cloth over his face. For some time his chest continued to heave under the torn shirt and his tied hands jerked spasmodically.

Captain Matyas put on his shirt and tunic again and sat down at his desk. He fiddled with a pile of documents and then asked Janos Habetler how he would have behaved if he had been down there under the gallows.

After a short pause Habetler answered that once on the Italian front he had tried to take a leather jacket off a dead enemy pilot, and almost bit the dust. That was his only sin. He had fought in the Big War and had been decorated and had never done anything against the law. When he had reported to the schoolhouse in Buda at the end of his leave, he had found that he had been abandoned. The company had vanished; perhaps Captain Matyas remembered.

The Captain nodded absent-mindedly.

"A hanging is no joke," he said. "I have watched many of them in their last moments; everyone behaves differently. The quiet ones react just as differently from one another as do the violent ones. Even when a man behaves as distastefully as this fellow did, I can't feel any contempt for him. Not long ago they hanged a Jew. He was mad at his Rabbi! He cursed him, attacked him. He even knocked the bearded old man off his feet, though everybody knows that a clergyman is at a hanging only because of his calling. Everybody laughed, even the executioner. I was the only one who did not. I understood the prisoner's state of mind."

The Captain paused.

"You, Habetler, would lament quietly and resignedly, you would walk to the scaffold with your head bowed. Not I. I would throw myself at the feet of the judges, I would plead for my life. They would have to drag me to the gallows like a pig. I've thought this out many times, step by step, and I find nothing shameful about it. Now I've put it out of my mind and it doesn't haunt me any more. My doctor and my mother say that I have a strong will, and that I am proving my manhood. That's the truth—despite my burdensome post, I have not had a drink in eight months."

Now the Captain turned his attention to Janos Habetler's future. He declared that the building trade was a precarious way to make a living. He dwelt on the difficult position of a construction worker, the low wages and the long winter lay-off. Janos was surprised that the Captain knew so much about the practical aspects of his trade.

Captain Matyas advised Janos to join the police corps. Although the police did not exactly welcome craftsmen to the force, he would see to it that Janos was accepted. After all, Janos was an honest, reliable fellow beyond even a shadow of political suspicion. He could stand up to any investigation.

"Be a policeman," Captain Matyas said. "You'd get a regular wage and a place to live. You could take care of your family without worrying."

In a small voice Habetler thanked the Captain. He said that he could never have dreamed that anything like this would ever happen to him. There is no happier man on earth than a policeman, he said; if it rains, if it storms, his family always has a roof over their heads and there is always bread on the table. And he would make a good policeman, he was used to the drill and discipline, and knew how to handle firearms. There was only one trouble. He couldn't read or write, and if anyone found out, it might be embarrassing for the Captain.

"Policemen are not selected for their scholarship," Captain Matyas replied. "What is your religion?"

"My foster parents are Catholic, but I was baptized a Calvinist at the foundling home. And my wife and little girl are Lutherans."

The Captain nodded.

"I'll talk to the right people tomorrow," he said. "Don't worry, I'll take care of everything. Go home now. I'll send word to you."

With that Captain Matyas dismissed his ex-corporal.

As Habetler left the building, Maria Pek waved to him. She was standing in the blazing sun in front of the cable-car terminal at the corner of Szinház Street.

They took each other's hand and walked down the sun-baked steps into the city. Once home in the tiny servant's room they quarreled violently.

Maria Pek shouted what she would do to the police and to the Captain as well. Any decent man works, she said, he doesn't wait for ripe plums to drop in his mouth. Habetler closed the window and begged her to keep her voice down, there was no need to make such a racket. What could he do? Where else could he find work? The Captain had told him not to worry, everything would be taken care of and he would be notified.

Maria Pek paled. She smashed her fist into her husband's face.

"I don't want them to take care of anything for me," she screamed. "Nothing, you idiot! By the time they finish with us we'll wind up begging in the streets!"

Habetler grabbed the claw-fingered, ugly hands and pinned them to her sides. They glared at each other. Maria Pek panted and gasped for air.

That evening after supper the doctor told them not to worry too much; the biblical seven fat years were about to begin for them. Habetler need not go anywhere, he must merely be patient, he would get a job and a place to live, that was certain, a high-ranking man like Matyas would keep his word under any circumstances. The doctor was ready to guarantee that personally.

And the doctor was not mistaken.

On August 21, 1920, Janos Habetler was summoned to the District Command of the Protestant Chaplain's Corps. After a short interrogation, Deputy Chief Chaplain Major Antal Borbás enrolled him as a civilian sexton.

Two days later the Habetlers were allocated living quarters. When Maria Pek held the requisition in her hand, her eyes filled with tears. They were assigned to the Lenke Avenue Barracks Settlement. The Doctor gave them an iron cot as a farewell present. Habetler carried it on his back while Maria Pek struggled with the laundry basket and Jozsi Stadinger's orphaned blanket. Door Number 183 in Barrack IX of the settlement was theirs. The new next-door neighbors, Endre Küvecses, a Transylvanian refugee, and his pretty, black-haired wife, gave them enough goose down to stuff a pillow. That first night, before going to sleep, Maria Pek turned to each corner of the room and prayed for a long time.

From the outside the barracks looked uninviting, but inside Maria Pek whitewashed the walls and scrubbed the floors with strong lye. She spread a carpet of burlap sacks and bought a few flowers. Cleanliness and the fragrance of flowers were always a part of their home.

Their wealth increased. By the spring of the following year there was a portable stove in the kitchen and in their room a table, two chairs, an alarm clock, and a mirror on the wall. Foamy white curtains hung from brass rods on the window.

Habetler got up at one o'clock every morning to go to the Central Market on Vamhaz Square, near the Danube waterfront. At dawn, barges loaded with seasonal vegetables and fruit tied up there. The produce, packed in baskets, was unloaded and trundled to the market stalls. The merchants accepted the goods on consignment. After they had sold everything they settled accounts with the grower.

This is where Janos Habetler worked. He was a porter for Jozsef Hunyorgó, a heavyweight wrestler and produce wholesaler. The market opened at two o'clock in the morning. At that hour Habetler went aboard the boat and fastened a hooked yoke to his shoulders. At times he hung as many as six baskets from it. And when Jozsef Hunyorgó hoisted a 200-pound sack of potatoes onto Habetler's back, Janos carried it effortlessly.

After this shift he went on to his regular job at the Protestant Chaplain's Corps, where he rested.

The District Command consisted of two rooms on the ground floor of Number 1 Veres Pálné Street. There God and country were served by Colonel Rezsö Taubinger, Archdeacon; Major Antol Bordás, Lutheran Chaplain; Captain Gábor Szabó, Lutheran Chaplain; Major Endre Tuba, Calvinist Chaplain; Captain Paul Koren, Calvinist Chaplain; and Janos Habetler, Lutheran Civilian Sexton. Within a year he had mastered his duties, which required patience, tact, and an ear for music.

Every day began the same way. Regimental orders of the day designated at what time services would be held that day in which hospital, jail, or garrison. Habetler would then carefully pack the black robes, the silver chalice, the psalm book, soap and towels, pick up the wooden valise, and accompany the Chaplain who was on duty. When the Chaplain had concluded the prayer and the sermon, it was Janos' turn. He would step forward modestly, fold his hands, and sing in a clear baritone:

"As the hart panteth after the water brooks,
So panteth my soul after thee, O God!"

On October 31, on the Day of the Reformation, he sang:

"A mighty fortress is our God . . ."

and on the Eve of the Old Year:

"In thee, O Lord, do I put my trust. . . ."

The pious in the military prison would sob loudly. The assembly always sang with him and they always finished with the Hungarian National Anthem.

On important holidays, there was Holy Communion. It was Habetler's task to buy the white bread and wine. He cut the bread into tiny pieces and whenever there was any wine left over, he took it home to his wife.

There were also weddings, christenings, funerals, death-cell vigils, and executions. He liked christenings best, because they were held in homes. The chaplains performed the ceremony over a silver christening chalice. Janos frequently got a tip from the new father. It was a pity that weddings were not held at home—the officers took their brides to the Lutheran Church on Rákóczi Avenue, on Deák Square, or to the Protestant Meeting House on Abonyi Avenue. Funeral services were always held in the Gyáli Avenue Military Hospital. Little time was wasted on enlisted men: only enough men to carry the coffin attended. With the officers, there was more work. A brass band marched behind the hearse on the way to the hospital, where the chaplain preached. Then they accompanied the hearse to the military cemetery. The band played again and the chaplain spoke again.

Janos hated important dead. They were given state funerals with great pomp and ceremony. They were laid out in the Kerepesi Cemetery or in the Great Hall of the National Officers' Club on Váci Street. Field Marshal Hermann Köves, hero of the 1914 War, was given his farewell in the Kerepesi Cemetery. The ceremony lasted two hours and a half. Major

Antal Borbás, who was on duty that day, cursed his luck for weeks afterwards.

Services for Colonel General Paul Nagy, Commander-in-Chief of the Army, were held in the Officers' Club. The Regent, Miklos Horthy, was there in person. Habetler talked about it many times afterward.

It was hot in the Great Hall. Giant candelabra flamed around the bier. The aristocrats dabbed their foreheads with their handkerchiefs. Colonel Rezsö Taubinger spoke the sermon listlessly. Habetler stood near one of the candelabra. Perspiration poured from his face, soaking his mustache, burning his eyes, but he did not dare reach for a handkerchief for fear that any move might be misinterpreted by the many secret police agents. And to wipe his brow with the back of his hand so close to the Regent would have embarrassed him very much.

An hour and a half later he happily staggered into the street. The procession marched the entire length of the Rákóczi Avenue, policemen in dress uniform leading the cortège. A guard of honor followed the caisson and a big brass band, under the leadership of Richard Fricsay, played a slow funeral march. At the cemetery a salute was fired. There was a pleasant breeze. Habetler felt good. He cracked his knuckles, helped Colonel Rezsö Taubinger take off the black robes, and walked back to Veres Pálné Street.

On days when there were no orders, the chaplains ate paprikas, rested, and drank beer in the Little Robber Restaurant in nearby Curia Street. Habetler checked on them every hour, and whenever one of them seemed on the verge, he fetched a horse cab and carted the chaplain to his home.

When Chaplain Captain Gábor Szabó was drunk he was always pleasant. He laughed, sang and hugged Janos Habetler, but Archdeacon Colonel Rezsö Taubinger was ornery. He often told Habetler to go to hell, argued and resisted, and once, on the way home in the carriage, badly scratched Habetler's nose. Even at home he continued to resist, Habetler and Her Excellency could hardly get him to bed. The pleasant, elderly lady was very much ashamed. To make amends she gave Janos Habetler a roomful of furniture from their attic.

"Take it, my dear man," she said gently. "I'd rather give it to you than sell it to a junkman for a few cents."

The next day, when the two closets, two beds, two night chests and the table were unloaded at the Lenke Avenue Barracks Settlement, the neighbors gathered to stare.

Maria Pek had been working at the Pannonia Export-Import Corporation in the subbasement of 15 Szinház Street for several weeks. Her attitude toward the job troubled Janos very much.

The firm had been established in the spring of 1921 to provide the Army with hay, straw, and oats for its entire complement of horses. The general manager was Colonel Móricz Balikovics, who rode noiselessly over the cobbled streets of Budapest in a beautifully equipped carriage with rubber tires on its wheels and rubber shoes on the hoofs of the horse—a rare sight in the capital. Maria Pek mended oat sacks, at four pennies apiece, and swallowed a great deal of dust. Her immediate superior was a silly young lieutenant whom Maria Pek, without batting an eyelash, swindled by adding twenty-five to thirty sacks to her count every week.

Habetler was afraid. He begged and beseeched her not to do it, he spoke of prison, and painted her downfall in somber tones. But Maria Pek would not listen. They bickered for months, until Habetler could not stand it any longer. In November he went to the office of the Pannonia Export-Import Corporation at 34 Arany Janos Street. Habetler mounted the carpeted stairs and very respectfully requested that Captain Imre Tasnády, the Managing Clerk, fire his wife. He explained that she was in the family way and that he had not been able to convince her that the dusty work was bad for her health. Captain Tasnády handed Janos his wife's two-weeks' severance pay and the next morning she was dismissed.

On January 4, 1922, Janos Habetler, Junior, was born.

Maria Pek gave birth without difficulty. At five o'clock in the afternoon she sent her husband for the midwife and by six the child was crying in the light of the kerosene lamp. It had a piece of thread on its finger. Mrs. Küvecses said that the child would grow up to be a tailor. Seven days later the baby was christened in the Deák Square Lutheran Church. That evening the Habetlers invited guests. Maria Pek fried fish and made cheese noodles. Everyone drank Brügecs wine out of a demijohn. Habetler got tipsy and kneeled in front of Maria Pek. He kissed her claw-fingered, ugly hand. Maria Pek blushed.

"Old fool," she said and patted his head. She laughed in embarrassment. István Kalauz, the godfather, made a toast. They sang and drank the health of baby Jani Habetler until dawn.

In March Habetler fetched Gizike from Brügecs. The little girl had scurvy on her head. Maria Pek fumed, swore, and cursed at her bitch of a mother-in-law. She didn't calm down for days. When in June five hundred undernourished children were to be sent to Holland for two months, Maria Pek refused to let Gizike go with them. No child of hers needed to be fed by strangers so long as she had any strength left in her arms, she said. She took in wash for the officers. A soldier brought their fatigues and linen all the way from the Citadel. On Saturdays she cleaned for Captain Vilmos Matyas' mother in Szép Street. She lived alone now that the Captain had been transferred to a teaching post at the Cadet School in Köszeg.

Saturday afternoons the Habetlers usually took a stroll to the Ringer Sanatorium, Janos carrying Gizike on his arm, Maria Pek pushing the baby carriage. They sat in the grass and watched the wonderful sick people promenading in the establishment's garden. A flowing-haired old lady was their favorite. She would waltz around, flapping her skinny arms like wings and singing: "I am beautiful, I am good, too, only I am a little bit false-hearted . . ."

After a while they tired of the show and moved on to the

nearby Linum Mills Soccer Field. One time they were in luck because the Third District team was playing a practice game and they could see the famous goalie Zsak in action.

Evenings they sat out in front of their door and watched the road. They observed the people coming home from work, among them the full-skirted, pigtailed peasant girls from Budaors who worked in the cotton mill on Karolina Avenue. When István Kalauz and Endre Küvecses, their neighbors, got home, Habetler brought out the cards and they played snap while the women gossiped and screamed at the children.

In the fall of 1923 the Budapest–Kelenföld Choral Society was organized in the Kris Tavern, on the corner of Villanyi and Abel Jenö avenues. They rehearsed there twice a week. Károly Kris was president, Béla Trafina vice-president, Endre Küvecses secretary, István Kalauz and Gyula Bugyi treasurers, and Janos Habetler steward. The choirmaster was Gyula Kapi, a singing teacher and church organist. By spring they had a reputation; Kris could hardly keep track of their engagements. They sang at weddings and funerals. Their best performances, though, were serenades. Holding lighted candles, they stood outside someone's window and sang softly, with feeling:

> *Oh, what stirs in the night?*
> *What disturbs your dreams?*
> *It is a little bird in the tree.*
> *It sings of love! . . .*

They did not accept money. After a concert, they were paid in wine at the Kris Tavern and sang:

> *I lift my glass to the dear company!*
> *Drink, drink, and God save you gentlemen . . .*

Janos did not drink but Küvecses drank all the more. When the cobbler got drunk he smashed everything within reach. But he rarely got that far, because everybody kept an eye on him. Usually he did not get beyond the quarrelsome stage. He kept accusing Janos of being in love with his wife Anna. He insisted that Janos and Anna go away and live together.

"You pimp!" he yelled. "Anna has eyes only for you. God strike you dead!"

The next day he sobered up, and sadly begged forgiveness.

The Choral Society had a fine repertoire. At funerals they sang:

> *Why is this multitude so sad?*
> *The color has left his cheeks . . .*

and beside the grave:

> *He is no longer of this earth . . .*

In June 1924, beautiful Anna gave birth to a boy. At Küvecses' insistence, and after many excited arguments and much weeping, the child was finally christened in a Calvinist church. Maria Pek was the godmother. She fried fish and made cheese noodles. Küvecses supplied five liters of wine. They drank it all.

That summer a Catholic kindergarten, the Pius Home, was opened in a small house nearby. Whenever the nuns passed the Barracks Settlement, they ostentatiously refused to acknowledge Anna's greetings. Anna was a devout Catholic and had been raised in a convent. She wept as she complained to Maria Pek that Sister Superior Ursula never even glanced at her child.

This bothered Maria Pek too. One afternoon she took the baby carriage from Anna and pushed it out into the middle of the road.

"Dear Sister," she said, "why don't you look at my godchild?"

"Because," the Sister Superior answered coldly, "if his

mother had to marry a Calvinist, the least she could have done to expiate her sin was to find a Catholic godmother."

Maria Pek became furious.

"Holy God, Sister," she said, "that Catholic woman's soul will not burn in perdition if her breadwinner is a Calvinist!"

The next day she was summoned to the police station. The desk sergeant warned her not to use coarse language with the nuns and sent her home. Janos Habetler was very much ashamed. He asked his wife very nicely to keep her mouth shut and not to provoke him, because soon he would lose patience and then there would be trouble. He repeated this as often as ten times a day.

In August, Maria Pek gave birth to her third child, a weak, bloodless little boy. The midwife did not predict a long life for it. And she was right. Eight months later István Habetler left them forever. On the child's last dawn Janos Habetler's foster mother arrived from Brügecs. She looked at the dying child and said that his clothes had to be buried right away. Maria Pek immediately dug a pit under the door and threw the tiny clothes into it, but it was too late.

He was laid to rest in the Farkasrét Cemetery. Captain Gábor Szabó spoke the sermon at the grave and the Choral Society sang:

He is no longer of this earth . . .

Tears streamed down Maria Pek's face. Her mother-in-law said to her:

"Stop crying, or you will flood the grave."

Maria Pek wiped her eyes and they walked home.

In September of the following year, Captain Vilmos Matyas' mother proudly told Maria Pek during the Saturday cleaning that her son had been ordered to Athens as a military attaché.

In October Colonel Rezsö Taubinger, Archdeacon, was relieved of his post and transferred to Szolnok. While conducting services at the Budakesz Officers Sanatorium he had twice dropped his psalm book, in fact he had dropped all sorts of things. He had belched loudly and repeatedly apologized to the assembled gentlemen. He was replaced by Colonel Balázs Dani.

Habetler met the new commandant under painful circumstances. The day the Colonel assumed his post, at exactly eight o'clock in the morning, he found the Civilian Sexton fast asleep at his desk. The Colonel woke Janos.

"How dare you sleep?" he asked severely.

Habetler paled and asked to be forgiven.

"Colonel, Sir," he said, "every night at one o'clock I haul vegetables for Jozsef Hunyorgó in the Great Market Place, because my family needs money."

Colonel Dani was silent a moment. Finally he declared:

"That is a fine thing to do. Yes," he said seriously, "you have a noble soul." And he gave Habetler a pengö as a gift.

With the money Janos bought candy for the children and a pint of sour white wine for Maria Pek. Sitting beside the wash tub, he told Maria Pek about Colonel Balázs Dani's kindness.

Later they walked to the Ringer Sanatorium to stare at the inmates through the wire fence.

"It's getting cool," said the Civilian Sexton. "Before long the rainy weather will come, then the snow, and they will lock these people inside and we can't watch them any more until spring."

That winter there was much snow. Habetler could hardly keep a path clear to the door. At the end of January Janos Habetler's foster mother came to visit. She stayed several weeks. Every evening she took Gizike on her lap and in the glow of the kitchen stove the old peasant woman told wondrous tales about the rainmaking wizard, the changeling child, and the hussar who returned from the grave and spoke beneath his sweetheart's window: "Lovely moonshine, do you fear me, my pretty violet?" At that point, Maria Pek would order everybody to bed. Outside, the wind howled and raged.

On May 8, 1926, Maria Pek gave birth to another little girl. She was christened Hajnalka. The Choral Society was rehearsing

> *The crane soars on high*
> *I can hear him sing*
> *Silent is my darling*
> *While I sadly sigh*

for the nationwide Sopron Song Festival.

Early one morning that summer, a bare-footed young Gypsy woman went from door to door, offering to tell fortunes for a few cents. She stopped at the Habetlers' too. A small lace doily caught her fancy. She flashed her healthy white teeth and asked for it as a present.

"You're a shrewd bitch!" Maria Pek laughed.

The Gypsy woman stepped closer.

"I don't want it for nothing," she said in a whisper, so that the neighbors would not overhear. "I'll tell you something important. A fatal truth. If you are not afraid, show me your palm."

Maria Pek opened her claw-fingered hand and the Gypsy woman said: "Not far from here lives a black-haired woman who has cast her bewitching eye at your husband and she will seduce him."

Maria Pek raised her fists and chased the Gypsy out of the house.

That year a sensational murder case was the main subject of conversation at the nightly card games. Finally the players asked Janos Habetler for authoritative official information. Readily the Civilian Sexton rolled up his shirtsleeves, lit a cigarette, and said:

"Captain Gustav Lederer's wife had a very close friendship with a rich pork butcher by the name of Kodelka. It's also probable that a love attachment developed between them. The butcher could visit the woman's home at any time of the day or night and her husband, the Captain, looked away, even though he knew that the woman was having a love affair with the butcher. One day, when the butcher probably had a large amount of money with him, the Captain and his wife murdered Kodelka and in order to dispose of the body they cut it up, piled the pieces into suitcases and baskets and threw them into the Danube. But then one of the baskets rose to the surface and was fished out. Since the butcher had disappeared, a search was made for him and that's how the crime was discovered, and also due to the fact that they were seen a great deal in each other's company. So it was discovered that a crime had been committed by a man of high station and his wife, and that he not only condoned the crime, but he even participated in it because he too was bedazzled by money."

"That's not how it was!" Küvecses argued. "It was Gustav Lederer who had an affair with the butcher's wife and that makes a difference because they were the murderers. Your story is all wrong!"

Habetler admitted that that was a possibility but one thing he knew for sure, that the very next night he would be with Gustav Lederer in the death cell, because Regimental Orders of the Day assigned him to assist Chaplain Captain Gábor Szabó.

Kalauz remarked that he would like to see how a man condemned to death behaves his last night on earth.

Habetler answered that "there's no telling in advance, every man behaves differently."

"Aren't you afraid?" asked Anna Küvecses.

"No, I'm not afraid," said Habetler. "I have no reason to be."

"Aren't you even afraid of nightmares?" she persisted. "Bad dreams can drive a person crazy!"

And she made the sign of the cross with her well-padded hand.

Gustav Lederer did not give them much trouble.

It was eight in the evening when they entered the Margit Boulevard Military Prison. In the prison commandant's office Captain Szabó, Chief Lutheran Deacon, donned his ministerial robes. After they had drunk a pony of brandy, a master sergeant led them to the freshly whitewashed cubicle which was called the death cell. Gustav Lederer, his uniform stripped of all insignia, smiled as he rose to greet them. He shook hands with Gábor Szabó and said:

"I've been expecting you."

Until midnight he was well-behaved. He sincerely repented his sin, tormented himself, prayed fervently. At nine o'clock a guard brought some cold roast, a nut crescent on a little plate, and a glass of wine. The condemned man excused himself, washed his hands in the basin, sat down at the table and ate calmly. Then he asked for the Bible. Toward midnight he began to show fear. A cloudy, distant light shone in his eyes, his teeth chattered, and nerves began to twitch on both sides of his face. Gábor Szabó signaled to Janos Habetler. The sexton nodded, stepped forward, and gently, softly, very beautifully began to sing:

"As the hart panteth after the water brooks,
So panteth my soul after thee, O God.
My soul thirsteth for God, for the living God:
When shall I stand and appear before God?"

The psalm did not have the effect that the Chaplain had hoped for; just the opposite. Captain Lederer went wild. He shouted curses, turned over the table, hurled the chair against the wall so violently that it broke. Gábor Szabó and Janos Habetler ran out into the corridor. Two guards overpowered the maniac and manacled his hands and feet. A few minutes later the prison commandant arrived. Captain Lederer apologized wearily. He pledged his word that for the remaining hours he would behave like an officer and a gentleman. They removed the chains and he lay back on the iron cot. Gábor Szabó read from the Bible in a slow, soporific voice. Gustav Lederer did not say another word until dawn. Then he said:

"Perhaps His Highness the Regent will grant me a pardon."

"We are all in the hands of God," Gábor Szabó replied.

At five o'clock in the morning Gábor Szabó and Janos Habetler went to get ready. In the commandant's office Habetler opened the wooden valise and handed Gábor Szabó soap and a towel, brushed his robes and cleaned his shoes. Then Janos washed his face too, combed his hair, brushed his dark-blue uniform, his black, gold-buttoned shako. At a quarter to six they returned to Gustav Lederer's cell.

The escort detail arrived at exactly six o'clock and lined up in front of the cell. Gustav Lederer was taken, surrounded by eight guards, to the prison yard. An officer with drawn sword led the detail. A long table for the court had been set up opposite the gallows; a number of officers sat there. As soon as the prisoner had mounted the platform, a colonel rose and read the indictment. He announced that His Highness the Regent had rejected the petition for clemency and called on the executioner to do his duty. At this point Gustav Lederer raised an arm.

"Your Excellency, Mr. President!" he shouted, but in the blare of the bugles no one heard what he said. When the trap was sprung, the bugles were silenced. A colonel of the medical corps examined him twice, then reported: "Death has ensued."

Gábor Szabó prayed loudly for the salvation of Captain Lederer's soul; the judges listened motionless, with bowed heads. The next afternoon at two o'clock he was laid out in the Gyali Avenue Military Hospital. Gábor Szabó said a prayer. Four soldiers, the Chaplain, and Janos Habetler accompanied the coffin as far as the hospital gate. From there it rode alone to the Rakoskeresztur Cemetery on a horse-drawn cart.

Gizike attended the Váli Avenue School, half an hour's walk from Lenke Avenue. She was a good little girl, but dull-witted. Only Maria Pek's frequent spankings kept her from failing. On her eighth birthday, January 20, 1928, Maria Pek made floating milk cake and island pudding and invited the neighbor children to the party. Habetler decorated the room with a Chinese lantern and set the birthday present, a brand-new pair of high-button shoes, on the table. Toward noon a violent blizzard arose. Gizike started home from school but got only as far as Fadrusz Street. Habetler found her huddled in the doorway of a tavern, crying and clinging tightly to her two little companions. That night she developed a fever. She was delirious, her lips were dry and cracked, perspiration bathed her dark copper hair.

Maria Pek screamed, "Dear God, this one will die too! Jesus, my God!"

Habetler rushed coatless into the storm, stumbling through deep snowdrifts, to fetch the midwife. The midwife washed the child with hot water, rubbed her dry, smeared lukewarm fat on her back and chest, wrapped her in a blanket, and made her drink tea with rum. Three days later Gizike was as healthy as ever. Only at times there was a ringing in her ears, but that was not an unpleasant sensation.

Every afternoon she and Jani and Hajnalka watched for their father. When they caught sight of him coming down the road they ran out to meet him, threw snowballs at him, and reached into his pockets where they always found candy.

Occasionally Habetler took his wife to the Kris Tavern. The tiny blonde woman would have a pint of wine and if the men whispered sly compliments in her ear or made indecent proposals, she always told her husband.

At the end of February Vilmos Matyas returned from his assignment in Greece. His new assignment was teaching at the Ludovika Royal Military Academy. He and his mother moved into a sunny, four-room apartment at 114 Fogarasi Avenue. Maria Pek went to do the cleaning and Janos Habetler moved and arranged the furniture, including the heavy potted lemon tree. At the end of the day the former Military Attaché thanked them for their help and gave them a hexagonal stone onto which was glued a colored panorama of Athens.

In the spring the people of the Barracks Settlement sat out in front of their doors again. The men played cards while the women talked and watched the children. Everyone laughed a lot. Armed with sticks, the boys waited for the pig-tailed peasant girls to leave the Linum Textile Mills. Then they circled around behind the girls, lifted their skirts above their heads and scampered away.

Another game was to throw pebbles at Sara Kohner. Sara Kohner was old and very ugly. Her eye teeth protruded from her mouth. Many people said that during the autumn holidays she drank the blood of Christian children. The authorities had even dug up the earth around her shack but nothing was found. One night after the lamps had been turned down Gizike, restless and jittery, asked why Sara Kohner drank Christian children's blood. Maria Pek answered to stop talking nonsense; all Sara Kohner drank was the soup from the soup kitchen. In June a pebble struck her head. For hours the old woman lay dead and bloody on the corner of Karolina Avenue. The event was feverishly discussed by everyone. At supper little Jani said: "Kaput, the old Jew!" Maria Pek slapped him, and Hajnalka and Gizike as well—it was her policy that when she punished one of the children, she punished all three so they wouldn't laugh at each other.

One August afternoon that summer, Hajnalka came down with lockjaw. Her body stiffened, her tiny mouth turned white, her eyes rolled upward like those of somebody who is about to die. The midwife said that it was tooth seizure and that the child should be taken to the Maria Street Clinic to get an injection. That was done. The physician examined her, gave her a shot, and told them to bring the child back in three days.

At the corner of Üllöi Avenue Maria Pek stopped and

pushed the blanket from Hajnalka's face with her clawlike fingers.

"She's dead," she said.

She covered the child again and they boarded a streetcar. All during the long ride home the people kept asking them what had happened. Maria Pek, holding the child tightly to her, slowly rocking her back and forth, answered, she is sick, very sick. Habetler nodded. The tears poured down his cheeks.

Afterward Maria Pek took her two surviving children to the Farkasrét Cemetery every morning. Jani collected bugs, butterflies, and frogs while Gizike played among the tombstones, stared at the graves. They even ate their lunch there. After work Habetler came to fetch them. By the time they reached Lenke Avenue the fireflies were already making sparks.

Time and again that fall Maria Pek sat in the kitchen babbling incoherently. When Jani asked for a slice of bread, she did not understand him. Gizike stood in the kitchen doorway whenever it rained, tears pouring down her face. If someone asked why she was crying, she would say that she was sorry for the dead in the cemetery and for the people who had no place to sleep. She and Jani shared the same bed, Jani by the wall, Gizike on the outer edge. One night she saw a skeleton and after that she saw it every night. She would stare at it with wide-open eyes, without the strength to close them. Sometimes it was at the chest of drawers, sometimes near her parents' bed, sometimes with a scythe, other times with a cross or an apple in its hand. She did not tell anyone about her vision. All the Habetlers knew was that she was scared and could not be sent out on errands after dark.

Christmas her grandmother arrived from Brügecs. Gizike climbed into her lap. The old woman patted the child's short copper hair and said that the skeleton meant that she would live a very long time. That night the skeleton did not come. Gizike never saw it again.

Maria Pek refused to go the Military Clinic. There was however a young doctor, the son of a master roofer on Karolina Avenue, who treated the residents of the Barracks Settlement free of charge. He even made house calls in the middle of the night. It was Endre Küvecses who called him to see Maria Pek. For four weeks the young doctor gave the emaciated woman arsenic and insulin injections every day. Then Maria Pek went back to her wash tub.

On June 4, 1930, at half past five in the afternoon, Maria went down to Ignáz Weisz's store to buy a red ribbon. At six o'clock she gave birth to a healthy little girl. They asked pretty Anna Küvecses to be the godmother. It was Habetler's wish that the child be named Eszter. Two years later, on August 25, they had another little girl, Hajnalka. Gizike cried and screamed: "Why are we always being born?"

At the end of April 1933, Janos Habetler was fired from the District Office of the Protestant Chaplain's Corps. Colonel Dani called the sexton into his office and thanked him for his exemplary diligence. He told Habetler that he could choose one of two positions, either at the National Military Physical Education Authority or at the Ludovika Royal Military Academy. The Colonel gave him two days to think it over.

"Look, Habetler," he explained, "His Eminence the Bishop has called our attention to an elderly Lutheran who is the father of five children. You are young and strong and healthy. You're fit for any kind of work."

On May 1, 1933, Janos was transferred to the Ludovika Royal Military Academy as a yardman. A sub-lieutenant explained that the cadets were to be addressed as "Sir" and the officers by rank. Janos, who was a duly appointed civil servant, was ashamed of his new assignment. He went to tell his troubles to Lieutenant Colonel Vilmos Matyas. Ten days later he was transferred to the Bureau of Maps. The chief of that section, Lieutenant Colonel Sandor Kogutowitz, was a skinny, malevolent man with glasses. Colonel Kogutowitz, a professor of cartography, was also a passionate stamp collector. Every Sunday Habetler had to be on duty to soak stamps. When Gizike was to be confirmed that Whitsun Habetler asked permission to take the day off. Kogutowitz said that holiday had been abolished by the Pope. Habetler paled and looked down at his shoes.

"I am not a Papist," he said quietly. And he did not report for duty that Sunday.

Kogutowitz would not have Janos back in the Bureau of Maps. For two weeks Janos served as a messenger in the office of the Commandant of the Academy, Colonel Gustav Jány. Then he was transferred to the museum as an assistant guard.

At the card game that evening he explained:

"The museum of the Ludovika Royal Academy is the depository of valuable patriotic souvenirs and other national treasures. As you approach the stairs you face a huge oil painting, the work of Árpád Bacs. It depicts the glorious victory of the Magyars over the Czarist armies at Uzsok Pass. Upstairs, in the main hall, there is another huge oil painting, about five by eight meters in size. It shows the dedication of the colors of the Ludovika Academy. Emperor Franz Josef I, the royal family, and the Lords of the realm are all recognizable. On a marble pedestal nearby, there is a reduced replica of the statue of Field Marshal Hajneberg, Commandant of the First Hungarian Cavalry Corps. In addition, there are letters displayed in a glass case: a letter from Louis Kossuth, the heroic leader of our nation's independence, and the letter Leiniger, one of the thirteen martyrs of 1849, wrote to his wife on the eve of his execution. Also, the gilded hammer with which the Sovereign drove a nail into the Academy's flagpole as well as the silver hammer used by the Lords of the realm. In a separate case there is the Genealogical Tree of the Academy, which lists the names of the Commandants throughout the past one hundred years. At our institution every new Lieutenant is presented with a gold signet ring with LA engraved on it. We are the custodians of the prototype of this ring. Since the uniform of the cadets has changed in the course of time we naturally preserve one of each. These miniature uniforms clothe little dolls. We also have the sword and belt of a duke, but I am sorry to say that I cannot tell you the name of the duke."

Janos' superior, Lieutenant Colonel Jozsef Rózsás, professor of history and German, editor-in-chief of the Year Book of the Ludovika Academy, was a good-natured, vain, and unbelievably stingy man. One day he pointed to the ankle boots he was wearing.

"You can have these," he said to Janos Habetler.

The civil servant waited, waited a long time, until finally he said:

"Colonel, Sir, I respectfully report that you said you would give me those shoes."

Colonel Rózsás answered, "I will, my friend, but I haven't worn them out yet."

He liked to have Habetler with him for appearance's sake. He would order Habetler to report to his apartment on Hengermalom Street in dark-blue dress uniform and gold-buttoned shako. Then with Habetler walking three paces ahead he would proceed to the popular restaurant at the Kelenfold Railway Station. The Colonel always ordered a large pretzel and a glass of beer. He would break the pretzel in two, drink half of the beer and give the rest to his subaltern.

Colonel Jozsef Rózsás wrote poetry. A few of his poems had been published in Budapest papers. The poem Habetler liked best had been published in a magazine.

One morning, the Colonel was bored. He sent for Habetler.

"Can you tell stories?" he asked.

Habetler pondered before answering, then said he would try. He began:

"When I was still a young man and used to go see the

girls, I had to walk through a big forest. Once I heard a Gypsy band playing in the treetops: 'When I was a bachelor and went to see the girls . . . I raised my walking stick to my shoulder as if it were a gun and shouted, "Bang, Bang!" whereupon all of the musicians tumbled out of the tree, all except the cimbalom player.' "

"Why did the cimbalom player stay up in the tree?" Colonel Rózsás asked.

Habetler answered: "Because, Colonel Sir, I respectfully report that I woke up."

The Colonel rewarded him with two days' leave.

Late one night Küvecses banged on the Habetlers' window. He spoke his usual challenge—he wanted to fight. Half asleep Habetler crawled out of bed, went to the door and tried to hush the drunken cobbler. But Küvecses was in a fighting mood. He was a crazy sight punching the air in the moonlight. Finally Maria Pek got fed up with the performance. "What in God's name is the matter with you?" she yelled, sticking her head out of the window. "A few glasses of wine and there you go spouting all sorts of nonsense, loud enough to rouse the whole neighborhood. And tomorrow when you've sobered up, you'll be asking us to forgive you. Go on now, get the hell home!"

Perplexed, Küvecses dropped his arms. He pondered a moment, then approached the window.

"Neighbor! Yesterday he took a walk in the woods with her. . . ."

"Who saw them?" Maria Pek countered quietly.

Then they glared at each other for a few seconds.

"Excuse me," the cobbler said very seriously and retreated through his own door. Soon he could be heard beating his wife.

Little Jani Habetler was a brawny, healthy child whose uncontrollable temper often caused his parents trouble. In the first grade at the Váli Avenue School he created a monstrous scandal. For some reason, the teacher slapped his face. Jani gnashed his teeth and pummeled the woman's stomach with his fists so hard that she doubled over and vomited.

When Habetler was told about the incident he paled with shame and couldn't eat his supper. He declared that he would rather hang himself than raise a murderer in the family. Maria Pek cursed the teacher.

"Only parents have the right to hit a child!" She screamed and flayed her son with fists and a wooden spoon.

In September a new red-brick school house was opened on Lenke Avenue. Jani attended school there five more years with results no better than his sister's.

His only passion was soccer. Whenever the family went to gawk at the inmates promenading in the Ringer Sanatorium's park, Jani refused to stare. It was in vain that the civil servant pointed out the new arrivals—the elegant man in the mohair suit who held an imaginary telephone in his hand and shouted excitedly: "Hello? Hello? The Africans have invented the bread tree! Available in lots of a thousand carloads!" or the lady dressed in blue who squeezed her beautiful face to the fence, winked, and begged someone to abduct her. The boy was just not interested.

"Oh, to hell with them! They stuff their faces with fried chicken and cucumber salad all day! Why don't they stop playing crazy?"

And he cursed and spat at them until Maria Pek chased him away.

Then he would run to the nearby Linum Mills Soccer Field. It didn't matter to him which team won; he watched every game intently, argued points of play expertly. Only when the Buda II team played did he lose his head. Even the slightest critical remark about the team he took as a personal affront. Not infrequently he resorted to his fists. He played too, kicking the rag ball with a great deal of ambition but little talent.

Sometimes he strayed away to pick violets or anemones on Sas Hill and gave them to his mother with an embarrassed grin.

Every Sunday Jani took dinner to Szörm. Szörm had a bushy beard and wore a white sailor cap. Sitting on the sandlot beyond Karolina Avenue, the two of them talked about ocean storms and wars at sea. Szörm said there is no Hereafter: people are eaten by the fish and that's all there is to it. He considered the Gregorian calendar ridiculous nonsense and could see no use for namedays. He made a seven-day calendar of his own on a piece of cardboard. It went like this:

"Monday: Lekvar noodles; Tuesday: dried peas; Wednesday: fast day—cornmeal; Thursday: dried peas; Friday: fast day—cornmeal; Saturday: horsemeat goulash; Sunday: Jani Habetler—everything good!"

Sometimes Szörm kicked up a row at the Soup Kitchen. He refused to wait in line and demanded a double portion. Stamping the ground with his bare feet he would shout:

"Don't you pick on me, you beggars! It was me who saved Miklos Horthy's life . . . on the *Navarra* . . . in a storm, in smoke, in a big battle!"

Everybody laughed: Szörm began to cry. He spat ugly insults at the ungrateful Regent.

It was snowing tiny flakes when a policeman on a bicycle came to take Szörm away. The crowd at the Soup Kitchen felt sorry for him. They watched in wordless silence until he vanished around the corner of Bocskai Avenue.

That evening after washing up for bed, Gizike said, "Now they'll lock the old man up in the Ringer. Then he won't be cold anymore."

Jani turned his yellowish eyes toward his sister.

"You stupid fool! They'll throw him in the tank, damn their lousy hides!"

He gritted his teeth with such fury that Habetler had to cover his ears.

Anna Küvecses bore two more sons, both black-haired as ravens, and in the fall of 1935 a little girl who died two weeks later. The cobbler had a hard time making a living. Very often he asked Maria Pek to buy groceries for him because the civil servant's wife had unlimited credit at Ignáz Weisz's store.

The daily card games at Habetler's continued throughout the winter. Maria Pek fed them garlic toast and rum-laced tea. The second day of Christmas the Choral Society honored the Doctor, whom they had elected an honorary member, at his father's home on Karolina Avenue. They lined up in his room and quietly, solemnly, and artfully sang Christmas carols.

In the spring of 1936 Anna Küvecses asked Janos Habetler to talk about the Ludovika Royal Military Academy. They were sitting out in front of the barracks. It was dusk. The nuns from the Pius Home walked by in pairs. Behind the many-paned windows of the two-story Linum Textile Mills the girls bent over their work. On the road a truck loaded with bales of wool stirred up the dust. Children in denim pants threw pebbles at it.

The civil servant carefully wrapped the cards, paused thoughtfully, and began:

"The area of the Ludovika Royal Academy comprises about sixty acres. His Excellency Baron Orczy presented it to the Crown so that the children of the country's most illustrious men might master the knowledge required of an officer in the Armed Forces. Stags, deer, countless birds and peacocks abound in its beautifully kept park. There are also goldfish ponds with statues and wild ducks. Besides these ponds there is also a lake large enough for rowboats. There is a Lutheran as well as a Catholic church. Commencement, when the Cadets are commissioned as Lieutenants in the Armed Forces, is held every August 20, the anniversary of the coronation of our first king, his Apostolic Majesty Saint Stephen. The highest dignitaries in Hungary attend in full dress. Of course, only the invited are admitted. When the personal representative of the sovereign approaches, clarions announce his arrival. Then the national anthem is played, followed by the solemn recital of the oath. The new Lieutenants say: 'I swear by the living God that I will be faithful to Hungary and to the highest warlord, that I will not ally myself with external or internal enemies and that I will remain faithful to the Magyar laws until death. So help me God!' Then they draw their swords, wave them in the air and cross them with great clatter and shout: 'For the Fatherland, until death!' It is very beautiful and moving.

"Then the best of the class makes a speech—I hear that this year it will be one of the two sons of Prime Minister Gömbös, because they are both exceptionally bright—finally there is a banquet with many toasts."

"And those who flunk?" asked Anna. "What happens to them?"

"In our academy nobody flunks," the civil servant replied. "The very stupid are sent to the provinces to serve as Quartermaster officers."

"And what do you do?" asked the cobbler. "Please tell us that too. Do you make sure that the officers don't steal the museum?"

"My position requires a man who lives a decent life," Janos replied. "I don't want you to think me boastful. I hate that kind of thing. I hand every penny of my earnings to my wife, even what I earn loading vegetables. I only drink wine on very special occasions and even then in moderation. And I could never but never be dazzled by beautiful or flashy things, because I do not touch what belongs to someone else.

"My assignment requires sober thinking too," he continued. "To make this clear to you, I will give you an example. My superior, the Lieutenant Colonel, sent a civil servant second class to fetch his two valises at the Eastern Railway Station and deliver them to the Colonel's home on Hengermalom Street. The civil servant used a taxicab and submitted the bill to the Colonel. The Colonel was very angry. He called the civil servant second class a Communist and ordered him on report. When he was asked how he had dared to take a taxi at the Colonel's expense, his defense was that the two valises were too heavy for him to carry to the streetcar stop. Well, that's no excuse, because if I had been given that order, there could have been no question of not delivering the suitcases to the Colonel's house by streetcar, regardless of the effort it took. Therefore it is clear that that Civil Servant—I don't say that he is a Communist, because that would not be true—is certainly not a thinking man. Of course he was immediately discharged from the service."

"I see," said the cobbler. He lifted jeering eyes at Janos Habetler's face.

"It's late," said Maria Pek. "Time to go to bed."

For a minute or two longer they listened to the whirring of the weaving machines behind the yellow panes of the Linum Textile Mills, then went into their houses to sleep.

Toward the end of summer Maria Pek attacked her husband in a most outrageous manner. With a glint of madness in her eyes she lashed out at him about Anna Küvecses. It was a weekday afternoon and the two of them were alone. The two littlest girls were in Brügecs for the summer, Jani had gone downtown to a movie, and Gizike was at the Ringer Sanatorium, staring with rapt attention at the patients, as she often did.

Habetler was shaving. He turned away from the mirror, put his razor down, and tried to hush his wife. He begged her to come to her senses and to stop yelling because he was a quiet, peaceful man who did not like rows. Normally, he said, he could not hurt a fly but if he was pushed too far, there would be trouble, big trouble. But the words just kept pouring out of Maria Pek. She called him a lousy son of a bitch and a goddamn liar.

"In the name of God, shut up!" Habetler said. "Or I'll leave, I'll go away forever."

"So why don't you leave?" Maria Pek laughed. "Take the black-haired strumpet with you."

Habetler grabbed his wife's blonde hair and twisted it around his hand. He pulled her onto the floor and began to kick her.

"Listen! Listen to what my husband is doing to me!" Maria Pek shrieked. "It's all because of you, you black whore!"

She struggled to her feet and flew to the Küvecses' door, smashed the glass with her fist, and cursed loudly.

Anna Küvecses sobbed hysterically and screamed that she was going to kill herself. She jerked open the kitchen drawer, but her hand found only a wooden spoon.

Habetler put on his dark-blue uniform, carefully set his gold-buttoned shako on his head and walked out. Two days later he came home. He was dead drunk: his face was tired and unshaven. Maria Pek put him to bed and drew the curtains.

"Be quiet," she said to the children, "your father is sick."

On October 1, 1936, the wreckers began to pull down the Barracks Settlement. The occupants were given fourteen days to find new quarters. The women wailed; the men huddled together to discuss the disaster. Policemen patrolled the alleys in pairs.

Like his neighbors Habetler was scared of high rents. The Central Market had been moved to Kvassai Avenue on the southern outskirts of the city, so far away that he could no longer earn extra money loading fruit and potatoes at dawn. After a few sleepless nights he sought out Lieutenant Colonel Vilmos Matyas. The Colonel gave him excellent advice. He told him to go on report and describe his difficult situation to the Officer of the Day and request to be assigned to waiting on tables in the Officers' Mess. He should also ask permission to take leftovers home for his family. The Ludovika Academy's new Commandant, Colonel Ferenc Szombathelyi, granted permission.

When Maria Pek heard the good news she began to laugh.

"We'll stuff ourselves!" she cried. "We'll have cake and whipped cream every day!" And she smashed a glass on the floor for good luck.

On their last evening in Lenke Avenue they went to the Kris Tavern. Everyone sang. Küvecses got drunk as a pig. He shook his fist, swore and whined about Transylvania. Then, stretched out on the floor, he buried his face in his hands and wept bitterly.

There were countless taverns in the Habetlers' new neighborhood, all of them alike. After their work people would drop in to talk and argue about anything and everything.

Yet the Harp Tavern was different.

It wasn't the small room or the dirty frosted lamp or the quality of the wine that made the difference. As in other taverns, the patrons talked over the day's events, pried into why Bela Sapadt had tried to kill himself by inhaling cooking gas, how Istvan Hires had won money at the horse races and who had made Juli Csele pregnant. In the Harp too, like in other pubs, things only calmed down when the innkeeper gruffly announced closing time.

The Harp was different from all other taverns because it was the haunt of Uncle Reich, the Jewish church singer. When his shabby figure appeared in the doorway, a merry glint lit the eyes of the dour innkeeper, who immediately began to prepare the herring with vinegared onions and Uncle Reich's usual white wine and soda.

One by one Uncle Reich placed coins on the counter. Then his dirty fingers tore the herring into small pieces and stuffed them into his toothless mouth. After the second spritzer the pallor left his face. He leaned back against the metal-covered bar, puffed at his cheap cigar, and pompously began to explain why migrating birds don't lose their way, what the shape of Cleopatra's bathtub was, or how parallel lines meet in infinity.

The innkeeper interrupted him: "If you know so much, could you tell us who stole the collection box from the Nagy-fuvaros Street Synagogue?"

Uncle Reich blushed: "It's not nice of you to ask me such a question."

"Not nice? And what are you always doing in the cemetery?"

There was a sudden uproar in the smoke-filled room.

"He's right! Tell us about that, you singer!"

He opened his eyes wide and glared at the shouters. Angrily he said:

"By what right does anyone suspect a citizen? Behold the effect of the Pan-German conspiracy! Don't you dare suspect me! It's true that sometimes I talk to strangers in the cemetery . . . but I have given alms too . . ."

He sat down at a table and drank a great deal of wine. He gave his orders grandly, bought rounds for everybody, sang, danced, even kissed Istvan Hires and said to Juli Csele:

"God watches over us, even in the darkest night."

The patrons applauded and laughed; good humor bloomed in the Harp. After a while Uncle Reich tired. He dropped his bald head on the table and snored until closing time.

Istvan Hires helped him home. In the drafty corridor he rattled the old beggar's door. Kato Reich, disheveled and drowsy, accepted the sweaty old man and put him to bed on his rickety iron cot.

The patrons said that Istvan Hires was in love with Kato Reich. The innkeeper joined in the talk:

"Istvan Hires just wants to get the girl into bed and that's all."

The patrons didn't argue. They agreed that every man in the neighborhood would like to take the girl to bed. Kato Reich was beautiful but unapproachable. And hopelessly in love with Jani Habetler.

Jani Habetler was not handsome, nor particularly intelligent. He was a stubborn fellow with an uncontrollable temper. When angered he would bellow at the top of his lungs and sometimes even smash his fist against the wall.

One spring day at the beginning of the holidays, when even the least religious communicant eats crisp unleavened bread and finds his way to a synagogue, Kato Reich asked Jani to marry her. She would be a faithful wife to him, she said.

Kato's proposal was completely senseless. Their different religions made marriage impossible, Jani explained to Kato very clearly.

In the neighborhood of Nagyfuvaros Street not only the taverns but the tenement buildings looked alike. As a rule they were three-story buildings surrounding a courtyard. An open walkway inside the courtyard gave access to the flats, as well as to a toilet on each floor.

It was on the third floor of such a building that the Habetlers lived. The family, which had earned the general respect of the neighbors, had a one-room-and-kitchen flat on the street side. They were warm-hearted, thriftless people. At their lavish table there was duck or chicken every day—for neighbors, relatives, a distant acquaintance or a passing beggar, regardless of creed or social status.

Bela Sapadt had painted the flat after Habetler built a dividing wall according to Maria Pek's plan, making the one room into two. In the room that overlooked the street they placed the two heavy wardrobes and the dining table which had been given them by Archdeacon Colonel Taubinger. Night tables flanked the beds. Maria Pek and Janos slept in one, Jani in the other. On the courtyard side of the new wall Hajnalka and Eszter shared a couch; with Gizike sleeping on a straw pallet. This half of the room also had a table, two chairs, a round stove, Habetler's green footlocker, and on a corner shelf jars of tomatoes, fruit, and cucumber preserves.

Everyone in the family had a job. Gizike earned nine pengös a week as a clean-up girl in the Cotton Industry's Ujpest plant. She got out of bed at four o'clock in the morning to reach her job at the far northern end of the city. Jani was an apprentice lathe operator in the Angyalföld Metal Finishing Plant. The two little girls attended the Csobánc Street Elementary School. At home they played make-believe and cut out dolls on the walkway. They often had fights and sometimes scratched each other bloody. Maria Pek did laundry which Habetler carried home from the Károlyi Barracks.

Sundays from early spring to late fall the Habetlers regularly went on outings to Népliget Park with neighbors and friends. The grownups sat on the grass while the children wandered around, played on the swings, munched cotton candy, and laughed at Zsuzsa Kaposztas, the idiot maid, the sideshow barkers, and the white-faced clowns.

Gizike was pretty: copper hair and clear bluish-gray eyes fringed with dark lashes, figure slender, breasts large and pear-shaped. She was waiting in line at the roller coaster in a tightly buttoned shantung dress when she was accosted by a strange man: for the first time in her life. He made a smart appearance with his black hair and white teeth. He said that he was a clerk in an instrument factory and an amateur boxer. He displayed three awards he carried in his pocket. When the Habetlers walked home at dusk he followed them all the way.

Two days later, Gizike looked out the window. She saw him pacing back and forth in front of the gray-walled synagogue across the street. This time he wore an eggshell-colored suit with a fire-red bow tie. Gizike and Kato Reich went downstairs and joined him. The three of them strolled around the neighborhood until Kato Reich excused herself. Then Gizike and the young man went to the Phönix Movie Theater where they kissed in the dark.

The next time he came, the following Saturday afternoon, he had tickets for the circus. Gizike invited him up to the apartment. Habetler, Kalauz, and the cobbler were engaged in a game of scat. Anna Küvecses was playing *"La Cucaracha"* on the phonograph. Istvan Hires was dancing with Kato Reich; Bela Sapadt and Jani were arguing loudly about a soccer match. Juli Csele was sitting on the garbage can eating a chicken leg and the two little girls were playing with empty matchboxes.

Maria Pek offered the man a glass of wine. "How old are you?" she asked.

"Twenty-five," he answered.

"You're past thirty," Maria Pek said. "Take care, my daughter. Men are sly foxes."

Gizike and the man left for the circus. He carried her pea-green coat on his arm all the way. After the show they strolled out in the park. He reached under the girl's skirt and started to fondle her. Gizike pushed him away and ran to the streetcar stop.

He took Gizike to the movies a few more times. On the way home they would stop to kiss in every doorway. Finally Maria Pek slapped her daughter. The suitor gave up and never came back.

Gizike told Kato Reich: "I like to kiss."

It was a fall evening and the two of them were leaning over the walkway rail outside the Habetlers' kitchen.

"I've never been kissed," Kato Reich said. "Sooner or later I will marry your brother. I want him to be the first."

"You mustn't even think of such a thing," Gizike said quietly.

"If he wants me to, I'll convert. My father will cry, but I'll go to the Lutheran minister and become a Christian. Then we could get married and I would bear him a little boy, because a boy is what he would like."

Gizike embraced Kato. They were silent for a long while.

Toward the end of that winter Gizike fell in love with Bela Szücs, a muscular young truck driver who worked for the

Grauer Liquor Distillery. He was an orphan from the Puszta, and now lived with his sister on Homok Street. Bela Szücs was in love with Gizike too. They went to the Kerepesi Cemetery to kiss undisturbed in the wreath-scented wind. They gazed fondly into each other's eyes in the shadow of the tombstones.

Gizike was happy.

"He has golden brown hair," she told Kato Reich, "and hazel eyes."

When Gizike was promoted to operating a power loom and her salary was raised to eighteen pengös a week, they decided to get married. But Bela Szücs' introduction to the family misfired. He greeted Maria Pek with a casual "Good day" and that spoiled everything. Maria Pek straightened up from the wash tub, wiped her claw-fingered hands and looked at the young man with her ice-blue eyes and said:

"I'll talk it over with my daughter." She never allowed Bela Szücs in her home again.

So he and Gizike met in secret. After a while Bela Szücs was called up to serve in the tank corps. They wrote each other faithfully for a year. By this time Istvan Hires was in love with Gizike. Every afternoon he sat in the kitchen talking to Maria Pek, telling her again and again that he would kill himself if Gizike married anyone else. He brought gifts, oranges and candies, and movie tickets for *Lilac Blossoms*. He worshiped Gizike to the point of absurdity. One day Maria Pek found Bela Szücs's letters hidden among some pulp novels in a battered suitcase. She beat her daughter bloody.

In the spring of 1938 Bela Szücs got sick. Gizike and Kato Reich went to see him in the Gyáli Avenue Military Hospital. They sat and talked in the hospital garden.

"Leave home!" Bela said to her. "I'll marry you."

"I can't leave my family," Gizike replied.

"You're a coward! Go away—I never want to see you again."

Then in September 1938 Hungary reoccupied Kassa.

Bela was ordered to rejoin his unit on the Czechoslovak border.

Istvan Hires still sat around in the kitchen, talking with Maria Pek. He still brought chocolate-covered cherries and often took Gizike to the movies.

Once Gizike said to Kato Reich: "He's such an idiot. He doesn't even dare hold my hand."

A few days later, on the way home from the movies, Istvan Hires stopped under a lamp post and said: "Listen, I want to tell you something . . ."

"Well, say it, then!"

"I mean, I want to give you something . . ."

"So, give it to me then."

"Close your eyes."

Gizike closed her eyes and Istvan Hires kissed her. It was more a peck than a kiss.

Gizike did not love him. She thought he was a dull wheedler and told him so more than once.

At her mother's insistence, Gizella Habetler married Istvan Hires on Christmas Day 1940. They vowed eternal fidelity in the Nagyvarad Place Calvinist Church. At the photographer's her new husband asked her to get out of her shoes—Istvan Hires was a short man. Maria Pek fried fish and cooked cheese noodles; everyone drank and sang way into the night.

In January Gizike ran into Bela Szücs. He was huddled in a doorway on Homok Street, waiting for someone. There was snow in his hair and on his eyebrows. He didn't say anything, he didn't even greet her.

That evening Mrs. Istvan Hires said to Kato Reich:

"He would not have loved me very long, anyway. He would have left me . . . but he was so handsome. Deep down, inside me, I was always scared of him . . ."

She bent down to pick up the coal shovel and noisily filled the enamel stove.

In February the next-to-youngest Habetler child, Eszter,

was taken to the White Cross Children's Hospital in great pain. Her joints were so badly inflamed that she could not move arms or legs. At the Harp the event was the subject of excited speculation. Everyone was sure that she would die since her fingers and toes had turned white.

Uncle Reich was of a different opinion. He argued that Eszter was well-nourished and that that would save her life.

Juli Csele started to cry. She said that she would pray for the little girl. She prayed twice a day, she said, once in the morning at the Rita Chapel, and once at night before going to bed. She implored God to help her bear a healthy child and to watch over Sándor Vargha's every step, and not to let the liquor in Uncle Reich's stomach burst into flame.

Everyone laughed.

"Who's this Sándor Vargha?" the innkeeper asked. "The father of your child?"

"That's him," Juli Csele said. "My intended. Every two weeks he walks all the way from Horthy Park just to see me —that's where he works. He's a very thrifty man, he's already saved up sixty pengös. When we have enough money, we'll have my room painted and we'll have it fumigated, because he has a very sensitive nature. Then we'll buy a real bed, a few things we need, and get married."

"Why aren't you working?" Bela Sapadt asked. "I'll tell you: because you're a lazy pig!"

Juli Csele shrugged.

"I can't stand hard work," she said quietly. "I tried, but I start to sweat right away, I feel faint, everything goes round and round . . . they even sent me home from the box factory. Besides, I've been after Uncle Reich to find me a good job. He knows a better class of people."

"That's true," said Uncle Reich, "very true. On my word of honor, I will certainly do my best."

At the beginning of March Uncle Reich did manage to get work for Juli Csele. An entirely new enterprise had come into being. It went under the imposing name of National Hygiene Institute. Quite unexpectedly Uncle Reich spoke to the director of the registered company personally.

Dr. Ernö Vajda, the director, was having his midday dinner in the Widow Salamon's excellent eating establishment when Uncle Reich politely, and without ever having seen the man before, wished him a hearty appetite and then alluded in a few words to his own miserable condition. Dr. Vajda looked up over the edge of his glasses and—offered Uncle Reich a job. He was curt, businesslike. He said that the National Hygiene Institute was important to the national health, the work he could offer was steady, a truck delivered the merchandise every morning, it was not piece work, it paid twenty pengös a week and there was no chance of rupturing oneself. Uncle Reich immediately recommended Juli Csele. He praised her clever hands, but he did not mention her blessed condition.

That evening Uncle Reich advised Juli Csele to dress in such a way that Dr. Vajda would not notice, at least the first day. Juli Csele could not hide her belly, but she promised to stand up straight.

This conversation took place Wednesday. Early Thursday morning Juli Csele went to the Frangepan Street. Dr. Ernö Vajda was standing at the entrance to the building. He led Juli Csele into the courtyard and showed her where she was to work.

The workshop was a wooden shed, housing a large tin-lined trough surrounded by empty crates. An old crone crouched on one of the crates, spitting pumpkin seeds in all directions. From time to time she let out a cackle. After a while Juli realized the old woman was drunk.

The National Hygiene Institute was a filthy enterprise. When a truck arrived, a great many spittoons were unloaded and the old woman began to clean them. Finally Juli Csele reached for the old crone's bottle, closed her eyes, took a big swig, rolled up her sleeves and went to work. As the day wore on, the two of them finished the bottle. They chuckled and sang.

One Saturday afternoon Sándor Vargha walked into the workshop. Juli Csele was bent over the trough. The old crone tried to attract Juli's attention by stabbing her gnarled fingers in the man's direction, but by the time Juli noticed Vargha, he was throwing up.

Before she could wipe her hands on her apron and move clumsily around the trough between the crates to help, Sándor Vargha had fled.

That afternoon Juli Csele drank heavily at the Harp. She was a well-behaved drunk, she didn't cry or quarrel. She just sat quietly, chin propped in her hands. After a while the tavern began to turn round and round so she started for home. On Matyas Place she collapsed. Some people helped her to a bench. The Harp's patrons rushed out into the street but they could only stare at her stupidly, in helpless fright. There was nothing they could do to ease her labor pains. She screamed, she pulled her hair, she bit her knuckles bloody. Several times Istvan Hires pulled her skirt down over her legs. Finally, an ambulance took her away.

Jani watched the scene leaning against the trunk of a locust tree in his black tee-shirt. He was boiling. He gritted his teeth and cursed. He called Juli Csele dirty names.

"Let the bitch croak!" he yelled. "I hope she dies! Filthy whore!"

A bald man in a linen suit stepped out of the commiserating crowd.

"Stop it!" he said. "Get out or I'll call the police!"

Kato Reich and Istvan Hires got scared. They asked the man to be quiet, to leave while he still could, before there was trouble. But the man wouldn't listen to them. He pushed Kato Reich's hand off his shoulder, and kept shouting. He said that fellows like Jani should be taught a lesson, they should be locked up because they were the kind who ended up cold-blooded murderers.

Jani looked at the man out of his yellowish eyes. He stepped away from his tree trunk. The man paled.

"Police!" he screamed, but didn't have the strength to run. He held up his fists defensively. Jani punched him in the face and the man fell to the cobbled street. Jani stomped on him until the police arrived; they could hardly pull him away. Finally Jani quietly went along to the Vig Street Police Station.

It was dark by the time Jani was released. Kato Reich was waiting at the corner of Jozsef Street. They walked to Matyas Place, sat down on a bench, and watched some filthy Gypsy children. Kato Reich asked what punishment he expected. Jani replied that it would probably be thirty pengös. Unfortunately, he was only too well-known at the Vig Street Station.

"As long as they don't find out about it at home," he worried. "You know my father. He would mope for days."

A few minutes later he blew up again. Eyes flashing, he called Juli Csele a vile, filthy, drunken bitch. He slammed his heavy fist on the backrest of the bench. The skin ripped open and blood spurted.

"That's no way to bring a child into the world," he shouted. "We're human beings, you can't do things like that. A child can't come into the world when the mother is drunk, like a sow dropping a litter! A child is a child, goddamn it!"

He stopped talking but kept clenching his fist. Kato Reich noticed that he was crying.

No one could find fault with Jani's work or his diligence. Several times Istvan Hires had inquired about him at the Metal Finishing Plant and was always told that the boy was a good and steady worker.

In his free time Jani pulled Bela Sapadt's tool cart, loaded with pails, ladders, brushes, rollers, everything that is needed for house painting. He helped scrape walls, mixed glue, handed Sapadt the tools, and eventually even drew the lines for hanging wallpaper. Kato Reich took him supper which Maria Pek prepared. Bela Sapadt paid him according to the size of the apartment and to his own mood of the day. Once they had turned off the lights and locked up the flat they had been decorating Bela Sapadt stopped in at the Harp. Kato and Jani always sat on the steps of the barber shop and talked.

"If I worked alone I'd be much better and faster," Jani said. He took the girl's hand as they sat in front of the shuttered shop. He smiled. "I'd paint the court apartments a very light color, blue and silver. You wouldn't need electric lights, even at night."

She smiled, too.

"Accept me," she said. "If you want I'll buy a light-blue dress with silver trim."

Jani lost his temper.

"I never want to hurt you, but you make me so mad when you talk like that that I hurt you despite myself, and then the next day I pick a fight with everyone. Please, let's talk about something else."

"Listen to me, Jani," she said. "I always listen very carefully to what you say. . . . Last year at the Electrical Worker's game you said my hair was fuzzy. I cried all night and I decided to have my head shaved to prove how much I love you. But then I got scared that you would never talk to me again. . . . We could be happy. . . . If I wasn't sure, I wouldn't talk about it any more. We would have a beautiful baby . . ."

"I can't marry a Jewish girl," Jani said. "I have a very bad opinion of Jews. It's impossible to like them. And that's not something I made up, everyone knows that!"

"I wasn't there, at Mount Olive." The girl smiled but there were tears in her eyes. "I was born right here, in Nagyfuvaros Street."

Jani's yellowish eyes flashed.

"That's not what I mean!" he said roughly. "My two little sisters' clothes are covered with patches. When they get out of school Jewish girls like Maca Stern, Rozsi Weiss and the

Schlesinger girl prance around in their patent-leather shoes and frilly dresses. Their mothers are as fat as pigs and sit behind the cash register and give Hajnalka and Eszter fly-blown cake. I despise them! I'd like to throw stones at every one of them. At their heads!"

He was silent for a moment.

"My mother's fingers are crooked and bent," he said quietly. "Do you know that she can't straighten them out any more?"

Kato Reich didn't move. Neither of them spoke for a long time.

"If anybody ever hurts you, tell me," Jani said nervously. "If anybody in this stinking world dares to hurt you, I'll kill him with my bare hands."

He took the girl's face between his strong hands and turned it toward him.

"Do you believe me?"

She nodded. She shook with soundless sobs.

Kato Reich went to every soccer game with Jani. It was a rough task. Jani was a wildly enthusiastic fan of the Iron Puddler's second-string team. He claimed that his team got pushed around because it was a workers' club. His behavior caused Kato many troubled afternoons. At the Puddlers–Pereces Championship Game he broke his wristwatch, which had been his confirmation present, in the frenzy of victory. But at the Latorca Street soccer field something much worse happened. During the Puddlers–Beszkart game he completely lost his head; he went wild, and shouted at the umpire, "Just you wait, you dirty bastard! You'll whistle a different tune when the Russians come!" The people sitting next to him moved away; nobody said a word. Kato Reich tightened her arms around his neck and squeezed her face over his mouth. Crying, she implored him to be quiet. Finally some spectators took pity on the girl and suggested that Jani take her home.

Eszter came out of the hospital in July. She was emaciated and pale, her health had barely improved. Every day Janos carried her piggy-back to the clinic where her joints were exercised and she was given painful injections of milk.

Maria Pek worked very hard. She kept the crowded flat —and her family—in impeccable shape. The only thing she didn't have to worry about was the cooking, because Janos still brought food home from the Ludovika Academy in small pails. Often Hajnalka waited for him at the gate of the Academy and helped him carry the containers.

Istvan Hires earned good money, sometimes as much as fifty pengös a week. He worked at the Magyar Precision Lab on Fehérvári Avenue. His skill and intelligence, his superlative ability were highly regarded. He loved his hands, which were long and beautiful with tapered fingers. He took great care of them and in conversation constantly used them to point and gesture.

After the wedding he asked his mother-in-law to figure out how much he and Gizike should contribute to the household every month.

Maria Pek laughed. "We live from day to day, my son. To hell with figuring and calculating. Everyone around here eats at our table, so why should I take your money?"

Hires lived a quiet life. After work he stopped in at the Harp to chat over a glass of wine, and after dinner he played his mandolin, almost always his favorite song, "Hawaiian Stars Are Gleaming."

One afternoon he was lounging on the couch when Juli Csele asked him whether he was satisfied with Gizike.

Hires shrugged.

"Everything would be great," he answered, "except that sometimes she irritates me. She just stares into space as if she were deaf, and I have to repeat everything twice."

"Make her change," Juli Csele said.

Eszter crawled out of her bed on the far side of the room. Leaning heavily on her canes, she went out into the kitchen and told her mother what she had heard. Maria Pek chased

Juli Csele out of the apartment. Then she turned on Istvan Hires:

"How dare you discuss my daughter with that filthy spittoon? Take care, Istvan Hires! Take care, for you don't know what God may still have in store for you!"

Istvan Hires did not answer. He went down to the Harp and bought some sour white wine. When he returned he kissed Maria Pek's hand and asked to be forgiven.

In August 1941 he bought a one-room cabin in Pesterzsebet twenty paces from the Danube. There was a boat and two pairs of oars, too. In October he was called up to the First Mobile Artillery Division.

Maria Pek baked chicken and cakes and prepared the green footlocker. At six o'clock in the morning Gizike and Jani accompanied him all the way to the entrance of the Count Andrassy Barracks on Hungaria Boulevard.

He had not been in the service a week before his sergeant sent him home to forage for soap. Uncle Reich helped—he took Hires to Mor Berger, a wholesaler of general merchandise. Hires made a deal: Mor Berger agreed to supply chocolate, candy, and razor blades at wholesale prices which Istvan Hires could resell to soldiers at a healthy profit. To Jani's disgust this wheeling and dealing became a regular thing; he had to carry the merchandise from Berger's place to his brother-in-law's barracks. Soon Istvan Hires had a desk job: first company clerk, then battalion clerk. By the end of his term he had made master sergeant, so he decided to re-enlist. Maria Pek objected.

"If you have to wear a uniform," she said angrily, "why don't you become a chimney sweep?"

"I know what I'm doing," Istvan Hires said. "I don't want to be sent to the front."

Early in December Hires invited the entire family to attend the festival of St. Borbala, patron saint of the artillery. When they arrived at the barracks a brass band was playing in the training area. Then one of the soldiers recited the St.

Borbala Scroll, a collection of couplets which ridiculed a few notoriously tough drill instructors, including some junior officers. Enlisted men and officers alike roared with laughter.

The day before Christmas Maria Pek rearranged the furniture and gave the house a thorough cleaning, as she did before every holiday. Sometimes, to the dismay of her family, she'd get the urge on an odd Saturday, too. Then she kept everyone busy pushing furniture, moving beds, and scrubbing floors and windows. The very air bristled with tension. Hajnalka kicked Gizike in the shins and the young woman limped tearfully to her mother to complain. Maria Pek slapped both of them.

"Please, not my head!" Hajnalka screamed. "Anywhere else, but not always my head!"

Gizike started to bawl, Eszter chimed in too, and the civil servant shouted desperately for quiet; the neighbors would think somebody was being murdered. Maria cursed and told him what she would do to the neighbors. Jani, seething with rage, picked up his father's footlocker and hurled it to the floor.

It was past eleven o'clock when finally, dead tired, they got to bed.

Eszter could not control her curiosity. She stole to the closet and searched until she found the package wrapped in pink tissue paper. Carefully she unwrapped it and saw in the snowy dawn that it was a book, *Great Times, Great Women,* by Mrs. Daniel, née Laura Lengyel. On the flyleaf there was a dedication: "To my little sister-in-law, with all my love, Istvan Hires." Eszter crawled back into bed next to her sister, buried her face in the pillow, and started to cry in furious disappointment.

Every Christmas the Civil Servant set the tree on his footlocker and decorated it himself. The girls helped Maria Pek in the kitchen while Jani hauled coal up from the cellar. Finally everything was ready and Janos was about to light the candles when Maria Pek angrily told her family to go and get Juli

Csele—that unfortunate cow should not be alone with her filthy brat on Christmas Eve. Jani went to get Kato Reich. Then the head of the family rang the Christmas bell and everyone entered. When they were all assembled in the flickering candlelight Janos began to sing, in his pleasant voice, "Silent Night." The others quietly joined in. After the songs the lights were turned on again and everyone kissed each other before scrambling under the Christmas tree for their presents which Maria Pek had labeled with little slips of paper.

Jani took Kato Reich into the other room and kissed her. He reached into his pocket for a little box lined with blue velvet. In it was a four-leaf clover on a thin gold chain. Kato gave Jani a necktie.

The girls spread a white tablecloth over Archdeacon Colonel Taubinger's table and began to fetch plates and glasses from the kitchen. Maria Pek ordered Kato Reich to go get her father and bring him to dinner.

"He's asleep," the girl said quietly. "He had some rum . . . at this time of the year he gets so chilled in the cemetery . . ."

Everybody insisted that she get him, so she and Jani went to wake the old man. Good-humoredly Uncle Reich crawled out of the rickety iron bed, washed his face and neck with cold water. Kato laid out a snow-white shirt and polished his muddy shoes.

Uncle Reich greeted the Habetlers joyfully. He wished them a happy holiday and asked their indulgence for not having brought a gift.

"I was offered a secondhand dragon-headed lamp," he said to Maria Pek. "I considered bringing it to you. Its eyes light up, blue, like the lamps in a hospital ward. It's an amazing piece. Then I didn't dare buy it . . . the old thingamajig reminds one of death."

Maria Pek said: "When you've had a bottle of rum, you always imagine such nonsense."

Uncle Reich blushed, as he often did, and tried to explain that he really had seen such a ghastly lamp. Everybody laughed, because they were used to the old vagabond's muddled stories. Maria Pek fetched a box of cigars from under the Christmas tree and gave it to him.

"Here, the Christ child brought this for you!" she laughed. "You old reprobate!"

There was golden beef broth, stuffed cabbage, fried fish, cheese noodles, poppy-seed and nut cakes. The demijohn of wine and the chitterlings came from Brügecs. After the second glass of wine, Uncle Reich began to smile. He declared that he believed in happiness and in the immortality of the soul.

Jani put his glass down. "Szörm said there is no Hereafter. People are eaten by the fish, and that's it."

Uncle Reich pondered a moment.

"Szörm did not tell you the truth, my boy. Perhaps he is dead and buried, but he still lives tonight."

He nodded.

"I have talked about this with my daughter many times," he continued. "Whenever she is sad, we discuss life's great problems." He rested his eyes on his daughter and smiled. Tears rolled down his cheeks.

After the holiday he brought the dragon-headed lamp. He asked for a rag, dusted the lamp, and stood it in the middle of the table.

"That's what it looks like," he said apologetically.

Janos was pleased.

"This is a very handsome gift," he said. "It must have cost you a great deal of money. I thank you for the esteem which you have shown to us."

Maria Pek put the lamp on her night table and turned it on. The dragon's eyes did not light up but even so she was delighted.

Eszter got well again and returned to school. Because of the time she had lost she was put in the same class with Hajnalka. She was wild. Whenever she was in a rage she rushed, headfirst, at the other children's stomachs. In 1942, at the Csobánc Street Elementary School her diligence and good conduct won her a scholarship of 120 pengös, donated by the Capital Savings Bank. The civil servant was very proud. He kissed his daughter's forehead.

"That was very nice of you," he said. And he boasted to everybody that in his entire life he had never earned that much money in a whole month.

In the fall Uncle Reich died. He was found at dawn on the back staircase. A huge crowd came to his funeral in the Rakoskeresztur Jewish Cemetery. After his body had been lowered into the grave and the dirt shoveled over his coffin, Jani took Kato's arm and led her away.

When they reached the gate of the cemetery, Jani took off his hat and stopped to give the beggars money. The sun was shining and it was warm.

"Kato, cry," he said.

He focused his yellowish eyes on her face and waited. Then they set off on foot. At the Brewery they took a streetcar to the corner of Nepszinhaz Street and Tisza Kalman Square. They wandered through the streets for a long time. At dusk Jani stopped beside the Municipal Theater.

"Cry," he said. "If you don't, I'll beat my head against the wall, I'll smash it to bits."

They looked at each other, then Kato Reich buried her face on Jani's chest. They both cried.

On the wall of the house at 27 Tisza Kalman Square there was a black glass plaque which said in gold letters DEUTSCHES HEIM. Well-dressed Germans lived on the third floor. Whenever Jani saw or heard them on the street, he turned white with fury and gnashed his teeth, as was his wont.

Once he chased a streetwalker out of the Harp because he had seen her with Germans. He could not explain the reason for his hatred. As his hostility developed to dangerous proportions —he cursed and insulted them everywhere, more and more wildly—the civil servant lost his patience and reprimanded his son.

"What have they ever done to you?" he asked. "Have they ever insulted you one single time? They don't even know that you're alive, and they don't care either. They must have the permission of the highest authorities to reside in our city among us. So I warn you, hold your tongue before you cause trouble!"

But Jani continued to curse them. He even started to listen to the Russian radio.

In the spring of 1943 he did get into trouble. On March 15, the anniversary of the 1848 Hungarian Revolution, there was a special broadcast from Moscow; they played old Hungarian folk songs, and then the announcer explained that while in 1848 it was the Russian Czar who had been Europe's policeman and who had hurried to the defense of the Imperial Austrian suppressors, now it was Hitler and the Fascist Germans.

The next day at Levente Youth Corps Training Practice, held in the yard of the Bezeredy Street School, Jani told some of the other boys about the broadcast. A few minutes later the instructor ordered Jani to him.

"What is the Russian radio barking?" he asked.

Jani was silent.

"Speak up," the instructor ordered, "or I'll knock your teeth out."

The boy paled.

"You're not strong enough. . . ," he said quietly.

In the corner of the yard somebody guffawed. The instructor stepped back.

"Company, attention!" he yelled.

He reported the boy. The civil servant was not told about the incident, but Maria Pek walked around the apartment dumbly, with a touch of madness; everything slipped out of her hands. Finally she put on her Sunday dress and went to see Lieutenant Colonel Vilmos Matyas at his home. She told him everything, word for word. Colonel Matyas listened to her story, nodded attentively, and offered her a drink.

"I do not like the Germans either," he said. "After all, my dear lady, I am a Magyar. A teacher of history and music."

He laughed and slapped his knees. Maria Pek realized that he was dead drunk. Quietly she asked whether he would help her son. The Colonel ran his hands through his gray hair; he was obviously trying to think. He grinned.

"Of course!" he said. "You may consider the matter closed. If necessary, I will go in his place, even to the gallows."

Maria Pek walked down the stairs with a numb heart. Kato Reich was waiting for her on the street.

"Pray day and night," she said. "Maybe your God is better."

Jani Habetler reported to the Vig Street Police Station. At the desk an officer looked at his summons.

"Wait," he told the boy.

An hour and a half later Jani was sent to the office of a police colonel.

"Do you feel guilty?" the Colonel asked.

"No," Jani said.

"Then why did you go to Matyas, if you don't feel guilty?"

The boy did not know what to answer.

"You're an anarchist," the police officer said. "Do you know what that means?"

"No," the boy replied.

"It's a disease," said the officer. "An incurable disease."

And he sent Jani home.

In October Jani was ordered to report to the 101–3 Mechanized Mixed Battalion, stationed at Camp Piliscsaba.

Maria Pek cooked and baked and prepared the green footlocker for her son. Monday morning Jani said good-bye to everybody, but he would not let anyone go to the station with him. The neighbors cried when he left the house.

At the Western Railway Station he met Gyuri Kalauz; he had come alone too. They shook hands. Some peasant women sitting in the waiting room were speaking Schwabian. Kalauz asked them what it was like in Piliscsaba. The women said not to worry, the food was excellent.

The company commander was First Lieutenant Jozsef Jozsa, their platoon leader Lieutenant János Kása, their junior officer Second Lieutenant István Kovács. From October through Christmas the new recruits were in basic training. They learned how to stuff a straw pallet as neat as a matchbox and how to make the red-white-and-green stripe on their blankets as straight as a ruler. The barracks were in apothecary order. If somebody forgot to close his footlocker, the noncoms dumped everybody's things on a big pile and everyone had to fish out his own belongings. The left-right, left-right, about-face began to come out of their ears. Every day at dawn they moved out to target practice with live ammunition. Afternoons they marched to a sandy exercise field where explosives of increasing strength were set off to get them used to combat conditions.

Jani got a letter from Kato Reich almost every day. She reported the soccer scores and told him that everybody at home was well, she was working too, the job paid pretty well, she had bought herself a dark-blue dress, but she wouldn't wear it until he got back.

At Christmas Jani went on home leave. The whole family was together again. Juli Csele and her little girl were invited too. Kato Reich looked pretty in her new dark-blue dress.

On the second day of Christmas there was company. The

record player blared, some people played cards, others sang. Everybody drank the Brügecs wine—Maria Pek had a hard time making enough sandwiches fast enough. Istvan Hires in his cups started an argument with Gizike. When he shook his fist at her, Eszter went wild, threw her arms around her sister, and screamed hysterically, "I won't let him! I won't let him!"

They had a hard time calming her. Maria Pek blew up too. She hurled a stream of curses at the sergeant and threw a glass at him. Janos turned white with shame, he implored them to stop their racket or he would tear the place apart with his bare hands. Anna Küvecses cranked up the gramophone; Katalin Karady's voice boomed out: "This was our damnation, the damnation of both of us. . . ." Gyuri Kalauz laughed and peace was restored. Later in the evening Bela Sapadt remarked that there was going to be a new law which would make it illegal for a Christian to kiss a Jew. Juli Csele was dumfounded.

"Whoever heard of such a thing?" she asked. "If I love someone I'll certainly kiss him, no matter who he is."

Bela Sapadt shrugged.

"It's the law," he said. "Anyone who breaks it is guilty of racial sin. But you needn't worry, Juli, nothing human would ever take you to bed."

Istvan Hires laughed: "That's for sure."

Maria Pek noticed the expression in Jani's eyes. Quickly she screamed for them to stop the stupid talk, to drink and eat instead. With a loud, forced laugh she began to tell a hackneyed, old funny story. But it was too late to save the situation. Jani crossed the room to where Bela Sapadt was sitting and started to make fun of the Ferenczváros Soccer Team. The housepainter laughed and kidded Janos about the Puddlers.

"That's a Jewish team," he said. "Like the MTK."

Jani said, "You're as slow as a turtle. You're absolutely worthless. By the time you dip your brush into the paint bucket, it's already time to quit."

Bela Sapadt was quiet for a minute.

"So what do you care? Did it ever cost you anything?" Sapadt pulled some bills out of his wallet. "Tell me and I'll make it up to you!"

He stood up from the table and glared at Jani.

"You tried to kill yourself with gas when your wife was being laid by everyone in the neighborhood, even Szilagy the barber," Jani said. "You couldn't even do that right."

Maria Pek got in between them. She slapped her son's face.

"So you're spoiling for a fight again! Why do you always have to fight? You monster! You curse of mankind! Oh, why did I ever bring you into the world?"

When Habetler and Endre Küvecses had dragged Jani to the other side of the room, Maria Pek turned her anger on Bela Sapadt.

"And you, you go straight to hell and tell your stories about laws there! And don't you ever set foot in my house again, because if you do, I'll kick you right out again!"

Kato Reich was standing at the Christmas tree with her back to the room. When Jani touched her arm, she winced.

"What a thin thread it hangs on." She pointed to a piece of silk candy trembling on the tree. She tried to smile. "Kiss me before you go away again . . ."

Jani knit his brow, cleared his throat. He could not speak. Finally he said, "Don't just stand here. Go help our mother. You're not a guest in this house!"

It was bitter cold when they went to Pesterzsebet, so cold that the blocks of ice on the Danube were motionless. Jani helped the girl over the frozen ground to Istvan Hires' little boathouse. He lit a fire in the pot-bellied stove, then crammed it full of wood. The stovepipe turned pink, then red. Kato took off her winter coat and sat down on the bunk in her dark-blue dress. The sun shining through the tulle curtain painted gay colors on her face.

Jani squatted at the stove.

"When I come back, you will be my wife," he said, "and don't think anybody can stop us."

The girl smiled. "I have always been your wife."

The boy was lost in thought. Finally he broke the silence. "I don't love you because you're beautiful, don't think that. I told Gyuri Kalauz that I love you because I can't help it. When I close my eyes, I see you. When I open my eyes, I still see you."

He picked up a chunk of firewood, turned it around in his hand and carefully put it down on the floor.

"You must not look at any other man," he said. "You must not do things many other women do. I told you the truth and if you ever lie to me, I'll throw you out."

"So be it."

After Christmas things got tougher for Jani and his buddies. Dressed in hot, uncomfortable rubber suits, they were trained to use flamethrowers, land mines, smoke screens, and poison gas. This kind of drill was more dangerous. Sometimes a land mine blew a soldier to bits.

In May they were sent to the front. After crossing the Tartar Pass in the eastern Carpathians they left the freight train at Dilatin. It was a bad beginning. During the unloading a Russian airplane attacked them. There were twelve dead the first day. From Dilatin they moved on to Porohi, where they spent two weeks laying land mines and building tank traps. The officers called the fortification the Arpad Line. They drew their supplies from the German depot at Nadworna, thirty miles away. One day only a horse came back. It was wounded; the broken harness trailed behind him as wild with terror he galloped into camp. Partisans had attacked the wagons. Gyuri Kalauz showed up the next night. The others were all dead.

Fear spread among all the soldiers camped on the north slope of the Carpathians. Even the terrain was frightening. The clouds floated low, catching in the giant pines covering the mountains; the streams were dark and full of shadows.

"An unfriendly area," Gyuri Kalauz declared. "It gives me nightmares."

Jani did not answer.

When they had to fall back, Lieutenant Jozsef Jozsa ordered them to destroy the village with flamethrowers and hand grenades.

There was no railway line through the Toronyai Pass, so they had to march to Okormezo. A few days later they were sent to the Carpathians again, to the Legio Pass. A road had to be built so that reinforcements could be moved to the front. It was a warm afternoon when they arrived at the Pass. They set up camp and posted guards. An overgrown trench, some rusty helmets and a few collapsed, unmarked graves were reminders of World War I. Gyuri Kalauz dug up one of the graves. A group of soldiers and officers stopped to watch him. He brought up a skull, an arm, and a leg bone from the pit and laid them out on the grass.

"I wonder what side he was on?" Gyuri asked out loud.

The soldiers stared listlessly at the crumbling bones. They were not in the mood for guessing games.

They felled trees, blasted rocks out of the mountainside, built roads over the Legio Pass, the Pantir Pass, and the Bornemissza Pass for the German infantry.

In August the retreat toward Budapest began. First they set up camp at Tarackköz, at the confluence of the Tarack and the Tisza rivers. A few days later the battalion marched off toward Ungvar, but a detachment including Jani and Gyuri Kalauz trekked toward Mandok under the command of a staff sergeant. Along the way Gyuri Kalauz traded nails and barbed wire with the peasants for chickens and ducks. Jani was tied to a tree for shooting a rabbit while on guard duty. At Hidasnemeti they boarded cattle cars bound for Fulek, then

Parkánynána. When they stumbled out of the train on November 3, they heard that the Germans had blown up the Margaret Bridge in Budapest. The detachment rejoined the battalion and the next day they proceeded to Esztergom and from there on foot to Piliscsaba.

Sunday morning the battalion commander, a major on horseback, gave the men a briefing:

"My battalion is not afraid to die for our homeland in the battle against communism," he said, "and will die for it too, if necessary! We will engage the enemy soon!"

No leaves were granted. Military police patroled the post.

Ten days later they marched across western Hungary toward Köszegdoroszlo. By this time everyone was to salute with outstretched arm and the shout, "Long live Szálasi!" The men in Jani's unit, grinning silently, still saluted the old way. They were building fortifications again. The local populace was ordered to help them dig trenches and tank traps. One morning Zita Szeleczky, an actress from Budapest, made an appearance, a white fur coat thrown over her shoulders. Jani flew into a rage. Gritting his teeth, he wanted to throw a hand grenade at the elegant visitors from Budapest. His buddies could hardly hold him back. Kalauz pulled him away and made him sit in the yard of a peasant house until he calmed down.

They were transported to the Komaram Citadel in trucks. The Russians were shelling the citadel from the other side of the Danube. Everywhere there were wounded and dead, blood and vermin. The next day they were moved to Many and on to Chapdi, where the infantry was thrown into battle. Within a few hours the entire unit was routed. First Lieutenant Jozsef Jozsa, Lieutenant Janos Kasa, and Second Lieutenant Istvan Kovacs were killed in this action.

Jani and Kalauz fled headlong through the vineyards. Then Gyuri Kalauz was hit and collapsed into the snow. Jani tore the pack off his friend's back, threw away his rifle, and carried him for more than a kilometer. Finally Jani buried him at the edge of the road. It was so cold that the tears froze on Jani's cheeks.

The next day the survivors were rounded up outside Chapdi and ordered to dig foxholes two hundred meters apart. There were two soldiers in each. By the end of the day the living were eight hundred meters apart. During the night the Russians surprised and disarmed them. That is how Jani Habetler was taken prisoner.

❖   ❖   ❖   ❖   ❖   ❖

In September Kato Reich gave birth to a healthy little girl. A linen band around her wrist said *Maria Reich*. Gizike took chicken broth, pastry, and stewed fruit to the pale, happy mother.

Gizike was expecting too. She bore a little girl in the same hospital a few days later. This baby was christened Agotha in the Calvin Place Church. Istvan Hires came home on leave; he brought his wife roses and told the family that the Germans had lost the war, now everyone had to try very hard to survive until it was all over.

"We'll see what happens then," he said.

Ten days later Hires' battalion office moved to Pet.

On October 28, Colonel Kocis, the Commandant of the Ludovika Academy, ordered the evacuation of the school. The Jewish forced-labor battalion packed the museum treasures into crates and trucked them to the Ferenczváros Freight Station. Lieutenant Colonel Jozsef Rozas sent for Janos Habetler.

"Here are six fillers," he said. "You still have four fillers change from yesterday. Go get me a copy of *Virradat*."

The Colonel read the paper while the paintings were being lifted off the walls. When all the display cases were empty, he laid down the paper and asked the assistant guard:

"When the Bolshevik tide sweeps away our sacred fatherland, what will you do?"

Habetler was baffled. The idea had never occurred to him.

On October 31, 1944, the Ludovika Academy Special pulled out of the Ferencvaros Railway Station. It was bound for Kormend. Then they rolled on toward Szent Gotthard. At half past ten the morning of February 2, they crossed the border into Germany. Lasznik was the first stop on German soil. Colonel Kocis ordered a Protestant service to be held under the open sky, in the below-zero weather, at the edge of a fir forest. Then they went on to Dresden.

The first two days there the soldiers unloaded the freight cars. On the third day there was an air raid. The city was destroyed. The next night and day were the most terrible Janos Habetler ever was to experience. More than 10,000 people died, including Colonel Vilmos Matyas and many other Hungarians. The Academy Special steamed out of the flaming city to Tirschenreuth. The museum treasures were stored in a cellar of the church under Colonel Rozas' supervision.

Janos Habetler shared a room with Colonel Vilmos Matyas' mother on the ground floor of Wetzerstrasse 214. They paid rent to their landlord, Otto Assenkammer, a one-legged soldier, with bacon, lard, canned goods, and rum. They had plenty. The elderly lady sniveled constantly. At night she clutched her jewelry box, refused to go to bed and often wet her pants. This aggravated Habetler so much that he did something he had never done before in his life. He drank half a liter of rum, called the elderly lady an old sow, cursed, and threw up all over the room.

Air raids were frequent in Budapest too. Several times a day in school the girls were led to shelter. But if the scream of

the alarm sirens caught them on the street Hajnalka and Eszter rushed home instead of seeking safety in an arched building entrance. In their own cellar Maria Pek would put her
arms around them and they felt safe.

Most of the day Maria Pek was alone with her grandchild Agotha. Tortured by horrible thoughts, she felt terrified
and defenseless against war. Gizike was not afraid. When the
streetcars weren't running she walked all the way home from
Ujpest after her shift. Kato Reich did not wear a yellow star.
Maria Pek would not let her. She went to see Bela Sapadt.
The housepainter had joined the Arrow Cross and wore the
green shirt. She asked him, "If I do not let her wear the star,
do you think she'll have trouble?"

Bela Sapadt's answer was "Rubbish! Nobody would harm
that girl!"

And indeed nobody did. In the box factory on Agtelek
Street where she worked the girls spoke to her affectionately,
the regulars from the Harp Tavern often stopped her on the
street to tell her how beautiful her little girl was. The innkeeper wanted to give her some money but she wouldn't take it.
She ate at the Habetlers'. Maria Pek took care of, bathed, and
kissed Kato's child with the same love as she did Agotha. She
tended her, played with her and when she cried she sang to
her, ten, fifty times, over and over:

Hopla, Hopla, Hopapa
Here we go with a Hopseesa!

When a government decree ordered all Jews to move into
designated Jewish houses and Kato Reich had to leave, Maria
Pek cried bitterly. Every single day she sent one of the girls
with dinner and supper. Twice Bela Sapadt went to visit Kato,
taking chocolate and a rattle for the baby.

The Shell Refinery was afire, blocks of houses were lev-
eled, and the streets were strewn with corpses. Maria Pek's
nerves gave out. Screaming hysterically, she attacked Gizike
and refused to let her go to work. Every time Hajnalka or Esz-

ter stepped outside, she pulled them back into the apartment by the hair. She listened for sounds from the street. That night she crept around the kitchen in a nightgown, barefoot watered the flowers, soaked dried beans, and tried to write letters. Finally she dropped the pen and folded her hands.

"My Lord, how can you do such a thing?" She spoke quietly and stared rigidly at the crack in the blackout curtain until the dawn shone through.

Unexpected, Janos Habetler's foster mother arrived to take them all to Brügecs. She clapped her hands impatiently.

"Let's go, let's go," she said, "or the truck will leave without us!"

Maria Pek grabbed a few things and ran down the stairs.

The truck sped along. Maria Pek held Agotha on her lap, the girls huddled together. It was already pitch-dark under the canvas when Maria Pek remembered Kato Reich.

"Dear God!" she said. "We left her!"

Nobody said anything.

It was quiet in Brügecs. Maria Pek took care of the household, in the evening wrote letters and crocheted pink dresses for Agotha and Kato Reich's baby. The Habetler girls enjoyed themselves. Gizike took Eszter and Hajnalka to the cemetery; they read the inscriptions on the tombstones. Hajnalka played with the peasant children and watched the geese bathing in the shallow pond. For the first time in her life Eszter showed interest in a boy, a pale, seventeen-year-old divinity student. The two of them sat under the bare mulberry tree and read classical Hungarian poetry. The boy had tuberculosis; he was drafted into the Levente Youth Corps where he caught cold and died.

❖   ❖   ❖   ❖   ❖   ❖

The Habetlers returned to Budapest in April 1945. Their building had been damaged. Maria Pek plastered the walls and painted the whole apartment. She dipped a skein of yarn in paint and slapped it against the wall to make a pattern. Painting lines was Hajnalka's job. Eszter, who was awkward and uncoordinated, proved completely useless.

Gizike worked at the Magyar Cotton Factory. Her name was always posted on the bulletin board as one of the three best workers in the plant. In addition to the flour, beans, dried peas, oil, and corn meal that she earned as a salary, she got frequent bonuses of cotton and synthetic materials. In July she started to work a night shift, too. She lost weight; by November she was down to 92 pounds. She collapsed. The District physician sent her to the Istvan Hospital in an ambulance but the examination showed there was nothing the matter with her. She was just exhausted.

Maria Pek searched the official list of the dead posted in the yard of the Gabor Bethlen Square Synagogue but she never found the names of Kato and Maria Reich.

Hajnalka and Eszter completed the eighth grade and then went to the Pedagogical High School.

At the beginning of February Endre Küvecses fell off a streetcar platform as it lurched around the curve at Boraros Place. He died in the street. A Calvinist minister held the funeral services at the Rakoskeresztur Cemetery. Anna Küvecses sobbed bitterly; her three sloe-eyed sons had to drag her away from the open grave. Maria Pek went over with her daughters and embraced the widow.

A Communist moved into Uncle Reich's apartment. He was a tall, gaunt man with a fat, thick-legged wife. The superintendent of the building announced that the new tenant would deliver a speech: everybody was to assemble in the courtyard. Saturday evening a kitchen table covered with a red cloth was set in front of the superintendent's door. The new tenant, poorly clothed and unshaven, climbed up on the table and in a slow, flat voice made the following speech:

"Comrades! First of all let me tell you that my name is Sandor Seres. I was born at Bonavolgypuszta Manor in 1903. I was eleven years old, Comrades, when World War One broke out. There were eleven of us children. When the War started I was taken out of school—I wasn't even allowed to finish fourth grade. Instead, I was sent into the fields of the manor. I had to work from sunup in the morning to sundown in the evening for a few fillers. Dear Comrades, my father was a railroad switchman whose pay was insufficient to support the thirteen of us. That's why from early spring deep into the winter I had to shiver in rags and shoes full of holes all day long. Besides, I starved a lot because the long work hours melted all the fat off your bones. Let us never forget this! Especially in the summer, during the harvest, we had to get up at three o'clock in the morning and often stay in the fields until eleven o'clock at night. Then, Comrades, when the Revolution of 1919 came, I was sixteen years old and I ran away. Then I was a tailor's apprentice. I am sure many of you remember what the life of an apprentice was then . . . that's another thing we must never forget . . . we must never forget that we had to do all kinds of household chores. Where there were little children —as was my case—you even had to wash the dirty diapers and even empty the chamber pots. Comrades, when I had finally finished my apprenticeship, the master tailor released me, but I could not find work. Alas, that is how it was! Finally I had to take a job at very low wages. Fate tossed people around, Comrades, and finally fate taught me how to work. I became a union man and participated in the wage struggle. We tried to organize our fellow workers but our employers discharged us because we contaminated the men. Indeed I was unemployed many times. So, Comrades, that is how fate taught me while still a young worker where I belong. When the glorious Soviet Army liberated me, a great stone rolled from my heart. I knew immediately what I had to do; my first duty was to join the Party and spare no effort, either now or in the future, to indoctrinate you. Before I finish I want to add that I do not speak to you with some infamous thought, with any ulterior motive. I did not join the Party to feather my own nest. I am only a simple worker, I toil in the garment industry. And finally I ask you to listen to the Communists, because I tell you with the purest heart that they have protected the workers in the past and they will protect the workers in the future, always and forever, in the working man's true interest."

The assembled tenants applauded loudly. Among themselves they decided that fate had sent them a stupid man, but they laughed at him without malice because he seemed to be gentle and sincere.

It was March when the elder Janos Habetler came back to the Nagyfuvaros Street apartment. After he had been thoroughly interrogated at the Defense Ministry and his identity verified, he was put on the B list: those who were not eligible for government employment. He was assigned to the newsreel theater as a ticket-taker. In April he was fired because he admitted soldiers without tickets. Next he shoveled coal in the boiler room of the Municipal Hospital.

In May Istvan Hires returned from Russian captivity. He went back to his job making experimental pieces at the Magyar Precision Machines Factory. Everything that left his hands was perfect and before long his name was known all the way up in the Ministry of Industry. He was promoted to foreman, then production manager, and finally chief supervisor of the production department. His monthly wages rose to 3000 forints. He got his wife a job in the factory too. Gizike was clever, hard-working, conscientious, and very amenable. She did so-called white smock work on the P.4 instrument carts. Later she was trained to finish cast-iron mondrels on diesel pumps with a variety of chemical pastes to a tolerance of one thousandth of a millimeter.

Istvan Hires managed to get an apartment to share on Dery Street, not far from the Habetlers. He bought a big double closet, a studio couch with a built-in lamp, a table, and four chairs. Juli Csele sold him a framed paste-up of butterfly wings for sixty-five forints.

Days Maria Pek took care of Agotha: after supper somebody would take the child home to the Hires' apartment. Chief Supervisor Istvan Hires was inhumanly strict. If Gizike did not set a knife and fork at the side of his plate he glared at his food, and waited until a knife, spoon, and fork were laid out for him even though the kitchen drawer was right in front of his nose. He checked Hajnalka and Eszter's math homework every day. Succinctly and efficiently he explained even the most complicated math problems but would not help them with any other subject, no matter whether or not they had understood or how late they had to work to finish. Once he brought some candy home for Agotha. She reached for it with her tiny hands but he put it back into his pocket and called Juli Csele's grubby little girl from the passage and gave it to her instead. To Agotha he said:

"The next time your father brings you a present you will thank him for it before you reach."

Maria Pek paled with fury.

"Oh, you think I'm not raising your daughter right?"

Istvan Hires did not answer.

"You have no heart," Maria Pek said. "I don't care how many men take orders from you or how much money you make, in my eyes you are a big nothing."

Istvan Hires smiled.

"Some day your son is going to come home. I wonder what you'll tell him?"

Maria Pek said nothing for a long time.

"I will tell my son," she said finally, aiming her ice-blue eyes at her son-in-law's face, "I will tell him that I have cried more tears than there is water in the ocean."

A few days later Maria Pek caught a bad cold while washing clothes in the drafty kitchen. Her fever soared and her skin burned to the touch, but she couldn't sweat. She refused to let anyone call a doctor.

"Bring me liquor!" was her demand.

Three days and nights she drank, slept, and babbled incoherently whenever she woke up. On the fourth day she got up at five o'clock in the morning, washed herself from head to toe, ironed white collars for Hajnalka and Eszter, a shirt for her husband and prepared breakfast. When the family, sleepy, frightened and amazed, came into the kitchen, she said:

"Fit as a fiddle, Pappa. The beautiful widow will have to wait a while longer!" And a happy grin lit up her wrinkled face.

The girls did well at school. This was entirely Eszter's doing. She badgered her younger sister to desperation; if Hajnalka made the slightest mistake in her homework, Eszter tore the page out of her notebook and made her do it all over again. Then Hajnalka would cry; the girls pulled each other's hair. Whereupon Maria Pek would slap them both until they sat down at the kitchen table again and bent over their books, often past midnight. Eszter was a stubborn and stingy tyrant. When they went to the indoor swimming pool, she hid their carfare and Hajnalka had to recite the next day's lesson while they trudged across town. With the pocket money she saved in various ways she bought skirts, blouses, stockings, and underclothes for both of them. She picked everything, too. If her sister tried to protest, she looked out of ice-blue eyes and said:

"Don't argue! Your taste is abominable!"

Eszter did have good taste.

On winter Sundays they sat huddled together and harmonized. Both of them loved music passionately and had an astonishingly good ear. Habetler, Hires, and Bela Sapadt played cards while Agotha played with Juli Csele's little girl.

One such afternoon Maria Pek was embroidering a sofa pillow with flowers and Eszter's initials. "Your dowry," she said to her daughter.

Eszter blew up.

"Don't say things like that to me! I'm never going to get married!"

Maria Pek smiled and rested her claw-fingered hands in her lap.

"Oh yes you will, my daughter," she said. "First you, then your sister. I want to see your happiness and my grandchildren."

The first party that Hajnalka and Eszter went to was given at a friend of Hajnalka's, a girl named Angyal. Her parents lived in Telepi Street near the Nandor Neruda Pharmaceutical Plant; the whole neighborhood smelled of camomile. Lajos, one of the Küvecses boys, escorted the two girls. Hot chocolate and cake were served. The dancers circled around a polar bear fur spread on the living room floor. Hajnalka was not asked to dance, she wasn't even noticed. She was given charge of the record player. Until eight o'clock in the evening she played "Like a sudden flame," and "The rhumba was my ruination" and gloomily watched the dancers, the coquettish girls who knew how to cuddle up to the pleasant, brazen boys from the Gymnasium, how to smile at them, admire them. After the party, Hajnalka sullenly trailed home after Eszter and Lajos. At home, she waited until Eszter crawled into bed to declare:

"Sickening nonsense!"

Some time later there was a costume party at Anna Küvecses'. Eszter went as a pageboy; Hajnalka wore a black-and-crimson-striped peasant skirt with a white linen blouse and braided her hair. She was full of energy, flitted about gaily, laughed very hard. She could barely catch her breath between dances. At that party she made her first conquest—his name was Dodi, he was the best athlete on the parallel bars and the best tumbler at Calvinist High School. He became her constant escort to parties and school affairs. All the other girls stared enviously at the muscular, broad-shouldered boy and at Hajnalka's cute pixie face.

The boys liked Hajnalka. They considered her a pal and if they left the room to tell a dirty story, they always said: "Hajnalka, you can come along!"

The other girls wailed and whispered and later insisted that Hajnalka repeat the joke, which she always did.

New Year's Eve 1948 the Habetler family was preparing to go to the House of Culture at the Magyar Precision Machine Factory. Hajnalka, who felt ill, did not want to go, but Maria Pek declared:

"The family must be together on New Year's Eve because then they'll stay together through the new year."

They had a table to themselves. Maria Pek was wearing a dark-blue high-buttoned dress with tiny tulle leaves around the neck. Her blonde, graying hair was braided and pinned in a wreath. Habetler wore a dark-blue, Istvan Hires a dark-gray pinweave suit, and Gizike a tailored suit of the same material. Hajnalka and Eszter had on black skirts and white blouses.

They ate jellied pigs' knuckles and frankfurters, Istvan Hires ordered wine in a quart bottle, which only he and Maria Pek drank. Occasionally the Chief Supervisor invited a shop foreman or an elderly worker to have a glass with them at the table; otherwise Hires remained conscious of his rank and only acknowledged the countless greetings with curt, polite nods. A blond, wavy-haired lathe operator did not take his eyes off Hajnalka; finally he screwed up courage enough to ask her to dance. A friend who was with him danced with Eszter. The four of them danced virtually without pause in the hall shimmering with confetti, streamers, and Japanese lanterns. At midnight the lights were turned off. The two young men solemnly wished the Habetler family a happy New Year. It was dawn when they walked the family home in the falling snow.

A few days later the young men called on the sisters. The next time they asked Maria Pek's permission to take Hajnalka and Eszter to the movies. Thereafter the four of them went out a lot; sometimes the young men met the girls on the street near the High School and took them for a walk on the Danube embankment. One day Istvan Hires sent Hajnalka to pick up a package in Kispest, an hour's ride from home. The blond boy went along for the ride. It was dark before they found the house. On the way back to the streetcar stop they kissed each other in the dark street. After that they kissed often.

The other lathe operator got into a silly argument with Eszter and she stopped seeing him. Hajnalka continued to go out with the other fellow. In the spring they saw *Hamlet*. The young man liked to hold Hajnalka's hand but his moist, clammy palms made her feel uncomfortable. Finally she dropped him unceremoniously.

Music and singing were major subjects at the Pedagogical High School. Habetler rented a piano from Bela Henz, who had been a tuner at the Ludovika Academy. Usually the girls practiced only the assigned exercises because they could not stand their own clumsy plunking. Sometimes, though, Eszter got carried away and played a Bartok folk song, most often her favorite, "They killed a fellow for his sixty forints." She would close her eyes, purse her lips, and tremble with excitement.

Hajnalka spent hours searching for chords, she liked their clean sound, but when she hit a wrong key, she was not displeased either. But dissonant sounds irritated Maria Pek.

"Hajnalka, can't you play anything else?" she would ask.

They sang a great deal too, madrigals, folk songs, opera, and jazz. They despised the popular dance music that came over the radio and got mad every time they heard the hit song "Rozsa." Whenever Hajnalka heard a pretty tune which appealed to her she improvised a modern arrangement for the melody. One day she met some musicians at a party given by a classmate named Lucie. That's where Hajnalka and Laci Sima met. He was twenty-six years old, of medium build, wore glasses, taught Russian and mathematics in a boys' school. He also played the trombone. He had his own combo with trombone, tuba, saxophone, clarinet, drum, and piano. A week later, Hajnalka saw him at Lucie's house again. Laci Sima had sensational news: he had made a jazz arrangement of the theme from Chopin's *Impromptu* in C minor. He handed out the sheet music. Hajnalka sang mezzo-alto, Eszter mezzo-soprano, Lucie soprano, Rudi bass, Laci Sima tenor. First they listened to a record of Bing Crosby's interpretation, then they tried to sing Laci's version. They decided that it sounded good.

On Sundays Laci Sima's combo played in a dancing school downtown on Molnar Street. It was there that the two Habetler girls saw wild, rhythm-crazed Western dances for the first time. When one couple was particularly good, the other dancers cleared a circle around them and watched until they were exhausted and another couple took their place. Whenever Hajnalka could find a partner, she jerked and panted, beside herself, rolling her eyes frantically. But Eszter would not dance. If a policeman or inspector approached, the orchestra slowed down to a sedate tango.

Hajnalka's dates with Laci Sima were always in espressos. He talked about school and his pupils. He told her that he knew no Russian; he would glance at the material prepared on his desk while quizzing his class; nobody noticed. Hajnalka told him about her preparations for her finals and raved about modern music. Then they kissed.

Maria Pek did not like Laci Sima. She said that he was a dirty-eyed debauched man who must have lied to many women in his life. It was not hard for Hajnalka to break off with him. Laci Sima had not touched her heart, he had merely been interesting company.

In the spring the school choir rehearsed Händel's Hallelujah Chorus. The short, fat Nikodemus twins, who were also in the choir, asked Eszter and Hajnalka for dates but the girls laughed. Shortly before graduation the school choir gave a recital at the Academy of Music.

Both girls graduated with honors. Proud Janos Habetler kissed them on the forehead. Sandor Seres congratulated them and made a speech in the kitchen. In his long-winded, soporific way, he described the misery of the people under the Horthy régime, dwelled at great length on the struggles of the poor, the strikes, the jails, and the hangings, and analyzed the defeat of Hitler and fascism. Then, unexpectedly, he spoke about the dignity of work and attempted to show the girls the magnificent promise of their future life.

"One must love work," he said. "No matter where fate throws you, you must never forget to remember that your parents had to struggle for a crust of bread in a villainous, people-oppressing world ruled by gentlemen. But now I can declare to you, it all belongs to you, the land, the factories, all of socialism-building Hungary. Our country now belongs to the men who emerged from the barracks and cellars of the slums.

And behind them are the thousands of landless peasants. Together they will bring about the death of imperialism through the power of the workers under the leadership of the Communist Party. Dear Hajnalka and Eszter, before you set out on your beautiful paths, let me tell you this, listen to me, a true Communist: Love the machines, learn the sciences, study the Marxist ideology, because it will give you faith and most powerful strength. If I may say so, it is the most exalted faith, more sacred than anything, than even the Bible because it redeems mankind and creates a paradise of abundance. And no working man can live without this faith, without it he would be in an unworthy and pitiful swamp. Do not forget that knowledge is power, but knowledge and well-being are not given free, one must study and struggle for it.

"Therefore, dear Hajnalka and Eszter, I counsel you from a sincere heart to live a simple, disciplined life, to fulfill the tasks that are entrusted to you with unswerving will and then you will create for yourselves, for your families, for your coming children and beautiful marriage a happy life in our magnificent socialism-building land. That is what I wish you now, both in my own name as well as in the name of my wife, on this occasion of your entry onto the road of life."

The girls listened to him seriously, politely. They only laughed loudly, heartily, after he had gone out of the door.

The graduation banquet was held in the garden of the Margaret Island Casino. The Habetler girls wore pale-green dresses with beige high-heeled sandals. They smoked and chattered at the long table. Later a tall, thin blond boy asked Eszter to dance. His name was Jeno Filato; he worked in an office and played the saxophone. After the banquet he walked the girls home and asked Eszter for a date. They met in a sweet shop. Jeno kissed Eszter's hand, ordered chocolate flips, and then began to describe how he imagined life with Eszter.

"I'd be a famous musician," he said, "known throughout the world. We'd attend receptions, me in a dinner jacket and you in silver shoes and a snow-white evening gown covered with jewels."

He spoke with a quiet smile, occasionally he raised an eyebrow ironically to show that all this was a silly game, a dream, but Eszter saw something touching in his eyes. That was the first time Eszter kissed a boy.

Hajnalka got a job as a clerk in a tractor factory, Eszter in a shoe factory. They each earned 500 forints a month. Hajnalka hated her job. She made up the payroll from worksheets, first in the casting shop, then in the Number 2 lathe shop. The shop was old and dirty and the windows were caked with grime. One had to go up four metal steps into a glass cage in which there were five flat-topped desks. Two were for the payroll clerks, three for the foremen. The plank floor was soaked with oil; thick casting dust was everywhere. Work began at seven o'clock in the morning. At half past three in the afternoon Hajnalka went home, slept for an hour, washed up and rushed out on a date.

Eszter made up her payroll in a sunny office where a fan circulated the air.

At the beginning of summer Istvan Hires bought an outboard motor for his rowboat. Occasionally the girls went out to spend Sunday but they did not feel at ease. Gizike was always crying and the atmosphere was strained. Besides, there was no place nearby to dance or listen to music.

Habetler developed an ulcer working in the boiler room, so he was transferred to a less strenuous job as a guard on a coal-delivery truck.

"What does the beautiful widow think of you now?" Maria Pek asked and went about preparing diet meals for him.

Jeno Filato and his friends became daily visitors in the Nagyfuvaros Street flat. They were young musicians full of dreams and illusions. They brought along their instruments and played until nine o'clock, Janos Habetler's bedtime. Fece played the piano, Filato the E-flat saxophone, Szeles the trombone, Ervin the tenor saxophone, and Laci Szeibor the drums. Fece, the bandleader, was talented and had perfect pitch. He wouldn't stand for any nonsense at rehearsals. When he turned his Mephistophelian face toward his friends and raised his thick black eyebrows, even the girls kept quiet. He had made a vocal arrangement of "Temptation." He was crazy about Hajnalka. They kissed in cafés. One day he showed up with two engagement rings, but Hajnalka handed them back to him with a laugh.

"Don't be silly!"

Fece put the rings back in his pocket. "It doesn't matter," he said. "Just let me know when you don't think it's silly any more."

Around this time girls began to wear their hair short, like boys. Hajnalka was one of the first to have hers cut. Her favorite outfit was a hobble skirt made of greenish herringbone with a light-brown leather belt. In the Inner City she bought a shantung blouse with fine hemstitching to go with it. That's what she wore to Jeno Filato's party.

Filato lived with his divorced mother in a comfortable four-room apartment; his father, who had been a textile wholesaler, had fled to London with a new wife. Everybody was there. They danced, sang, and listened to long-playing records. Later Fece spoiled the mood by getting drunk and moaning about his love troubles. He made such a fool of himself that Hajnalka got fed up and set her cap for Ervin. She followed him from room to room, making eyes and flashing her teeth, snuggling close in his arms when they danced. But Ervin was reluctant because he loved and respected his friend. Hajnalka started this game around midnight. Toward dawn they were kissing in the hall. The next day Ervin confessed everything to his friend. They shook hands and Fece wished Hajnalka happiness.

Ervin had blond hair, snow-white teeth, a boyish grin, and dreamy blue eyes. He and Hajnalka loved each other very much. They hid in sweet shops and played a game they had invented. One of them would kiss out a song on the other's mouth until the other guessed the title. One day Ervin unbuttoned Hajnalka's blouse and kissed her naked breast. Neither of them could speak for a long time.

Sometimes Ervin and his band got to play at factory dances when a regular band couldn't be found. The two girls always tagged along. Wherever they went Ervin played "Stardust" especially for Hajnalka—he could make his saxophone talk. And Filato stared at Eszter from the bandstand. He was very much in love. He wrote a song and dedicated it to her. One summer evening he sat down at the Habetlers' piano and sang it. Janos Habetler liked it very much and said so several times. Istvan Hires shrugged and called it sentimental trash. Eszter screamed at him, they quarreled loudly until Maria Pek came in from the kitchen, slapped her daughter, and told Istvan Hires to get out his mandolin and show what he could do! Then they all sat down to supper. Later in the evening Sandor Seres, the Communist, dropped in. Maria Pek smiled and poured him a glass of wine.

"Did you come to preach to us, Sanyi?" she asked. "We're always glad to listen to you but you really ought to shave. It's not nice to make speeches looking like that. If I were your wife, I'd thrash you."

"I'm very tired, dear Maria," Sandor Seres answered seriously. "I rest very little, believe me. Fate taught me where I belong and I cannot pause in the Party's incessant fight for truth."

"Who is the enemy?" Maria Pek asked. "Tell us, Sanyika. You know, sometimes I think that you yourself don't know. You rave and storm and talk into the wild blue yonder until you yourself don't know why . . ."

Sandor Seres sat on the edge of the sofa, straight as a ramrod, his knees pressed together. He drank to the Habetler family's health in small sips.

This is how he replied to Maria Pek:

"You see, my dear Maria, I am a stupid man, I know that's what you all say about me after I leave here. You say it, Maria, not because you want to hurt me, but only as a joke, so that your family can laugh at me. That doesn't matter, I never claimed to be smarter than anyone else, I only try to fight for truth in the position the Party has assigned me to. And that is not easy, indeed it is very difficult. To illustrate, let me tell you about one of my battles.

"I had a colleague who was dismissed because there was a labor surplus. He said the factory belongs to me, I work for myself and yet dismissed myself, even though I don't want to quit. I overheard him and asked him what he was saying. First I began to explain by repeating exactly what he had said, that the factory was his, he worked for himself and yet he had dismissed himself, even though he did not wish to leave his job. He agreed that what I said was indeed exactly what he had said. Then I politely asked him what he had done for the factory to think that the factory belonged to him. Because in my opinion, only he who does something for the community can consider the factory his property. He answered that he was not a greedy man, he did not want to deprive anybody of the chance to do voluntary community work. I replied that there was no need to take anything from anybody, everyone would have a small share if everybody did something. But he who does not want to do his share can easily defend himself this way. A man like that should not claim that the factory belongs to him, he should be happy that the community suffers him in society. If everybody did his share of community work, it would not happen that certain conscientious and devoted men don't get home until after midnight, as late as one o'clock in the morning. People who get enough rest work better the next day than those who do their share of community work after their regular working day.

"This story got around. The union sent a delegate and I was chosen to speak to him. When I told him what had happened in full detail, I was praised and told that not everybody could have explained so well."

"You are a stupid man, Sanyika," said Maria Pek. "I'm afraid you don't understand anything about politics either, because what you have just told us is a huge piece of nonsense. You sit here as if you had swallowed a stick and talk gibberish. Better have another glass of wine instead, and sing along with us."

Sandor Seres refused the second glass of wine. He stood up.

"My dear Maria, I am in a very difficult position. Your only son, who participated in the war of aggression against the heroic Soviet Union is now enduring long captivity. How can anyone move your maternal heart to the most beautiful of causes now? But once your son returns in good health and the tears no longer flow from your eyes, you will understand the policies of the Communists. I can only tell you that happiness is waiting for you. Your family came from below, from the depths, just as I did, just like all poor people, but you will see the dizzying perspectives for a good life of your daughters and of your coming grandchildren and then you will ask me, 'How did you come to be so clairvoyant?' and I will answer, 'Fate taught me where I belong, to the Communists, because they create for the working people peace and well-being.' "

He apologized to the Habetlers for the intrusion, shook everyone's hand, and left.

❖   ❖   ❖   ❖   ❖   ❖

Late in the fall Jani Habetler came home. After he washed up, Maria Pek admitted the neighbors who noisily crowded into the kitchen. Sandor Seres introduced himself and shook hands with the returned P.O.W.

"Work awaits," he said. "You stand before a great and glorious future in the magnificent socialism-building People's Democracy of Hungary."

The elder Habetler bustled around Jani, laughing and crying, rushed down to the Harp for wine, urged everybody to drink, and very soon was tipsy himself. Hajnalka and Eszter arrived. They eyed the strange, muscular man; they seemed embarrassed, ill-at-ease, as they kissed their brother.

Finally Maria Pek ordered the neighbors out of the flat, fried fish, made cheese noodles. After supper she aimed her ice-blue eyes at her son.

"Kato Reich is dead," she said to him. "The little girl's name was Maria."

The elder Habetler shook his head.

"Such a pity, such a pity," he muttered drunkenly. "I liked her father too. They were very decent, lovable people."

Gizike burst into tears.

"Father, keep quiet," she shouted. "Please shut up!"

Silence fell over the family. Finally Jani said he was tired. Maria Pek made up the beds and everyone went to sleep.

Next day the girls bought Jani a suit, a shirt, a tie, and a pair of shoes. A few days later he began to operate a lathe in the Anyalfold Metal Plant.

❖   ❖   ❖   ❖   ❖   ❖

New Year's Eve the Habetler girls threw a party. Maria Pek baked and cooked. The old people drank wine and played cards while the young ones danced and sang. An hour before midnight Maria Pek said to Jeno Filato:

"Go and get your mother. It's not right for her to be alone on New Year's Eve."

The boy kissed both of her claw-fingered hands. He and Eszter left to fetch his mother in a taxi. It was immediately obvious that the bejeweled lady with dyed blonde hair felt out of place in the Nagyfuvaros Street. She held court on a chair, haughtily shaking her head when offered something to eat or drink; she refused everything. Juli Csele and Bela Sapadt made an effort to be nice, but she looked at them so coldly that they slunk away. Jani, sitting in the corner on his father's footlocker, did not take his eyes off the woman. Finally he stood up.

"A curse on any woman," he said loudly, "who has never put her hands even in cold water!" He went out, slamming the kitchen door so hard that two glass panes crashed to the floor. The girls whimpered. Istvan Hires laughed loudly. Maria Pek went over to the woman.

"What are you preening about?" she asked. "Take off your blouse, and I'll wash it for you."

Jeno Filato, blushing to his ears, took his mother by the arm and left without a word. Maria flung a shawl over her shoulders and went out to look for her son. She found him leaning against the shutter of the barber shop across the street from the Harp, watching the slow snowfall. Wordlessly he went home with her and took a seat among the card players. The old men were arguing in wine-laced voices, cursing each other's good hands and childishly rejoicing over every trick. Once in a while Istvan Kalauz turned to Jani and asked stupidly:

"You say he's dead?"

And Jani would nod in reply.

At the other side of the room the young ones were making a racket.

Eszter jilted Jeno Filato. In reply he sent her a reed from his saxophone, broken in two, with a note that he was going to kill himself.

❖   ❖   ❖   ❖   ❖   ❖

Winter passed, and spring. At the end of summer Istvan
Hires asked his mother-in-law not to let Agotha play with Juli
Csele's little girl. An ugly quarrel broke out. Maria Pek ac-
cused her son-in-law of snobbishness.

"Who do you think you are? What do you take yourself
for?" she shouted. Jani took Hires' side. He said that Juli
Csele was a bitch and a thief who was bound to wind up in
jail. And her daughter would be no different.

Juli Csele worked in the chocolate factory and stole like
a magpie. When she didn't feel like going to work, she drank
strong black coffee mixed with salt, which gave her a high
fever. Then, while officially on sick leave, she spent the day at
the flea market, trading. Occasionally she made a deal but she
never had any money—it just slipped through her fingers. One
day Sandor Seres rebuked her. He was sitting in the Habetlers'
kitchen, ramrod straight, his face pale, anger flaming in his
eyes:

"Under the old system, anyone who damaged capitalist
society was punished right away, much quicker than today."
Seres stopped a minute, then continued in a loud, threatening
voice. "The capitalist watched over his wealth much more
closely than a great many people now watch over the wealth
of the People. People like you only worry about their own personal affairs, what they have to pay for out of their own pockets. Filth like you don't care how much the property of our
People's Democracy costs, as long as they don't have to pay
for it. When I was employed in industry, I was as careful
about the People's wealth as I am now, because I feel that if
we do not respect and take care of it, we are cheating ourselves."

Maria Pek turned from the stove to look at Seres.

"You lucky man," she said. "You don't work in a factory any more?"

"No I do not, dear Maria," he answered proudly. "A few days ago the Party lifted me out of the shop. I have been assigned to a strictly confidential field of work. I want you to know this right away, because I cannot answer any questions about my present activities or give you any other information."

Maria Pek smiled.

"Well, then I won't ask, Sanyika. So now you have become an important man, a Baron of Democracy. Some day maybe we'll even see your name in the newspaper and we will be proud and happy that you honor us with your visits. But, my dear Sanyi, I think you ought to shave more often and change shirts more frequently, too, so that in the end we won't have to be ashamed for you."

Sandor Seres was obviously deliberating how to reply.

"My dear Maria," he said finally, "you are right. Even though you constantly mock me, I know very well that you like me and that your sarcasm is not malevolence but well-meaning affection. And I am not angry with you. I believe that as a consequence of my educative efforts you will one day join the ranks of the Communist warriors, because that is where you belong, and your proletarian steadfastness will be a great help to the People's Democracy. And in connection with the problem previously mentioned, I wish to remark that a Comrade in competent authority called my attention to my appearance and I will act accordingly."

And sure enough, a few days later he came to see the Habetlers dressed in a well-cut suit, a silk shirt, and a neat tie, freshly shaved and well-groomed. From then on that is the way they always saw him.

Old man Habetler tried to tease Seres. Smiling broadly, he pricked him with hidden allusions to the Peace Bonds which every worker had to buy, to daily assemblies in the factories to listen to articles from the Party newspaper, *Szabad Nep,* and putting on a pious face naïvely asked Seres to explain the difference between the gentlemen of the old regime and the party workers and functionaries of the present. Sometimes Janos overshot his mark and Sandor Seres got angry and stayed away for days on end. One late-summer evening he said to Janos Habetler:

"Listen Janos, let's you and I talk openly, man to man. You consider yourself a smart man, even though you have never read a single newspaper or book in your whole life. You can barely read and write. Well, I don't consider myself a smart man, but I can tell you that this deficiency is not your fault, it is the crime of Horthy fascism which oppressed the people. I suffer from this burden too, as do many others of older-generation workingmen. I do not consider myself smart, but while the Germans were still fighting on Soviet soil, we who were already organizing the unions knew that when the situation in Hungary changed, every office and position would be held by men of our kind, and we knew that these people would be entirely different from those of the old régime. And that's what has happened! So what are you griping about? What in the name of God is bothering you? All your life you bowed to gentlemen. Is that what you miss? Why are you always sarcastic with me? I'll tell you why! Because you are a stupid man and you know nothing about the changes that have occurred in this world! And take notice! There can be no jeering at Marxist ideology, there can be no jeering at the new social order or at the Communists, in the ranks of whom I fight hard, untiringly, without sparing any effort, for the total happiness of your daughters, your son, your grandchildren to come."

Janos Habetler could not answer him. Maria Pek showed

Sandor Seres to the door. But they never said a word about the regrettable incident.

In the fall, gentle, blue-eyed Ervin was drafted and the crowd drifted apart. The day before he was to leave he came to say good-bye. Hand in hand he and Hajnalka wandered through the city. At dusk they stopped at the corner of the Boulevard and Rákóczi Avenue and watched traffic. Hajnalka said:

"Every week I will write you that I will love you until I die."

They had chocolate liqueur in the nearby Homer Café and kissed.

In midwinter a dance was held at the tractor factory. One of the Nikodemus twins was on the saxophone, the other on the trombone. A dark-haired man in his mid-thirties was at the drums. He looked good to Hajnalka. She made eyes at him and every time she danced by he returned her smile. During intermission the twins greeted Hajnalka and Eszter joyfully; they said proudly that the little combo was theirs and that they were getting to be known and were asked to play in more and more places. The drummer joined them and introduced himself. His name was Miki Mummel. He asked Hajnalka for a date.

They met every Wednesday afternoon in the Youth Espresso from six to eight, at the same dimly lit corner table upstairs. On their first date Miki Mummel told Hajnalka that he was separated and that he had a little girl ten years old. Then they kissed.

Miki Mummel was a colorful man and a good storyteller; though he used vulgar words, with him it was not repulsive. He spoke a great deal about the relationship between man and woman, he explained that if two people were in love, physical love was a natural consequence. Occasionally he recited poetry to Hajnalka, mostly François Villon. He spoke about the absurdity of life and lightly, as if he were joking, said that whenever Hajnalka was tired of being a virgin she should just let him know. Hajnalka would answer laughingly:

"Okay, I'll remember that."

They kissed on every date.

Hajnalka loved the fall of snow. Looking up at the clouds with her head tilted back, she felt as if she were floating toward the sky. She and Miki Mummel liked to hold each other tight and pretend that they were flying out of the world. They pelted each other with snowballs and laughed a lot, but Hajnalka always said good-bye at the corner of Republic Square; she would not let him walk her to her door. Hajnalka went dancing very often and kissed many boys. She recounted all of these passing adventures to the drummer. Mummel thoroughly examined the knight of the day; they had a great time making fun of him.

In March Miki Mummel shot off his mouth about politics somewhere and could not find a job anywhere except with the State Circus. Sadly he complained to Hajnalka that he had to create confusion while the trapeze artist swung up under the roof.

Every Sunday Hajnalka wrote a letter to Ervin, pressing her lips under her signature to make a red seal.

She and Eszter met two good-looking industrial draftsmen at a tea dance. Szilard Gulyas was blond, Laci Peres dark. They shared a room in the five-room apartment of a pensioned schoolteacher who was completely deaf. They invited the Habetler girls and their friend Angyal to a party they were giving. There was black coffee, liqueur for the girls, cognac for the men. It was a large room; an enormous Oriental rug covered one of the walls. A radio stood on a low coffee table in the corner. There were also four armchairs, several hassocks, a wrought-iron standing lamp, and a sofa with a coffee-brown cover. The first time the girls were there, they met a pudgy bespectacled medical student named Willy, a self-employed leather goods manufacturer, and an elderly man whose profession nobody knew. They played cards, listened to the radio, and told funny stories. Often there was a large and mixed group of people milling around the draftsmen's apartment, men and women appeared at the door, drank a cup of coffee or a cognac, exchanged a few words about films, fashions, praised the movie *Via Mala,* and then surrendered their places to others. The girls were fascinated by this restless coming and going.

Sometimes Hajnalka was alone with Szilard Gulyas in the apartment. She straightened up and aired the place, and once even made supper with whatever she could find in the kitchen cupboard. It was the first time in her life that she had made a meal by herself and she liked it. Szilard Gulyas talked about his parents. He told her that they lived in the provinces and that his father was a county official. He asked whether she could picture herself as the wife in an apartment like this. Hajnalka smiled and answered maybe. Then they kissed.

One fall evening the usual crowd of people dwindled; the Habetler girls, Angyal, Gulyas, Laci Peres, and Willy were alone in the apartment. Everyone was in a gloomy mood. Hajnalka wanted to go to Buda because she had heard that Ervin was playing the saxophone at a dancing school on Kapas Street.

"Let's go listen to 'Stardust,' " she begged her sister. "I'm sure he'll play it for us."

Eszter did not feel like going out in the rain. She and Laci Peres were curled up in the corner of the room. Angyal dimmed the standing lamp, sat down in an armchair, and gave her mouth to Willy. Hajnalka was at the window looking down into the dark street. Gulyas touched her hand lightly.

"Come on, let's not disturb them."

Gulyas did not turn on the light in the other room. They sat on the sofa. Hajnalka listlessly let herself be kissed in the dark. Nor did she protest when the man pushed her down on the sofa with a hard movement. A few minutes later her body contracted with pain. She said nothing, she did not cry as Gulyas' trembling hands turned on the little shaded light, she just stared at the man rigidly. Then she fixed her hair and walked back into the living room.

"Let's go!" she said to her sister.

On the street, Eszter, frightened, asked her, "What happened?"

Hajnalka turned her green face to her sister and shrugged.

"Jesus Maria!" said Eszter.

They walked home in silence. The elder Habetlers were at a grape harvest festival and Jani was already asleep. The sisters undressed and climbed into bed. Hajnalka fell asleep instantly. Eszter looked at her sister, stroked her short, boyish hair, and wept silently.

They never had anything to do with that crowd again.

❖   ❖   ❖   ❖   ❖   ❖

A few weeks later Miki Mummel, who had been in the provinces, phoned Hajnalka at the tractor factory. They arranged to meet in the Youth Espresso. Wryly, slightly bitterly, Hajnalka recounted her painful, silly experience. Mummel was furious. He slammed his fist on the table, called Gulyas an animal, a barbarian, a son of a bitch. When he had calmed down, he said that if he had been Gulyas, Hajnalka would have experienced great joy. They made a date to meet again in the Hauer Sweet Shop. Hajnalka knew that one of Mummel's friends lived in the Hauer building, so she arranged with Angyal to appear at six-thirty and ask her to go to the movies. Miki Mummel was in the Sweet Shop at six o'clock on the dot. He made small talk while Hajnalka waited for him to begin to maneuver. A few minutes before Angyal was supposed to come she asked:

"Why did you pick this place to meet?"

Miki Mummel looked surprised. He lit a cigarette and said:

"A friend of mine lives upstairs. I want you to come up with me."

Hajnalka looked hard at him for a moment.

"All right," she answered.

Just then Angyal arrived. Waving movie tickets, she began a clumsy story about what a hard time she had had finding the place. Then she bawled out Hajnalka for having forgotten that they had planned to go to a movie.

"Now come on," she said with transparent anger, "or we'll be late."

Miki Mummel smiled superciliously.

"Sell the ticket," Hajnalka said. "I can't go tonight."

And she went upstairs with Miki Mummel. Mummel's friend kissed her hand, asked her indulgence; he had something very urgent to do, he said, they should make themselves at home, there was cognac and coffee, they could leave the key with the superintendent. With that he left.

There was a painful silence.

Hajnalka asked:

"Don't you think this is a bit ridiculous?"

They stared at each other sadly.

Afterward Mummel lit a cigarette and said:

"You've been spoiled, little girl, spoiled forever."

❖   ❖   ❖   ❖   ❖   ❖

Every year before the blossoming of the acacia Maria Pek and Janos Habetler went to Brügecs. It was a spring Sunday. Gizike fell asleep on the couch, Jani had taken Agotha for a walk. Istvan Hires was bored, poked around in his notes, then asked Hajnalka and Eszter if they felt like music. The Corvin Restaurant had a good band. During supper Istvan Hires told them he had decided to buy a co-op apartment, he needed 20,000 forints; he would raise the money somehow. Two men sitting at an adjoining table stared at Eszter. One was dark and of medium build, the other blond and slender. Hajnalka was bored. She yawned and said it was time to go home and sleep.

As they were leaving the blond man stopped Eszter at the coat room. He apologized for being so forward and introduced himself.

"I'd like to see you sometime," he said.

The next day they met in the lobby of the Bristol Hotel. They danced and talked. The blond man told her that he was in charge of a construction project in Miskolc and that he owned a motorcycle with a sidecar. He asked Eszter where she worked, where she went for fun, how she spent her time altogether.

A week later they met again in the Hotel Astoria but they had nothing more to say to each other, so they just sat. Eszter decided that she would not date the blond man any more. A few days later he called long distance from Miskolc. He said that on Sunday he was coming to Budapest with a friend, he would meet her at the Emke Restaurant, could she bring her sister along.

Sunday evening in the Emke the friend, a dark, medium-height man introduced himself. His name was George Zentay. He sat at the table silent, his eyes glued to Eszter's face; whenever she looked back at him he smiled self-consciously. After a while he invited her to dance. He asked her to accompany him to the bar, he would like to introduce his father. The elder Zentay sat with a group of old men. He kissed Eszter's hand and declared that he had never seen such a beautiful girl. He introduced her to his friends as "my son's fiancée."

George Zentay left the bar to get Hajnalka and his friend. The elder Zentay made room for them, ordered "chocolate flips" and cognac, bought each of the girls a bouquet of roses. He danced with them and told amusing stories.

The following Sunday Eszter met George Zentay in the Palma Espresso. She was a half-hour late, but George Zentay was not angry. He looked at the girl with shining eyes and said: "I was afraid you had forgotten."

He ordered black coffee. He told her that he was a work-quota inspector in Miskolc; he was separated from his wife.

Eszter was amazed. "Such a child and already married?"

George Zentay did not reply. He began to talk about books, about Ferencz Herczeg, Cronin, Dostoievsky.

"They are good friends. Often they keep me company all night long."

Later they took a taxi to Buda, to the old Firenze Restaurant. They drank Cinzano. Zentay told her that his father had been an inspector of police. His mother had committed suicide. His stepmother drank secretly. Once, when he was still a schoolboy, she had come to his room naked and kissed him on the mouth. The despair in his sad face was touching. He took Eszter home in a taxi. They arrived at the house a few minutes after the front door had been locked and they had to ring for the concierge to let her in.

The first time Zentay met the Habetler family was on Eszter's nameday. He brought a basket of red roses, an album of sheet music, and a volume of Paul Geraldy's poems. They were in love. Every Sunday they rode to the country on Zentay's little Csepel motorbike.

That summer Hajnalka was assigned a vacation at Lake Balaton by the tractor factory where she worked. Eszter and George Zentay spent their vacation at Lake Balaton too—Eszter at Foldvar, Zentay at Balatonfenyves. One Saturday evening the three of them got together in the garden café of the Balatongyongye. Zentay brought along his vacation roommate Laszlo Dittera and Dittera's sister Margit. The young man had black hair and green eyes, he was twenty-three years old and was the son of a pensioned railway official.

Dittera was interested in abstract things, like yoga, hypnotism, spiritualism, graphology, and astrology. He danced with Hajnalka and asked if they could see each other in Budapest.

They met in the Youth Espresso. Dittera was wearing a steel-gray suit and a black onyx signet ring on his finger. He brought along a childhood friend who had gone to the Piarist High School with him. The blond, girlish-faced university student listened to his friend with wide-eyed admiration. Laszlo Dittera was saying that Christ was the greatest of all hypnotists. He explained to Hajnalka that when Jesus had changed water into wine at the wedding feast at Cana, it was mass hypnosis. Christ said: Now you are drinking wine—and the guests experienced a sensory delusion. Dittera went on to explain the resurrection of Lazarus by the fact that in the East there were still magicians who have themselves buried and then dug up after a specific time and are still alive. It was a matter of total concentration, he said, he practiced it too, but his experiments were rarely successful because other thoughts always crowded in. One must think of only one thing, that was the secret. He promised Hajnalka that one day he would show her the yoga postures, especially the one for withdrawing from the world, and he would teach her yoga breathing through the stomach.

After a while the girlish-faced student took his leave. He kissed Laci Dittera and nodded politely to Hajnalka. After he had left, Hajnalka talked about her family, music, and men.

They walked to Republic Square, where they sat on a bench and kissed.

❖ ❖ ❖ ❖ ❖ ❖

Eszter got engaged at Christmas.

George Zentay sublet a furnished room in Nagymezo Street from a National Fuel Enterprise official. On his birthday, Zentay asked Maria Pek to let the girls stay out until morning; they wanted to go dancing somewhere, he said. The three of them and Laci Dittera went to the little furnished room. Zentay had prepared smoked salmon, caviar, salami, and ham sandwiches. He uncorked a bottle of sparkling wine. Half of it spewed on the ceiling. They listened to music on the radio and then Zentay asked the girls to sing. They harmonized, "In a little Scottish town . . . are celebrating" and "Summer Time," and old Hungarian folk songs. George sang along; Dittera didn't because he was tone-deaf. It was well after midnight when Hajnalka declared that she was sleepy. Zentay spread a blanket and some cushions on the floor. Hajnalka and the Greek-faced boy lay down beside each other, fully dressed. Eszter huddled next to her fiancé on the narrow bed. They turned off the little lamp but they could not kiss for very long. Soon the dawn filtered in the window, a tram rattled somewhere. Eszter fixed her hair and said:

"It's morning, let's go home!"

At the end of February Dittera asked Maria Pek to let Hajnalka stay out late, there was going to be a party at his sister's fiancé's home, a small family gathering; it would not be over until after the house door was locked for the night. Jani lifted his yellowish eyes to the pretty boy's face but said nothing.

Margit Dittera's fiancé lived in Lonyai Street. His name was Gyula Szuhapa; he was an antique dealer permitted to operate in the private-enterprise sector. When the pale, moustached man of fifty opened the door, a shudder ran down Hajnalka's back; she felt as if she were looking at the face of a waterlogged corpse. . . . He took them into a large, high-ceilinged room. At the far end, in front of heavy drapes, a single shaded lamp supplied dim light. Everything in the room took on a brownish hue: the antique furniture, the sofas, the Oriental rugs on the floors and the tapestries on the walls. In the corner a pretty, bright-eyed airline stewardess was tending a tape recorder. Near her store-bought *hors-d'oeuvres* and drinks were set out on a low table. The girl-faced university student, his attractive, bespectacled girl friend, Margit Dittera, thin and thirty-five, and the antique dealer with his drowned face sat around on sofas and hassocks. Szuhapa was discussing sixteenth-century art. Dittera asked the antique dealer to show him the small reclining Buddha he was holding up. He and Hajnalka looked at it closely. The antique dealer smiled and remarked to Hajnalka that under a total dictatorship, Buddha should be a model to them all, his wisdom was silence. He kissed the girl's hand and presented it to her. Later Hajnalka crouched beside the tape recorder and helped the stewardess select tapes. At the sound of "Moonlight Serenade" she beckoned to Dittera. They folded back the rug and everybody danced. Dittera kissed Hajnalka's neck.

"This music is concentrated eroticism," he smiled.

Hajnalka closed her eyes and nodded: "Umm, you're right."

Next Ravel's *"Bolero"* swelled out of the machine. At the first bars, the stewardess swung her hips softly, began to dance alone in the dim light, with slow, beautiful movements, for her own delight. When the last muffled drumbeat had died away, she turned off the tape recorder.

"This dance should be danced naked, with veils," she said.

The antique dealer poured cognac for everyone and said he thought they should stop dancing and play a game instead. The players were to discard an article of clothing at every loss —playing for winnings would be boring.

They all settled down on the rug and rolled dice. Luck was with Hajnalka for some time. Dittera and his blond friend had already lost their ties and shirts, they were half-naked. On her first unsuccessful throw Hajnalka took off her shoes, then her stockings, then her garters. By this time, the drowned face had shed his socks; his flashing white underpants were only partially covered by his shirt. Every time Hajnalka looked at him, she had to laugh. After the next throw she turned serious. She got to her feet slowly and went to the far corner of the room, unbuttoned her collar, pulled the zipper down her black dress, and stepped out of it; returning to her place on the rug, she squatted there in her slip. Next, the stewardess took off her dark-blue tunic with the airline emblem on its sleeve; under it she was wearing only a sheer blouse. Then the bespectacled university student wiggled out of her dress. Margit Dittera was sitting in her underpants and bra. The antique dealer stared at Hajnalka. The girlish-faced young man snuggled up to Laci Dittera and caressed his back.

"Your skin is like velvet," he said.

It was Hajnalka's turn. She threw the dice and looked up frightened. She broke into a loud nervous laugh. Margit Dittera looked at her.

"Well, kids, I've had enough of this."

The drowned face got angry. It wasn't fair to spoil seven people's fun, he said. Margit Dittera made a gesture for him to be quiet, took his hand, and led him into the other room. The beautiful stewardess disappeared behind a brown door with the bespectacled university student. Bewildered, the girl-faced boy glared at Dittera, then followed the others. Only the two of them were left in the dim room. Hajnalka put Ravel's *"Bolero"* on the tape recorder and put her arms around Laci Dittera.

At the Nagyfuvaros Street apartment Jani Habetler made a scene—out of boredom, according to the girls—every afternoon. He watched his younger sisters wash up, comb their hair, make up, then he was up and at them.

"Where are you going now?"

"Out!" Hajnalka snapped.

"To the espresso, eh!" Jani thundered. "What in the hell do you do there all the time?"

Hajnalka pounded on the kitchen table.

"We sit!" she shouted. "We just sit!"

"We sit! We sit!" Jani roared.

Maria Pek burst into laughter.

"What else do you want them to do, for God's sake? Why don't you go with them?"

"By all means, do that!" said Eszter. "Come with us!"

Jani glared at her. "Me? Me, in a place like that?" he sneered.

In the evening he stirred up his father.

"The concierge had to unlock the door for them again last night," he exclaimed furiously. "All night they hang around with thieves, smoking like chimneys and drinking chocolate crap. That's no way for nice girls to behave! It's not decent!"

Maria Pek called him a fool, and they quarreled and shouted at each other. Finally Janos Habetler Senior declared that it was wholly improper and very saddening for the neighbors to be able to gossip about how the girls were allowed to stay out until after eleven o'clock at night. In serious tones he said to Maria Pek:

"I will not stand for this. Please tell your two daughters that if they are one single minute late tomorrow, there'll be trouble."

The next night the girls got in a few minutes after the house door had been locked. Habetler slid out of bed and slapped Eszter so hard that she fell to the floor. Then he hit Hajnalka. Maria Pek screamed, pushed her husband out of the room, then turned on her daughters.

"You asked for it," she yelled and shook her bony fist. "Now get to bed!"

Sobbing, Hajnalka turned to Jani.

"Now are you satisfied?"

Jani was lying on the divan. He looked at his youngest sister out of his yellowish eyes.

"I'd like to kick you both in the seats of your pants," he said.

Laci Dittera was a very attentive man. Whenever Hajnalka had a new hairdo or wore a different-color lipstick, he always noticed, kissed her hand, and praised her good taste. They kissed and hugged everywhere, in espressos, on the street, and at night in the building entrance. Everybody teased them. Once old man Zentay remarked that if they loved each other that much, they ought to get under a roof now and then. And he offered his own furnished room. A few days later Hajnalka smiled at Dittera and said:

"Well, why shouldn't we?"

Old man Zentay lived in Corvin Allee. He took them up to his room and left, saying that he would return around nine o'clock. For a while Hajnalka and Dittera kissed and petted in an armchair. Then Hajnalka asked the young man to turn around. She undressed, lay down in the bed and pulled the cover up to her chin. When Dittera crawled in next to her, she pressed her face against the wall. For a long time they lay side by side, smoking. Later Dittera said:

"It's no good this way, planned in advance."

"No," said Hajnalka. "It's no good."

They dressed and went out into the street. Hajnalka never saw the handsome young man again.

That summer George Zentay took Eszter and Hajnalka on a day's excursion to Siofok on Lake Balaton. At Szekesfehervar he got out of the train to buy a cold drink. When he came back, another man was with him; they had spent six months together in a select industrial training school. He was good-looking, modest, and shy; he was on his way to the Rest House of the enterprise where he worked. In the evening, on the way back to Budapest, he shared a compartment with them again. He stared at Hajnalka out of big, wondering, childlike eyes. Before they left the train he asked her whether they could meet again. Hajnalka laughed and said "Of course."

They met in the Youth Espresso. The young man's name was Miklos Szuha. He told her that he lived with his parents, who had been landowners, and that he was a job analyst for the Concrete-Road Building Authority. Unfortunately he had the wrong ancestors. No matter how hard he worked, he was constantly harassed and screened. His father was ill and his mother worked for the Home Industries Co-operative. They had a hard time making ends meet. He wished that he did not have to live in constant terror of losing his job. Hajnalka felt very sorry for him. On the way home they kissed.

Soon Miklos Szuha sat in the Habetlers' kitchen every night from seven to ten o'clock. Hajnalka loved him. She felt she was stronger, she sensed that he needed her. For the first time in her life the idea of having a child crossed her mind, a child by him, because he was handsome, clever, and honest. One night she mentioned the idea to Eszter, who said it would be a good mixture. In the same café where Ervin, the blue-eyed saxophone player had first kissed her breast, Hajnalka told Miklos Szuha that she was not a virgin.

"An evening turned out badly . . ."

Miklos Szuha kissed her.

"Marry me," he said.

At Christmas, at Eszter's wedding to George Zentay, Miklos Szuha brought engagement rings. After the holidays he asked Maria Pek's permission to take Hajnalka to a three-day pig-killing at his relatives' in the country.

Hajnalka never forgot those three days. They went to Siofok on Lake Balaton, where they rented a room from an old woman. The snow fell in fat flakes; the whole world seemed like a white dream. They spent most of the time in bed. Evenings they had their supper at the Fogas Restaurant and danced cheek to cheek. People sitting at the other tables looked fondly at the couple in love. They returned home half a day late. Maria Pek did not ask questions. She gave her youngest daughter a mighty slap.

They were married in February. Maria Pek made soup, boiled beef with horseradish, onion gravy, gooseberry and currant sauce, fried fish, chicken and pork, cheese squares, and several kinds of cake. Everyone in the building ate, drank, and sang. Istvan Hires made a beautiful toast and then Bela Sapadt wished the newlyweds great happiness on behalf of all of the neighbors. George Zentay took pictures with flashbulbs. After a few glasses of wine he pulled off his tie and began to sing in a thick voice:

"Hey, ho, fisherman, fisherman . . ."

Eszter looked at him sharply. "Shut up," she snapped.

Jani beckoned Hajnalka away from the table. He stuffed a wrist watch and 2000 forints into the pocket of her black suit.

"Buy some pots or something," he said, embarrassed.

Hajnalka stood on tiptoes and kissed her brother's cheek.

Toward the end of the evening old man Zentay blurted out that his son had been married before. Maria Pek paled. She said that if there weren't so many people present she would beat George Zentay to a pulp. Around midnight the newlyweds asked Maria Pek's permission to leave.

"It is not proper," Maria Pek replied sternly. "You will please wait until the guests have gone."

Then she broke into a smile. She called Janos. Hajnalka kissed her parents' hands. With tear-filled eyes, the old couple watched their youngest child leave home on Miklos Szuha's arm.

❖   ❖   ❖   ❖   ❖   ❖

A few days later the Habetler family had an unexpected surprise. Late one evening Sandor Seres knocked on the door. He and his wife had come to say good-bye.

"We are going away," Sandor Seres said. "We are taking an airplane to Rome and from there to Tel-Aviv, which is our final destination. Boris and I felt that we should not depart without saying farewell. We must not leave you in anger, dear Maria and Janos. We are now going to work for Socialism in the midst of Imperialism, you must work for it here at home, in our beautiful People's Democratic Fatherland. Since the Comrades have given us permission to write letters, I will give you our exact address, if you wish. You must follow the instructions carefully. First you must put the letter in two envelopes. The outside one is to be addressed as follows: Post Office Box 114, Post Office 72, Budapest. But on the inside envelope, in which you must put our letter, you write my name, Comrade Sandor Seres, Hungarian Legation, Tel-Aviv. That way you will only need a domestic stamp. Your letter will be delivered to us. If anything is not clear to you, I will be glad to explain once again whatever you do not understand."

Maria Pek wrote down the address and wished them a good trip. They kissed good-bye and said farewell.

Eszter had moved into her husband's furnished room in Nagymezo Street. Zentay was working in Budapest now, at the Milling Machinery Enterprise, but he frequently had to make inspection trips to the provinces. He earned 1330 forints a month, Eszter 700. The first month they were married they bought a radio. Otherwise they lived on a very strict budget. Sundays they would go to the country on Zentay's motorbike. In the third month of their marriage George Zentay came home drunk. When he climbed into bed with an imbecilic grin on his face, his breath reeking of wine, Eszter pulled away from him.

"You're disgusting. Don't touch me," she said. "I'm going to leave you."

Zentay guffawed.

"Then leave, my pet, leave."

In the morning he was sober. He kissed his wife and left on an inspection trip.

Eszter got dressed, went to Nagyfuvaros Street and said to her mother:

"I'm coming home!"

Jani helped her move her things; it took three trips to get everything. When Zentay returned from the provinces he stared at the empty room stupefied. He did not dare go to the Habetlers' because he was afraid of his mother-in-law and of Jani's yellowish eyes. He watched for Eszter across the street from the Habetlers' building. Finally she came out and he asked her to go to the Youth Espresso with him. After a short conversation Eszter angrily declared that she would not go back to him. Two days later Jeno Filato appeared at the Habetler flat, his face beaming. He kissed Eszter's hand and asked her to go dancing with him. In Nagyfuvaros Street Zentay waylaid them. Filato was frightened, but Eszter aimed her ice-blue eyes toward her husband and told him to stop his threats or she would call her brother.

For a week George Zentay sent his wife roses every day, then he telephoned her at the shoe factory and asked her to go out with him. They met in an espresso. Over a glass of Cinzano, Zentay quietly, sincerely begged her to forgive him. He swore that he would never get drunk again. He courted his wife with pretty compliments. He said smilingly, "I certainly won't let the prettiest girl in Budapest slip away from me."

Eszter went back to him. The next day old man Zentay was banished from Budapest, deported to Obat Pusta. Maria Pek sent him packages of food by way of George Zentay, who took a train to visit his father once a month.

When Eszter got pregnant Maria Pek ordered the young couple to eat at her house. For nine months she cooked for daughter and son-in-law, refusing all the while to take any money from them. Eszter gave birth to a little girl. It was a normal birth, but the child died in the hospital. On the death certificate it said that the cause of death was cerebral hemorrhage, but Eszter insisted that somebody had dropped her baby. Everyone in the family went to the funeral, except Eszter. She stayed home crying and shrieking hysterically, tearing her hair. Nine-year-old Agotha, who was assigned to watch her, cowered on the edge of the bed in fright.

❖　　❖　　❖　　❖　　❖　　❖

Hajnalka and Miklos Szuha lived in a large furnished room on the first floor of a private villa in Buda. It was a bright square room facing a garden full of flowers. Hajnalka sang all the time. They loved each other very much. And they both longed for a child. One Sunday night Miklos Szuha's father died in his sleep. Miklos did not cry; he just stared at his wife with big, frightened eyes. He was not allowed to help with the funeral arrangements. Hajnalka and the widow rushed from bureau to bureau collecting the necessary papers. The whole Habetler family went to the funeral. Maria Pek sent a wreath of real flowers. Miklos Szuha stood unsteadily beside the open grave. He would not let go of his mother's hand. Hajnalka took him home in a taxi. For a long time they sat silent at the table. After a while Miklos obediently ate his supper, got up, and went to the window and stared out into the garden. Hajnalka straightened up, washed a few things, and they went to bed. Miklos Szuha kissed her neck, her breasts, touched her thigh.

In the sixth month of their marriage Hajnalka became pregnant. It was a difficult pregnancy; she felt sick all the time.

At Maria Pek's insistence Hajnalka gave up her job at the tractor factory and she and her husband moved into the smaller half of the divided apartment on Nagyfuvaros Street. When the child began to move in her belly, Hajnalka felt better. At night she and Miklos Szuha felt the baby's kicking with their fingers and looked at each other in the half-light. Hajnalka laughed and said to him:

"You will love us, won't you?"

The man just kept nodding and kissed her blotchy face.

In the last stage of her pregnancy Jani fretted constantly; he admonished her to move and not get lazy, but at the same time he would not let her do a thing; he grabbed everything she picked up from her hands. Toward the end he was so restless that he squabbled and quarreled with everybody until Maria Pek finally threatened to chase him out of the house.

"What will you do when your own wife has a child? You'll kill the whole family!"

They looked at each other. Maria clamped the poppyseed mill to the table and began to turn the handle with her ugly, claw-fingered hands.

Hajnalka was in labor from nine o'clock Sunday night to four o'clock Monday morning. Jani and Miklos Szuha did not leave the hospital until it was all over. She gave birth to a healthy little boy, who was to be named Miklos. When mother and child were discharged from the hospital Miklos Szuha took them to his mother, who lived in Rakosfalva in a one-room flat in a house surrounded by a garden.

❖ ❖ ❖ ❖ ❖ ❖

Istvan Hires had saved up 12,000 forints, borrowed the rest from some co-workers at the plant, and made a down payment on a co-operative flat under construction in the suburb of Zuglo. In the summer he took a week's vacation and went to stay alone in his boathouse. On Saturday Gizike decided to take Agotha and join him. She got up at dawn, made a roast, and took a train to Pesterzsebet. In the doorway of the boathouse she stopped short. She sent Agotha to play by the river. Then she stepped into the room and drew the multicolored curtains. A girl about twenty years old was sitting on the pull-out cot. Gizike saw that under her slip she was naked.

"Who is this piece of trash?" she asked her husband.

"I resent that!" the girl said. "I am Istvan Hires' fiancée."

Gizike picked up the girl's dress and stockings and flung them at her.

"Get out!" she screamed. "And make it fast! The faster the better!"

The girl took her time. She asked Istvan Hires to pull up the zipper on her back. Gizike boiled. She hurled the girl's pocketbook out the door.

When she had left, Gizike asked quietly: "How could you do such a thing?"

Istvan Hires sat down on the edge of the bunk and smoothed back his thinning blond hair. He lit a cigarette.

"I did it to shake you up. When a man struggles to make a living, he wants to laugh sometimes, but all you do is stare into space or sleep."

"You shook me up all right," Gizike said, "but I hate you, you rat."

And she took Agotha home. Istvan Hires came back Sunday night. Gizike was still fuming. She told him that she had been warned several times at the plant about her husband's whoring around. Twice he had been seen with a beautiful Gypsy woman in Petofi Sandor Street.

Istvan Hires put down his paper.

"Who said that?"

"Somebody reliable."

"It's a lie."

"You mount every lousy, dirty carcass in the plant!"

Istvan Hires slapped her. Gizike crashed to the floor. She did not cry. One side of her face and her ear were red. At the corner of her mouth, the skin was torn open. Istvan Hires' eyes filled with tears.

"You see, that's what happens when you talk such nonsense," he said. "You just don't think . . ."

Gizike stayed on the floor staring up at her husband.

There was a letter from Sandor Seres. His letters were always events in the Habetler household because they brought tears of laughter to everybody's eyes. This time, too, everybody sat around the kitchen table, and it was Eszter who read the letter aloud because she could keep a straight face, even at the most ridiculous parts. Besides, she could imitate Sandor Seres' slow drawl perfectly:

"My dear Maria and Janos: This is to let you know that we received the letter you directed to us, which made us very happy. By answering our letters so faithfully you prove that there was never any truly deep difference in our views, such that often in a hard political argument you still always understood me. In addition to the good Communist People's educational work, I would like you to know, my dear friends, that we are doing well, which we wish you too, from the bottom of both our hearts. We are very happy that you are in good health too. Here it is still very hot, which Boris can't stand very well, because the longer one is here, the more difficult it becomes to bear the climate. And the heat of the climate weakens Boris and she perspires very much. Otherwise everything is well. What we are doing now we do for ourselves. The way in which we do our work determines the fruit. Therefore we must strive to accomplish whatever the Party entrusts us with. Once everybody realizes this we will quickly put an end to the Imperialists. This is the only way we can strike a last blow toward the final triumph. If only everybody realized this! Dear Janos, I am very happy that you see me as I really am, that I do not try to put on airs in front of anybody. In this way I prove that we self-respecting Communists differ from those who strive only to reach a top rank, and then forget that it was the Party which by the mandate of the people entrusted them with their specific tasks. But he who forgets this is easily discovered and put in his deserved place.

"You write, my dear Janos, that your Peace Bond did not win in the lottery. The most important thing however is that we should continue to be able to work in peace, which is worth more than winning any lottery. Because it would be in vain to draw the first prize if we cannot assure peace. We would not be of any use to the working people. All I can say on this subject is that even if not a single ticket is ever drawn, our state assures a secure living for everybody, and human rights too. Which is worth more than anything. And there is still a chance that with luck your ticket will win. With a clear conscience I can declare that if we take our fate in our own hands, as we should, there is every possibility of maintaining a peaceful life.

"Dear Janos, you write that Hajnalka is out of work. That is not pleasant but you must not despair. I am quite sure that the Trade Union will see to it that she gets another job. Because in the eyes of our Party, youth is the greatest treasure, on which it can build the future best. And the Party does consider youth a building block, so you have no reason to despair because of a few imperfections. I am sure that this problem will be solved shortly. About the results achieved by our soccer team, all I can say is that they have secured us great fame throughout the whole world with their wonderful scores. And with this I end my letter. I remain, with the greatest love from the far distance, in the hope of meeting you again. Before long we will return home. We kiss the entire family. *Boris and Sanyi.*

"And every honest tenant in the building. I will not write names, those to whom I refer will know anyway."

The letter was a success. Even Eszter burst into laughter when she read the sentence, "This is the only way we can strike a last blow toward the final triumph." What Gizike liked was "There is every possibility of maintaining the living of a peaceful life." According to Hajnalka the high point was "The heat of the climate weakens Boris and she perspires very much." And old man Habetler said gleefully: "Such a stupid man, such an unbelievably stupid man!"

George Zentay disagreed.

"He's smarter than any of us," he said. "The reason he writes so much rubbish is because his letters are censored. He'd have to be crazy to risk his job abroad."

Miklos Szuha smiled.

"I think you're mistaken," he said in his quiet way. "The man is incredibly stupid. I think he is some sort of messenger at the Legation and his wife cleans and cooks, a kind of maid of all work."

"If you don't mind my saying so, Miklos," George Zentay replied, "you don't have much of a sense of reality. I don't claim that the guy is a genius but I do maintain that for a man with only four years of school he has made a brilliant career. Out there he is paid in foreign currency, in Palestine pounds. When they return home loaded with packages, you will understand what that means. One thing is certain, that silly Bolshevik line of his gets him places much faster."

He smiled.

"You know, kids, some day I'll set a trap for him, so help me God! I'll fill him full of good Brügecs wine and we'll see what his politics really are!"

"He doesn't play politics at all," said Jani, who was working on Colonel Rezsö Taubinger's chest nailing new hinges on the worn doors. "If you get him drunk, he'll just sing folk songs."

Hajnalka laughed.

"Folk songs? He'll chant sentimental ditties dreadfully off key!"

"Well, and so what?" Jani said with a sardonic grin. "That's still better than tenor sax or alto. And chocolate flips and all sorts of other things."

Eszter looked up from the table.

"What's bugging you now?" she demanded. "Join the Party if you're so impressed! Go stick your head under the cold water faucet!"

The unpleasant smile did not leave Jani's face.

"Shut your trap!" he said. "If you don't shut up, I'll smash everything in sight . . . the preserves, the furniture, the room, everything. I'll break them into a thousand pieces and spit on them."

Janos Habetler stood up from the couch.

"What do you think you're doing?" he asked. "You're not in Siberia any more. With the Russkis. In my home you will behave like a decent man, or else I'll beat you to death with my own two hands."

There was quiet in the room. Jani put the hammer down on the table.

"Papa, why do you have to butt in?" he asked. "You're the stupidest man in the entire Eighth District, Papa. Tell me, Papa, how much is six times nine?"

Janos Habetler stood rooted in his place, glowering at his son with tears in his eyes.

"When I am laid out in my coffin," he said in a trembling voice, "you will remember what you just said. But then it will be too late. Your stupid father will not say anything to you from the world of graves."

The girls began to sob loudly, hysterically. Maria Pek rushed from the kitchen and punched her son in the face. Then she grabbed his arm and pushed him out the door. Their shouting could be heard clearly in the room.

"You dare attack your father?" Maria Pek screamed. "You snake! You turn against your family, against your sisters? You Cain, you . . ."

"What right do they have to laugh at a messenger's letter!" Jani roared. "If a messenger and a washwoman believe in something, only idiots laugh at them! And what do the people who laugh at him believe in? What? Tell me that, Mama! Tell me!"

After a while he calmed down. He helped his mother wash the dishes and scrubbed the kitchen floor. Then he cowered on his father's footlocker late into the night. At last, with a shamefaced grin, he wished his parents good night and crawled into bed.

Hajnalka found a job as a bookkeeper in the warehouse of the Construction Glass Enterprise. She commuted from Rakosfalva to Pest on the six o'clock suburban electric every morning.

Sundays she slept late. Her mother-in-law slept in the kitchen with the little boy and took care of the household. After dinner Hajnalka fetched water from the town pump, washed clothes, and hung them out in the garden to dry. Miklos Szuha tinkered; he made a lampshade and a pair of slippers and a wallet out of waste leather. In the afternoon they crawled into bed and made love until suppertime. Sometimes Hajnalka asked her husband to talk, to tell her about his adventures, women, love, or at least what he would have liked to be. Miklos Szuha puffed on a cigarette. Finally, with flashing eyes, he answered, "Pilot."

Once Hajnalka brought theater tickets but Miklos Szuha would not go out in his secondhand checkered suit.

In the spring Hajnalka met a good-looking man who took the train to work at the same time she did every morning. The man nodded politely to her a few times, then introduced himself. From then on he never stopped talking. He told funny stories at which Hajnalka flashed all thirty-two of her healthy, sparkling-white teeth. He also spoke about serious things; he told her it was a shame that people laughed at the foot-kissing scene in the movie *The Red and the Black*. Real lovemaking, he explained, requires a great deal of imagination and a complete lack of inhibitions; a good lover is never speechless in bed. Hajnalka liked the morning conversations on the train.

One August afternoon she ran into the man on the Number 6 bus. He was carrying a black patent-leather suitcase and a blanket; he was on his way to his weekend house.

"Are you doing anything right now?" he asked.

"No," Hajnalka answered, "nothing special."

"Then why don't you come along?"

In the Buda hills they had some horrible black coffee and cognac in a garden café. The garden was empty, loudspeakers blared canned music. Later they walked up a steep street to his weekend place. Hajnalka liked the little white house, the handkerchief-sized yard, and the abundance of summer flowers. They went inside and the man closed the shutters. Sometime later a button popped off Hajnalka's dress.

That evening Hajnalka did not kiss her child good night. She did not even eat supper. She said that she wasn't feeling well, got into bed, and drew away from her husband.

The widow liked Hajnalka; she was grateful to her because her only son seemed happy. When Hajnalka was rushed to the Uzsoki Hospital for an appendectomy, the widow cried.

Eszter was expecting a baby again. At her mother's insistence she and George Zentay moved into the Habetler flat. Maria Pek washed, cleaned, and cooked. Every two weeks she took preserves, meat, and pastry to Hajnalka in Rakosfalva, kissed her grandchild, and returned home by eight o'clock in the evening. George Zentay chased around in search of an apartment. Everyone in the family teased him; only Juli Csele believed that he would succeed. She said she had never seen a more clever or hard-headed man than Zentay.

Jani Habetler did not like his brother-in-law. One evening after supper Zentay went down to the food store, bought himself some sliced ham, and started to eat it at the kitchen table. Jani went out and bought some more ham and gave it to his sister.

"Eat!" he ordered.

The pregnant woman looked up at him. She did not dare refuse.

A few days later she gave birth to a healthy little girl. George Zentay took them home from the hospital to a two-family apartment with bath in Kispest.

Christmas, New Year, Easter, birthdays, and namedays were all celebrated by the entire family in Nagyfuvaros Street. Maria Pek would clean house and rearrange the furniture;

Janos, Jani, Gizike, and Eszter tidied up. Hajnalka helped her mother with the cooking. Everyone quarreled and shouted until all were hoarse. In the evening the husbands arrived with the children, and flowers for Maria Pek. They kissed her claw-fingered, ugly hand and then everyone sat down to a big party supper at Colonel Rezsö Taubinger's table.

Old man Zentay liked to tease Maria Pek at these feasts.

"My friends," he began one evening. "I met a beautiful woman a while ago. Her husband is always out of town. She lives in a beautiful apartment. She's a lady."

"Aren't you afraid the gentleman will come home?" Maria Pek asked.

"Oh, he's got better things to do!"

"And how old is the lady?"

"Forty," the senior Zentay said. "The best age. But she doesn't look it. She's madly in love with me."

Maria blushed.

"A lady? Hmph! She sounds like a slut to me!" She dismissed the lady with a scornful wave of her hand. "And you say she's madly in love with you? What do you give her?"

Old man Zentay winked.

"What she wants."

Laughter broke out all around. Maria Pek banged her fist on the table, called the old man a rascal and cursed loudly.

After supper Habetler, old man Zentay, and Bela Sapadt played cards while Miklos Szuha, Istvan Hires, and George Zentay talked. Istvan Hires expounded on production problems and politics, bitched about work quotas, the régime, and his wife. George Zentay said that Eszter had a big mouth too, sometimes she drove him to the limit of his endurance. Miklos Szuha smiled quietly.

Istvan Hires looked at him.

"You're lucky," he said seriously.

"Yes," Miklos Szuha replied. "I have no reason to complain."

Jani romped with the children. He lay down on the rag rug and let them ride horseback and climb all over him. The women helped Maria Pek with the dishes. Later Maria Pek made the beds, put mattresses and straw pallets on the floor, kissed her grandchildren good night, and sent the entire family to sleep.

Miklos Szuha was dismissed from the Concrete Road Building Authority under pretext of reorganization. For a long time he couldn't find another job until finally he got work loading paving stones in a freight yard. Then Hajnalka got him hired on the transportation crew at the Construction Glass Enterprise. The work there was too hard, the other men were strange to him, and their practical jokes crude, but with the 17,000 to 18,000 forints he earned a month, he made out all right financially. Every payday the crew met in the Coach and Horn Restaurant after work, the crew chief collected 100 forints from each of the men, they all drank wine and sang. Miklos Szuha did not dare stay away. Twice he took Hajnalka along; they stole away quickly.

By nature an untalkative man, Miklos Szuha became taciturn. When his shift was over he went straight home and did not leave the room again. He played with his son, read about aviation, solved an endless number of crossword puzzles. After supper he made love to his wife, and they both slept deeply, tiredly. He bought a short-wave radio, some kitchen furniture, a portable broiler, a yellow corduroy jacket with brown pants; he had identical brown sport shoes made for himself and Hajnalka.

On her job Hajnalka kept inventory of finished merchandise and packing materials in a glass-enclosed room at the rear of the courtyard crowded with huge crates ready for shipment.

From the charts she kept she calculated the gross weight of the materials each loader handled. There were two desks in the office—one was for the stockroom manager—a cabinet, and a safe where the diamonds and tracing wheels used for cutting inlaid glass in the adjoining workshop were kept. Once a month Hajnalka worked overtime, often until ten o'clock at night. On those days Miklos Szuha went home alone and she would calculate the payroll with the shipping-crew chief. The crew chief was a tall, balding, muscular man of about forty. He wore overalls and a blue beret. The loaders respected his tremendous strength, his superior attitude, and the open-handedness with which he paid for rounds of drinks. When they had washed up and changed out of their work clothes, they sat at a table in the canteen and played Twenty-One. With loud laughter and daring bets the crew chief almost always won, ordered food and wine for everyone to be brought from a nearby restaurant. Whenever someone got married, he collected money from every loader and contributed 500 forints out of his own pocket.

On Hajnalka's nameday he covered her desk with roses. The card read *With much, much love from the crew*. Of course, Hajnalka helped him a great deal. The two of them struggled for hours over the payroll figuring overtime and the weight per square meter and the distance the various types of glass were transported. Once in a while they tampered with the charts so that no loader's earnings were either too high or too low. Whenever they worked late the crew chief went to get supper from the restaurant and later black coffee.

"I don't want you to work for nothing!" he said. With his chin propped in his hands he looked across the desks at the short-haired woman figuring in the light of the office lamp.

The first time he kissed Hajnalka on the back of the head she sat up, put down her pencil; they stared at each other. At ten o'clock he took Hajnalka all the way home to Rakosfalva in a taxi. One summer evening she pushed the game too far.

When she wriggled out of his embrace and started to lock the adding machine in a cabinet, the crew chief tore off her blouse. They wrestled. Finally the man went out to cool himself off with cold water, and returned and quietly asked her pardon.

Two days later, in bed, Miklos Szuha said to his wife: "You're having an affair with my crew chief."

Hajnalka paled. She answered that she was not having an affair with anyone; they had kissed three or four times, but that was all. Miklos Szuha did not speak for a long while.

"Get your clothes on. We're going to see him," he said finally.

"What good will that do?" Hajnalka asked.

"Put your clothes on!" Szuha repeated.

The crew chief lived in Ujpest. He was sitting in the kitchen; his wife opened the door. With suppressed anger Miklos Szuha demanded an explanation of the chief's relationship with his wife. The crew chief was amazed.

"Relationship? There is none!"

Hajnalka began to cry.

"Guszti, don't be stupid, I told my husband that we kissed."

"You're dreaming!"

Miklos Szuha declared that Hajnalka had admitted everything, it was silly to keep on denying it. The crew chief answered that it certainly was silly, in fact the whole thing was silly because there was nothing to deny. And his wife just stared, like someone who has suddenly landed among madmen. Hajnalka took Miklos Szuha's arm.

"Let's go," she implored.

For almost three hours they walked the dark streets toward the center of town. Near the Eastern Railway Station Miklos Szuha said that naturally the child would stay with him. Hajnalka burst into frantic sobs.

"No! Only not that!" she begged. "You can't do that!"

Miklos Szuha told her to control herself, there was no need to make a scene. He lit a cigarette.

"How could you do such a thing?" he asked, pale with hatred. "I didn't deserve it. With that piece of dirt. And your child, how could you still kiss him?"

He fell silent, looked up at the darkened roofs, at the stars. Then he turned his sad brown eyes to Hajnalka.

"What am I to do now?" the woman said softly.

For a week they did not speak. Sunday night in bed he put his arms around Hajnalka. Tears filled her eyes. She kissed his hand.

."Thank you," she said.

She loved Miklos Szuha very much.

❖　　　❖　　　❖　　　❖　　　❖　　　❖

Early in 1956 Sandor Seres and his wife, loaded with elegant new luggage, returned to their old one-room apartment in Nagyfuvaros Street. The other tenants feverishly discussed the thrilling event. A storm of rumors arose. There were whispers about expensive clothes, jewels, and yards of fabulous materials. Juli Csele said that they had brought home a thousand pairs of nylon stockings, and a tape recorder in which they carried a tiny box full of valuable platinum needles used by dentists in the private sector. Bela Sapadt claimed he knew about two BMW motorcycles which he said were hidden in the Party garage. Of course the Seres' financial condition could not be estimated exactly, since people become very shrewd in such situations, there is never any trace of the smuggled goods. However, an upturn in the Seres' finances was obvious. They bought a big double closet, some modern tubular furniture, and a short-wave radio set. Bela Sapadt painted their apartment. He told the patrons at the Harp that out of curiosity he had asked for a wage of 800 forints and they had paid it without even trying to bargain.

"Comrade Seres is rolling in money," Sapadt said, "money earned by the sweat of the brows of the Hungarian people. Some day he'll have to answer for that."

The patrons in the Harp sipped their wine but made no comment. They switched to talk about Sunday's soccer game.

Sandor Seres paid no attention to the spiteful gossip. He acknowledged the greetings of the other tenants politely and visited the Habetlers often. Sitting straight as a ramrod on the kitchen stool, he stubbornly, untiringly tried to convert Maria Pek.

"Dear Maria," he would begin in his drawling voice, "do believe me, an honest Communist, that there is an enormous difference between the old gentlemen's order and the People's democratic system. And you must admit that that's true, because you yourself arrived on the threshold of Socialism from the sad condition of a domestic servant. It is the duty of the Communists to prove the truth with concrete examples, because otherwise it is all just demagoguery. So I will give you a concrete example. One of the sons of your old and dear friend Anna Küvecses has been commissioned a Lieutenant in our glorious People's Army at the Ludovika Academy. Her other son has become an electrical engineer. I don't know about the others. This example proves that we are living in a beautiful chapter of history."

Maria Pek offered him a glass of wine.

"I'll tell you what I think, Sanyika!" she laughed. "I think you're a bad preacher! People say you are hiding pounds of gold. Now you have become a baron! A Baron of Democracy! You are as elegant as a dandy and you let other people do the work for you. Is that right?"

Sandor Seres turned as red as a poppy. He gulped his wine, put the glass down. He twirled the empty glass and said quietly:

"Dear Maria, it is not right for you to say such a thing. I have always worked, ever since I was a child. I have always completed the tasks entrusted to me by the Party in a manner worthy of a Communist. I have never missed a single day of work, not even a single hour. I have never been late, ever. I have been lifted out of the plant because my untiring efforts were noticed and because if anyone had to face up to certain people for the sake of truth, I always did."

And coolly he took his leave.

A few days later, while on an inspection trip in the provinces, George Zentay's motorcycle skidded. Hours later he was found unconscious at the side of the road and taken to the Nyiregyhaza Municipal Hospital. His broken bones were set immediately but the pain persisted even after he was returned to Budapest. New surgery was necessary. Eszter rushed desperately from doctor to doctor, until finally a well-known surgeon at the Anna Koltoi Accident Hospital agreed to undertake the difficult and dangerous operation. It was months until he could leave the hospital. He was brought, still bedridden, to Nagyfuvaros Street. Since Eszter was working, Maria Pek nursed him, washed him, fed him, emptied his bedpan. She also took care of their child as well as Gizike's little girl Agotha.

By October George could get around on crutches; he and Eszter moved back to their own apartment in Kispest. Hajnalka helped them carry their belongings on the streetcar. After dinner she and Eszter went out to the bathroom to do the laundry; every week the two of them washed the family's pillow cases and feather-bed covers in the washing machine. In the evening the telephone rang: a young physician who lived in the same house asked them to tell his sister that he could not come home, he had to stay at the hospital overnight. Later they heard Party Secretary Gero on the radio. George Zentay said that the speech meant trouble. He phoned some acquaintances but the garbled, contradictory reports only made them more uneasy. All night long they heard shooting from the direction of Pest. The next day, heeding the instructions that came over the radio, they did not leave the house. In the evening Istvan Hires appeared. His clothes were wrinkled and dusty, his face stubbled, his eyes feverish. They asked him what was happening in town.

"Revolution," he answered.

"But what's all the shooting about? Who's shooting? At what? Why?"

Istvan Hires smoothed back his hair. He pondered a moment, then said:

"I am a member of the Petofi Circle. We felt the time had come to demonstrate. We announced it to the workers and we led them. I took part in the demonstration at the Petofi Memorial, at General Bem's Statue, and at Radio Central too. That's where they started shooting at us first."

He washed up. Hajnalka fried eggs. Eszter put clean sheets on a bed for him; they tried to persuade him to lie down. He insisted that he had to go on.

"But there's a curfew!" Eszter said. "Are you crazy?"

Hires shrugged. "I have to go!"

He left. Zentay said quietly, "Oh Lord, why do I have to be a cripple now . . ."

Eszter covered her sleeping child. She prayed and began to pace up and down the room, moaning hysterically. "What will happen to the family?"

Hajnalka begged her to stop. They quarreled violently. Then they both started to cry.

Thursday morning Hajnalka set out on foot for Nagyfuvaros Street. There was a thick fog. As she neared the city, she had to duck into doorways more and more often to avoid the whistling bullets. She stared stupidly at the corpses on the street. She couldn't make any sense out of it all.

At last she reached the Habetler flat. Maria Pek sobbed bitterly as she embraced her daughter. Hajnalka assured her mother that Eszter and the children were safe and well; Istvan Hires was alive too, he had come by but had to leave again.

"To see the red-coated whore. . . ," Gizike threw in.

Everybody looked at her but nobody asked questions.

Old man Habetler wandered around the city all day; wherever he could he joined the food lines. Bela Sapadt and Juli Csele brought four demijohns of schnapps from a looted warehouse and offered some to everybody in the building. Juli Csele's daughter ran up and down the stairs, reporting excitedly that on Republic Square they were hanging Communists and spitting on their thingamajig.

Someone had scribbled *Hajra, Fradi! Death to the Communists!* on Sandor Seres' door. Seres stared at the door, then wiped the chalk marks off with his handkerchief. He found his wife inside sobbing wildly. She had put on an old flannel dress and tied a peasant kerchief around her head. A zippered suitcase stood open on the table.

"Sandri, let's get out of here!" she begged. "The entire neighborhood has gone crazy! The Gypsy children on Matyas Place have a machine gun and some streetcar conductors beat a man to death in front of the Harp; they dragged him out of one of the buildings in his pajamas. Sandri, the people are drunk, they're shouting horrible things and nobody will help! Sandri, please, let's get away from here!"

Sandor Seres paced up and down the room. Finally he locked the door and fastened the window.

"Where can we go, Boris?" he asked. "I was chased out of the office too. . . ."

"Out of the office? Who . . ."

"Jeno Schleiffert . . ."

They sank into the armchairs and stared at each other blankly.

At dusk Jani Habetler came to get them. He pounded on

the door with his fist and shouted very loud. "Uncle Sanyi! Mother's made fish soup! She's expecting you!"

They ate supper in the kitchen. Boris picked the fish bones from her lips with stubby fingers and praised the taste of the food, she had never eaten anything so tasty, she said, not even in Bonavolgypuszta where she was born.

"Eat, dear Boriska!" Janos Habetler encouraged. "Help yourself! Please, have some more, as much as you feel like! I'm very happy that you like our modest little supper."

Boris thanked him profusely for the encouragement and called Janos Habetler a dear man. Then she looked around in fright.

"They wrote *Death to the Communists* on our door," she said, trying to smile. "Why did they do that? Did we ever do anything to hurt anybody? We hardly even talked to the neighbors."

Hajnalka lit a cigarette.

"Nobody wants to hurt you, Auntie Boris," she said, weary. "It must have been some kids' idea of a joke."

In his slow drawl Sandor Seres complained about Comrade Professor Jeno Schleiffert, to whom he had expressed the opinion this morning that things were going from bad to worse and that the cause of Popular Democracy must be implemented in the strictest manner, to take effect immediately. Maria Pek made an angry gesture for him to be quiet.

"Eat, Sanyika, and don't always talk politics. You don't know anything about it. Always the Party this and the Party that! Try and find the Party now!"

She raised her ice-blue eyes to Sandor Seres' face.

"God knows what might be dug up against you. I know what I'm talking about . . . I saw a stonecutter dragged to White Guard headquarters . . . he was my cousin . . . he never came out again . . ."

Sandor Seres scratched his unshaven, silver-bristled chin.

"I don't know how to answer you now, Maria," he said

slowly. "There was a time when I believed that only people of our class would be leaders in our new society and that everything would be different. That's what we kept insisting in our study cells. Alas, mankind has suffered a truly great disappointment. I have lived my life without opportunism, I was not like many others for whom joining the Party was important only so that they could feather their own nests. And today I am still a messenger in the Ministry of Foreign Affairs, who because of his lowly function is not very highly regarded. And Boris is a cleaning woman, she has forty meters of corridors, six offices, and the lavatory to clean. And now, you see, dear Maria, we still have to be afraid. Everyone in the building looks at us suspiciously as though we were thieves."

Boris fiddled with her wedding ring.

"Maybe they're just letting off steam, maybe it's only talk . . . after all, they know us."

Jani shook his head.

"They've gone crazy. It's the shooting and the machine guns. Sometimes here, sometimes somewhere else. Strange people climb up on the roofs—nobody knows who they are—and shoot! It drives you crazy!"

"Yes," Boris said. "This morning they shot a milk can out of a woman's hand . . ."

Sandor Seres pulled at his tie.

"There is big trouble . . . the Comrades must realize that . . . it's already such a great misfortune that even the Comrades at the highest levels must be able to recognize that clearly . . ."

Jani looked at him and grimaced.

"You might just as well go and find yourself a lamp post!" he said gruffly. "You're as good as dead anyway."

Maria Pek paled. She raised her bony fist.

"Are you howling again? So soon?" she screamed. "You animal! You mad wolf! Howling again?"

Jani guffawed.

"I am! And why not?" he roared. "Aren't I right? They've left him and that's that! He can dangle from a lamp post or roast in Auschwitz for all they care! They've forgotten about him! If he gets killed, they'll say it was just his tough luck!"

Hajnalka covered her ears.

"Jani, stop it!" she begged. "For God's sake, don't we have enough trouble? All we need is your circus! Always your circus!"

She dropped her head on the table and sobbed. Old man Habetler closed the kitchen door, drew the calico curtains, and with an embarrassed smile begged the couple's pardon. He offered them more cheese noodles, brought a demijohn out of the other room, and filled their glasses with Brügecs wine. He wished his guests and his own family good health, happiness, and a long life and clinked glasses with everyone.

Around nine o'clock there was a knock on the door. Bela Sapadt came in and sat down on the trashcan. His eyes flashing with drink, he talked a blue streak. He told how they were digging up the ground on Republic Square in front of Party Headquarters, they were looking for a Secret Police bunker where more than a thousand innocent prisoners were locked up. Old man Habetler offered him some wine and declared that he did not believe that anything would result from the search; indeed he considered it nonsense, because in his opinion the Secret Police did not need to build any sort of bunker. This is how he reasoned:

"I must tell you quite sincerely that I have never concerned myself with politics, and for this reason I do not claim that I understand anything about politics, because that would not be true. I'm interested only in the fate and happiness of my dear family and I have always worked for them without sparing any strength or energy. Yet even I can see that such an enormous construction for more than one thousand people

—145—

would have been an amazingly great waste of money on the part of the Secret Police, since there is more than enough prison space owned by the competent authorities."

Bela Sapadt shrugged.

"What do they care about money?" he said. "The Communists don't pay the bill nor do the loud-mouthed mercenaries who travel abroad, nor the murdering Secret Police, but the working people. There was no need for a subway either, absolutely none, but they built one anyway."

He lit a cigarette. Then he said he had important news: Within three days UN troops were going to arrive to free the Hungarian people from Russian oppression. It was international law.

"The UN?" old man Habetler said in amazement.

"Exactly!" nodded the housepainter. "They will introduce the eight-party system with upper and lower house. Or maybe they'll restore the old Apostolic Crown Kingdom."

He smiled.

"What do you say to that, Comrade Seres?" he asked. "In historical perspective? What do your study cells teach for times like this?"

Sandor Seres did not answer immediately. He sat on the kitchen stool as straight as a ramrod.

"In the seminars we were taught," he said slowly, "that if someone commits an act against the System, he will get his just punishment. I must add that, alas, this is not very noticeable now. Capitalist society took better care of itself. But in historical perspective, this is my answer to your stupid question."

The housepainter took a drag on his cigarette. He winked.

"And three days from now? When the blue-uniformed soldiers parachute into Hungary? What will you preach then?"

Sandor Seres glared at him.

"I refuse to answer you," he said, the blood drained from

—146—

his face, "because you are part of the hooligan element. I spit on you. I am addressing my wife, who is scared of your face and of the people shouting in the street. The situation is such that it will be very difficult for me to calm her, because the events are happening before her eyes. I only went to school four years. I am not an educated man. How can I explain why I am an optimist? Because that is the truth and if someone were to look inside of me, that is what he would see."

He poured himself some wine, drank, then he continued more calmly. "When in forty-one Germany attacked the Soviet Union, one of my relatives, a young boy, asked me who would win the war, the Germans or the English or the Americans. I answered that the Soviets would come, which terrified him greatly, because his teacher had used the Russians as bogey-men. I told him not to believe the teacher, because he was not telling the truth. When the Russians come, I told him, we would no longer be slaves in a gentlemen's world, but we would be able to work for ourselves. We would be human beings. Whereupon he asked, will it really be like that, God-father? I replied that when the time came and if I happened to be around, he would tell me that I was right. And that's what did happen. He said, 'You were right, Godfather, only tell me how you came to be such a clairvoyant man. I am very proud of you.' I told him that Fate had taught me where I be-long, because we are either the vermin of the lords or else we must rule and bring into being the happiness of the poor peo-ple. He was one of the first to join the Young Communist League and later he volunteered for the police, where he was asked what conviction had sent him and he referred to me. He said that I had convinced him where he belonged. That's how he became a member of the Secret Police and that is how he died a few days ago."

Nobody said anything. Janos Habetler filled the glasses again and they all drank the Brügecs wine. Sandor Seres got very tipsy; he declared that he was dizzy and that he had to laugh. Maria Pek advised him to lie down, she would make up a bed for him on the couch. He and Boris should stay for the night. But Sandor Seres protested. He declared that he had his own apartment but he would like to urge the Habetler family not to be afraid because there was no power on earth which could prevent their happiness since the cause of Socialism was the final truth. Boris kept wiping her pale, sweaty face with a handkerchief. She and Jani took Sandor by the arm and carried him downstairs. In the corridor he laughed loudly and sang lustily, "Dilia, my Dilia . . ."

The neighbors looked out their doors and smiled.

Next afternoon Istvan Hires turned up. He washed up. Maria Pek gave him a clean shirt and something to eat; he slept for an hour. Then he sat in the kitchen and studied his brother-in-law's face with a serious, reproachful look and slightly ironic smile. Jani stepped over to him and tore the insurgents' red-white-and-green ribbon off Hires' lapel.

"Are you playing games again, Istvan Hires?" he asked. "You're a Party member! Why don't you re-enlist this time? Or isn't it good business now?"

Maria Pek screamed at Jani to shut his trap, it was none of his business. Istvan Hires was already long gone but mother and son were still quarreling violently.

Hajnalka set out for Rakosfalva in the afternoon. Her father walked with her as far as the Eastern Railway station. She kissed him good-bye and continued alone in the drizzling rain. She arrived home thoroughly soaked. In the kitchen she hugged her little boy and broke into tears.

"Mommy, why are you crying?" the child asked.

"Because there is war."

The widow heated water for her and Hajnalka washed from head to toe. She had just crawled into bed when Miklos Szuha arrived. He had gotten a ride on a truck from the provinces where he worked for the Land Survey Bureau. They embraced for a long time. After a while Hajnalka asked where all the conversation was leading. Miklos leaned out of bed and groped for a cigarette.

"You ought to join the Communist Party. That might make life easier for us, because things in this country aren't going to change. And if they should, my mother will vouch for you . . ."

Hajnalka could not see his face in the dark.

Istvan Hires was shot on a windy, ugly November afternoon not far from the Chain Bridge. He was taking a duck to Buda in his knapsack. The bullet shattered his hand. He ran about 200 meters until some passers-by stopped him and called an ambulance, which drove through winding little streets past the Mathias Church to Szikla Hospital. A few days later Gizike visited him. The electric lights were on in the long, crowded ward. She found her husband and sat down on the edge of his bed. They did not talk. Istvan Hires closed his eyes; he said he was feverish and would like to sleep, she should go home. Perhaps Gizike didn't hear what he said because she stayed, sitting with back bent, eyes darting, and absent-mindedly fluffing her thick graying braids. The red-coated woman arrived, bringing the fragrance of lavender to the bedside. She scrutinized Gizike with curious embarrassment. Istvan Hires' expression was hateful as he watched his wife walk away, worn and tired. A few weeks later Hajnalka and Eszter brought the wounded man cookies, lemons, and cigarettes, but they did not sit down to talk because he was feeling feverish and said he wanted to sleep.

He was discharged from the hospital at the end of February; Janos Habetler went to fetch him. They met in the corridor. Istvan Hires stopped, greeted his father-in-law embarrassedly; the red-coated woman touched his arm and led him away.

Later he was interned at the Kistarcsa Detention Camp.

Every visiting day Gizike took him food and cigarettes but she never saw the red-coated woman again.

Hajnalka worked in an Atex State Textile Trust store. The manager was a clever, sociable man. All kinds of people dropped in to visit with him: good-natured tailors from the private sector, sad young actors, a falsetto-voiced boxer, a fat man who sold wolfhounds, and other odd characters. They brought black coffee from the espresso next door, gossiped, and admired the new cashier's beauty. Hajnalka was happy and relished every silly compliment.

At the beginning of summer another clerk joined the staff. He was a very blond, slender, sinewy young man of twenty-two who had just completed an enlistment with the Security Police. Hajnalka bewitched him the first day. From then on the young man constantly hung around the cashier's cage. He told her that he liked to wrestle and read books on criminology. He proudly displayed his new silver-monogrammed cigarette case. Whenever he paid Hajnalka a compliment she laughed and told him not to talk so much because he was very stupid. One day after closing when she had to take twenty kilos of cherries to Rakosfalva, the young man lugged the two duffel bags. They chose side streets; the young man set down the cherries and they kissed.

In the fall Hajnalka met a tall dark-haired dancer from the People's State Ensemble. He walked her to the train station; he spoke about foreign travel and the joys of dancing. One afternoon in November they dropped in at a sweet shop on Jozsef Boulevard. Time flew by. When Hajnalka looked at the clock it was past eleven; she panicked.

"Are you in trouble?" the dancer asked.

Hajnalka shrugged.

"My husband is out of town. Sometimes I spend the night at my sister's."

They danced at the Poppy until midnight. Then they took a taxi across the river to an old one-story building in Óbuda. They had to ring a long time before the concierge let them in. The dancer's apartment was at the far end of the courtyard. They shed their coats in the foyer. The dancer led the way through a dark room to another smaller one. Couches stood at right angles along two walls and against another wall there was an empty serving cart next to a worn armchair. Hajnalka sat on one of the couches. The man took off his tie and jacket and sat next to her. They kissed. He began to unbutton her black jacket. His face, his eyes changed and a disagreeable expression appeared around his mouth. Hajnalka pushed him away and sat up.

"If that's the way you feel, why did you come here?" the dancer asked.

And he laughed.

In the morning Hajnalka had to stop on the cobbled street to ask a kerchiefed woman the way back to town.

In the middle of winter Eszter phoned her sister. She was desperately angry. She complained that Zentay came home drunk every night. Hajnalka said that she did not know how to handle Zentay—whenever he had a single drink she flew off the handle and made a scene. She constantly felt sorry for herself and humiliated her husband at every family gathering.

"You always take his side!" Eszter shouted into the phone. "I know very well how to handle my husband! If I let him have his way, he would be drunk day and night."

And she slammed down the receiver.

A few days later Hajnalka called Eszter to ask how Zentay was behaving. Eszter replied that he was being very nice.

"Just imagine, the idiot came home with two sweaters," she said. "You see, when he's nice, I am too."

Ten days later Eszter broke her umbrella over George Zentay's head and tore out a handful of his hair. Zentay punched her in the face so hard that he knocked out one of her teeth. Eszter told Hajnalka about it in the Youth Espresso. Hajnalka stared at her sister aghast.

"My God! In front of the child? Have you two lost your minds?"

Eszter burst into tears.

"I can't stand it! I can't stand the sight of him, of his dumb face when he's drunk!"

Every other Sunday all of the grandchildren were taken to Nagyfuvaros Street. Eszter poured out her troubles. Maria Pek seethed with anger.

"I can tell he's been drinking every time he comes home from the provinces!" she yelled. "He guzzles water by the gallon! He craves it! That pig gets drunk at every stop!"

Gizike stepped into the fray.

"That's not fair. Everybody condemns him without looking at his side. Eszter has plenty of faults too; she's bossy, she's constantly bitching, she insults him at every chance. The poor man is never right and he never has a single moment of peace."

Jani sneered.

"There she goes again, defending somebody else," he taunted. "The defense counselor, the unhired adviser, the girl with the big heart!"

He pushed his face close to Gizike's.

"You stupid cow!" he roared. "They told me the truth—that time he fell off his motorcycle he was dead drunk too! Do you know what they do on those inspection trips? They get girls to dance on tables!"

"Shut your trap!" Maria Pek shouted.

"Why should I? He wouldn't even offer his pregnant wife a slice of ham!"

Old man Habetler intervened. "There will be no such improper behavior in my family. I will have a talk with him."

"You won't talk to anybody!" Maria Pek shouted. "What's there for you to talk to him about? It's none of your business! It's between the two of them!"

Gizike turned to her younger sister.

"You're an idiot! Why do you have to discuss your problems here?"

"What do you mean?" Maria Pek demanded. "Where else should she go to complain?"

"Anywhere but here!" Gizike replied. "They tear that poor guy apart and then they give his wife the worst possible advice to boot."

Maria Pek shook her bony fist.

"Shut up, or get out of here!"

Gizike collected her things and dressed Agotha.

"I'm always wrong in this house," she sobbed. "I'll get out, all right. I'll leave and I'll never come back again!"

Maria Pek rushed out and locked the kitchen door.

"Oh no, you won't," she screamed at her daughter.

Everyone helped set up table and they sat down to stuffed cabbage. They laughed, they clowned, they teased Jani about when he planned to get married. Jani blushed.

"There wouldn't be enough room around for all of us," he stammered. "Ain't there enough fighting now?"

Maria Pek laughed.

"Arguments don't mean anger, and as for your wife, we'll be happy to make room for her." She paused. "I want to live long enough to be at your wedding."

Janos Habetler raised his glass.

"Though I do not have a fondness for wine—I daresay that in my whole life I have not drunk as much wine as your mother does in a week—I raise my glass to my dear, good wife, to my beloved children, to my adorable grandchildren, to my most dearly loved family."

"Are you forgetting the beautiful widow?" Maria Pek asked. "What about her?"

Habetler kissed her.

"Oh, leave her in peace!" he laughed. "She probably has a bellyache."

The whole family laughed at this because Anna Küvecses went from clinic to clinic, complaining sometimes about her heart, sometimes about her stomach. Yet she was strong and healthy, the doctors told her sons each time.

❖　　❖　　❖　　❖　　❖　　❖

George Zentay brought his wife a big basket of flowers and material for a winter coat. And he applied for the addiction cure. The happy reconciliation was celebrated in the Corvin Restaurant. They invited old man Zentay, Miklos Szuha and Hajnalka, and at Maria Pek's insistence they dragged Jani along too. Old man Zentay ordered dinner, wine, and afterward cognac for everyone.

"To your mother's health," he said. "May she be happy in our midst and enjoy a long life. I do not know how to express my gratitude for what she did for me during the time I was deported."

The wine went to Jani's head quickly. He grinned and said he felt dizzy. The others wanted to help him home but he would not hear of it. He kissed his sisters, shook the men's hands, and left. On the corner of Nagyfuvaros Street he bumped into Juli Csele.

"What's the matter with you?" she asked.

"I'm drunk," he answered, laughed, and leaned against a lamp post. Snow was falling in fat flakes.

"Is something bothering you?" she asked.

"No, nothing special." He knitted his brows. "Do you believe in dreams? I dreamed of a big ocean—it means something bad—death, I think. Or a big fight. According to my mother a dream always tells the truth but I didn't tell her about this one."

Juli Csele shrugged.

"I don't believe in that. Uncle Reich didn't either, remember."

Jani thought hard.

"You're a whore," he said without anger. "And a thief. Your soul was washed away in the spittoons."

Juli Csele pulled off her gloves and lit a cigarette.

"And your soul?" she asked.

For a minute Jani was silent.

"You'd take your clothes off for anybody . . . you lie and you cheat and you steal . . ."

Juli Csele nodded.

"I'd take them off for you too. If you want me to, I'll even pay you for it. I have plenty of money now, but I hate to spend the night alone." She shrugged. "Come on, I'll put on my housecoat, it's Chinese silk. You can admire it, it has black, yellow, and green dragons all over it . . . they're disgusting things, but I haven't been afraid of them for a long time now . . ."

Jani looked at her.

"You're an animal," Jani said quietly.

Juli Csele smiled.

"Of course! I'm a dirty slut! Even though my ancestry is the very best, as good as gold! You don't have to grin like that. Whether you believe it or not, I could be a doctor. Or a judge! . . . Why not? . . . That idiot Seres swears I could . . . just imagine how amazed the other tenants would be . . . I would attend the opera regularly . . . on my honor . . . my husband would be polite and smart, if there were something I didn't understand, he would explain it to me . . . You know, Jani, there are so many things that one doesn't understand . . . isn't that so?"

She waited for the man to say something, but he just watched the falling snow, silent and intent. Then she started to laugh.

"Oh, well, what the hell! So I have no diploma, so I don't go to the opera. I love liquor, money, and men, which isn't so bad! Believe it or not, one silly guy swore that I have eyes like a little girl. I thought I would eat him up! I just stared at him and bawled! The silly fool! I told him I was madly in love with him. Bah! You can't be in love with all of them! . . . but they need that kind of lie . . . You know, Jani, my boy, I have to lie, because it makes it harder for them to stay away. . . . Of course it's a lot of baloney. Don't you fall for that line!"

They went to the Harp and drank until closing time. Juli Csele helped Jani up the stairs. He did not want to make a racket, so he sat down on the kitchen floor and took off his shoes. When Maria Pek came out into the kitchen and turned on the light she found him lying flat on his back, his eyes open, mumbling incoherently.

❖   ❖   ❖   ❖   ❖   ❖

Istvan Hires was released at Christmas. He went straight to the Habetlers'. He kissed Maria Pek's hand and thanked her for the family's kindness. He was received affectionately. Under the Christmas tree there were three handkerchiefs and a carton of cigarettes for him, as there were for the other husbands. After supper Gizike drew him aside and said:

"While you were in trouble I stood by you. Now you are free, you can work, I don't want you any more."

Istvan Hires adjusted the black sling on his arm and left. Everyone looked at Gizike. Hajnalka walked up to her.

"What happened?" she asked.

Gizike told her what she had said. Tears rolled down Hajnalka's cheeks.

"You shouldn't have done that, Gizike. He just got out. Where can he go?"

Eszter began to cry too. Concerned, old man Habetler asked:

"Have you thought this over carefully, my daughter?"

Gizike's reply was resolute:

"Yes, I've thought it out. I know what I'm doing. When I discovered what a bastard he is, you wanted me to come home, but I said that my glass wasn't full yet. I waited, I suffered at his side. Without him I could never have gotten an apartment. Now he doesn't need me any more, and we don't need him either."

Then they talked about other things.

On New Year's Eve, to everyone's surprise, Jani brought a stranger to dinner. The family had never been so happy. The new guest was a delicate blonde girl; her name was Piroska Cira. She and Jani worked in the same plant. Old man Habetler rushed to help her with her coat, steered her to the stove, and pulled up a chair for her.

"Sit here!" he said. "Make yourself comfortable in our modest home."

The girls offered her food and drink, Maria Pek raised her ice-blue eyes to Piroska's face and exchanged a few words with her. Later George Zentay took pictures. Piroska Cira took her place at the family board, smiling diffidently. After midnight Jani collected the children, put coats and caps on them.

"Don't let go of the child's hand!" Eszter warned him. "She'll run out into the roadway and we've had it!"

"What kind of idiot do you take me for?" Jani countered.

"Are you trying to be smart? You have no idea what she's like! Let go her hand for a split second and she'll manage to get in front of something."

"Then I won't take her!" Jani thundered. "I'll leave her home!"

Maria Pek rushed over.

"Stop it!" she shouted. "Of course he won't let go her hand! Get out of here before you drive us all crazy!"

An hour later he brought the children back laden with balloons, paper hats, and trumpets. They made an infernal racket.

Miklos Szuha's silence got more and more on Hajnalka's nerves. For hours on end he worked crossword puzzles, entertained himself with mathematical equations. After supper he would make love to her and immediately fall into a deep sleep. In February they took a vacation. Jani came to Rakosfalva to paint their apartment. Hajnalka cleaned up the mess, did a housecleaning, washed and ironed. In the evening she crawled into bed and gave her tired body up to lovemaking. The two weeks went by very slowly. She was glad to go back to work again.

One rainy afternoon she ran into Ervin, the saxophone player, on the street. In their happiness they threw their arms around each other. They sat down to talk in the Youth Espresso. The young man told her proudly that he had a small combo, they had just returned from Bulgaria, they had a good contract, they played at a beach resort on the Black Sea, they had made good money. Hajnalka told him about her little boy and her job as a cashier in an Atex store, and that her husband was often out of town on his job as a technician for the Surveying Bureau.

"He's crazy about mathematics!" she laughed.

Then they reminisced over old memories. Hajnalka smiled.

"Do you still play 'Stardust' sometimes?" she asked.

Ervin kissed her hand.

"Come over to my house," he said. "I'll play it for you . . ."

Thereafter they saw each other two or three times a week.

Maria Pek was not well. She had trouble breathing and was wracked by a dry choking cough. Though she still took care of the household, she hardly ever went out any more. Old man Habetler did the shopping at the Teleki Place Market and Jani scrubbed the kitchen floor, washed the windows, and even did part of the laundry. Janos Habetler climbed the four flights of stairs more slowly too; sometimes he had to stop for several minutes, holding his hand over his heart. The district physician examined him and warned him to take it easier and prescribed several kinds of medicines which Janos swallowed dutifully.

When the acacia began to bloom Maria Pek went to Brügecs for a rest. Janos' foster parents were not alive any more; Maria Pek stayed with the oldest daughter, who lived in the little old shack. Old man Habetler went to see his wife every Saturday lugging a knapsack full of bread, meat, cauliflower, and green peppers. The peppers made Maria Pek angry.

"Why do you bring green peppers to the country where they grow, you foolish old man?"

"Just look at them! Look how beautiful they are!" He showed them to her. "I picked only the finest."

Maria Pek crocheted bedspreads, shifts, and bloomers with a pretty peacock stitch and traded them with the peasant women for chickens, eggs, sour cream, farmer cheese, and vegetables which she carefully divided and sent home to the children every Sunday night. Monday afternoons the old man delivered the packages to each of his daughters.

In the middle of summer, on the train to Brügecs, Janos felt sick. His face turned white as a sheet, beads of sweat formed on his forehead. When he got off at Felsö Akác he felt a sharp pain in his heart. He walked a few steps, but then he had to sit down at the side of the road. The crippling pain did not stop.

"I have to make it to the house!" he thought in panic.

He struggled to his feet and slowly continued toward the house. Maria Pek was working in the vegetable garden and rushed out the gate to meet him.

"Sweet Jesus! What's wrong with you?"

"My heart is kicking up." He took off the knapsack and smiled. "But I feel better now."

During the night he took sick again. He gasped for air; his face contorted with pain, he lost consciousness. Maria Pek was alone at his bedside. It was morning before their relatives returned to the isolated house from a wedding. Wailing loudly, they rushed away to fetch a cart, laid Janos Habetler on a bed of straw, and so made the nine kilometers to Felsö Acác.

The village doctor was called out of church. He gave Janos an injection and phoned for an ambulance. Not much later, with Maria Pek by his side, Janos was taken to the Istvan Hospital in Budapest.

Bela Sapadt telephoned Eszter and asked her to notify the other two children. When Hajnalka and Eszter arrived, Maria Pek was sitting on the kitchen stool staring at the sun shining through the curtains. She was alarmingly composed.

The three women rushed to the hospital. Janos Habetler lay motionless on his back without a pillow. His face was drawn and waxen, perspiration poured down his body, his mouth was open, he gasped for air. They stood at the foot of the bed and called his name. But he did not recognize them. Eszter sobbed hysterically. Hajnalka dragged her out into the corridor and shook her.

"Pull yourself together or go away!"

Hajnalka put 200 forints in an envelope, found the doctor in charge, and gave it to him. The physician adjusted his glasses and said compassionately, "I'm sorry I can't say anything encouraging. It's a miracle he's been able to hold on this long."

Tears ran down Hajnalka's cheeks.

"Will you be with him during the night?"

"There will be a resident physician on duty. But I will be back at dawn. Your father won't be left alone."

Later Jani, Gizike, George Zentay, and Piroska Cira arrived.

Jani was crying. He pulled 500 forints out of his pocket.

"You take care of it!" he said to Hajnalka. "Give something to everybody. I'll bring more tomorrow!"

Hajnalka gave 200 forints to the resident on duty and 20 forints to every nurse in the ward. The family stayed around in the corridor until ten o'clock at night, listening to Janos' horrible wheezing. Finally, after they had been asked to leave several times, they all went home with Maria Pek.

The next morning Hajnalka and Eszter hurried to the hospital together. The chief cardiologist asked them to sit down and explained at length, in great detail, their father's thrombosis.

"It is very serious," he said sadly. "I can give you no reassurance."

The sisters had a good cry, then hurried to Nagyfuvaros Street. Maria Pek was sitting on the kitchen stool. They kissed her. Hajnalka smiled.

"Thank God he got through the night—perhaps everything will be all right now—that's what the doctor said . . ."

Maria Pek looked up at her daughter and burst into stormy sobs.

In the afternoon Hajnalka and Eszter returned to the hospital. Janos recognized them.

"My little girls," he said softly. "My little girls . . ."

And tears welled in his eyes.

Hajnalka bent over him.

"You mustn't cry, Papa," she said, in tears too. "You mustn't talk or move or cry. You have to rest so you can come home soon. Meantime we'll come and feed you every day."

They spoonfed their father for weeks. He was very weak —Hajnalka had to plead with him to swallow each mouthful of chicken broth. Eszter was useless at the bedside. Her hands trembled, she got in everybody's way and quarreled with her father if he so much as moved his big toe. Ervin, the saxophone player, waited for the sisters on Nagyvarad Place every afternoon and escorted them home to Nagyfuvaros Street.

On visiting days the whole family was at the hospital. Every Sunday old man Zentay, Miklos Szuha, Sandor Seres, Boris, and many of the other neighbors went to see Janos. Istvan Hires always brought chestnut purée, kissed the old man, then went out in the corridor to smoke and talk with the men. He had bought his co-op, and gossip had it that Juli Csele was living with him but no one asked him about it. Maria Pek's health deteriorated very much—she had to be taken to Janos' ward in the elevator. If the elevator was not running or if they could not find the operator, after a moment of stormy argument, Jani would carry her up the stairs in his arms. When autumn set in she could hardly breathe; she couldn't leave the apartment. When the others were at the hospital Piroska Cira stayed with her. After a while Piroska slept there; she and Jani went to work together every morning. One day Maria Pek asked her son severely when they were planning to get married. Jani kissed her.

"If Papa is home by Christmas, we'll get married then."

One Saturday night early in November in bed, Hajnalka told Miklos Szuha that this would be the last night she would spend with him. She did not want to take anything except the child, her clothes, the Peace Bonds, and the little Buddha which was a girlhood souvenir. Miklos Szuha was stunned. He begged and pleaded with her all night not to leave him. In the morning Hajnalka said she would pick up the child and her things on Monday. She got dressed. Miklos Szuha stayed in bed.

"Are you going to the hospital this afternoon?" he asked.

"Yes," she answered.

"I'll see you there," Szuha nodded. And he took a deep drag on his cigarette.

That Sunday morning Hajnalka went to see her mother. Maria Pek was home alone, cooking in the kitchen. Jani and Piroska had gone to Brügecs to get wine. Hajnalka kissed Maria Pek's shriveled face and sat down on the kitchen stool. She lit a cigarette.

"I'm leaving Miklos," she said.

The rolling pin in Maria Pek's hand stopped still.

"What happened?" she asked.

Hajnalka cogitated a moment.

"Our marriage went to pot," she said. "I can't say exactly how, I can't say he did this or that. I'm just bored to death by him . . . it's no good, no good . . . I might not have noticed if I weren't in love with someone else . . . with Ervin . . . the saxophone player . . ."

"Good heavens! What are you saying? Your Miklos is an honest, decent man who loves his family. Have you thought it over carefully?"

"I have thought it over, Mother, and the reason I came to see you is to ask whether we can come back home?"

Maria Pek was silent. With her gnarled hands she adjusted her black kerchief.

"When will you bring the child?" she asked, and returned to her baking board.

At dinnertime Eszter arrived with husband and little girl. Eszter said "To hell with Miklos Szuha, to hell with his eternal crossword puzzles. Here it is November and neither Hajnalka or the boy have winter coats."

She turned to her younger sister.

"How much does your husband make?"

"I don't know," Hajnalka replied.

"What do you mean, you don't know!" Eszter shouted. "You gave him every penny of your salary! How much did he contribute to the household? Six hundred forints! Tell Mama that it was you who supported the family! She had to worry about pocket money for cigarettes and busfare, Mama, and on Sunday she washed and ironed and he never even took her to a movie! She'll be better off without him."

Eszter looked at her husband as if to ask for support but Zentay just kept on eating.

After Maria Pek had prepared Janos' soup and began to do the dishes, Eszter and Hajnalka set out for the hospital to feed their father. Later in the afternoon Anna Küvecses and her son, now a lieutenant colonel, Gizike, Agotha, then Istvan Hires came to the hospital and finally somber-faced Miklos Szuha.

Janos Habetler was feeling better, but he was not allowed to talk much yet. At five o'clock visiting hours were over. The group stopped in the hospital entrance. It was raining outside.

"Who's going which way?" George Zentay asked, turning up the collar of his raincoat. "We're going to Mother's."

"I'll come along too," Istvan Hires said.

"Me too," said Miklos Szuha.

Anna Küvecses and her son said good-bye. Gizike said that she and Agotha would come later, they had something to do.

They all sat around in the Habetler kitchen. Everyone

felt the tension, glared at each other and smoked. Maria Pek, perched on the kitchen stool, cleared her throat.

"Papa's getting along quite well," Eszter said. "Now we have to see that he doesn't move around too much. We had to talk ourselves hoarse to make him understand."

There was silence again. Hajnalka watched Miklos Szuha's face. She burst into a loud nervous laugh and stood up. She spread out her arms and made a mock bow.

"Well, the family council is assembled," she said. "We can begin. Let's get it over with. I think everybody knows that I have left Miklos because I don't want to live with him any longer. I don't want anything from him, all I will take with me is my child."

Istvan Hires stubbed out his cigarette.

"What did he do to you?"

"Nothing," Hajnalka answered. "But that's not the point."

Szuha spoke: "But she did something to me."

Maria Pek looked at him.

"What did she do?"

"She was unfaithful to me. With my crew chief. She came home in a taxi."

Zentay stared at the sink. Eszter's hand trembled. Hajnalka, white as a sheet, looked at her husband with eyes narrowed into slits. Istvan Hires smiled discreetly. Maria Pek focused her ice-blue eyes on Miklos Szuha's face. She made a ball of her trembling, claw-fingered hand and slammed the table with her bony fist.

"Do you mean my daughter is a whore?"

Szuha paled.

"I didn't say that . . ."

"Charming, I must say!" Hajnalka laughed. "That's a hell of a thing to bring up now! Why did you go on living with me then? Because it wasn't like that! You know very well that it wasn't like that!"

—165—

George Zentay spoke quickly.

"Look, that's not the issue. What we have to discuss is what's going to happen to the child. That's the important thing."

Not soon after that the company broke up. Miklos Szuha pulled his wife aside. Softly, timidly he asked her:

"Are you coming home now?"

Hajnalka stared at his big brown eyes. Suddenly she felt sorry for him.

"No, Miklos," she said. "Tomorrow I'll pick up the child and my things."

Miklos Szuha dropped his head. He left with Istvan Hires.

Jani and Piroska returned from Brügecs at nine o'clock with four demijohns of wine. Maria Pek poured herself a glass. She addressed her son.

"Your sister has come home," she said. "Tomorrow she's bringing her child too. They're going to live here."

Jani bent over and untied his shoelaces.

"There's room," he answered and went to bed.

Jani Habetler's wedding took place Christmas Day. Maria Pek started cooking at dawn. She cut up ten chickens and a mirror carp which had been gasping in a bucket of water. Hajnalka kneaded dough, Gizike peeled potatoes and cleaned a huge pile of vegetables, while Eszter washed the pork and beef and prepared the sauces. They wouldn't let Piroska set foot in the kitchen.

"You'll get enough of it once you're married," Maria Pek told her. "More than enough."

Jani sat at the festive table in a dark-blue suit, his wife in a dark-blue dress. They drank the strong Brügecs wine.

George Zentay took pictures, then Janos Habetler asked for attention. He was in bed, propped up with pillows. He was almost bald now, his few remaining hairs quite white. His thick neck still suggested his former strength but his skin was etched with deep wrinkles. A little wine was poured into a glass and Gizike took it to him. He sat up straight and began:

"My dear children, from the bottom of my heart I wish that you may live the same way I have lived with your dear, adorable little mother. Even if sometimes we had a small fight or even a big one—I must admit that we did, because I have always despised lies and liars, a person like that is a nothing in my eyes—but your dear mother always knew how to smooth things. And I don't mean to boast, but all my life I gave your mother all my earnings without holding back a single penny because I was completely untouched by any kind of unwholesome passion. So I lift my glass to my dear wife, to the newlyweds, and to my entire dear family, with the wish that you all be very happy always."

And tears rolled down his cheeks.

After midnight the mood brightened. Old man Zentay announced that he was going to get married, too, to a widow worth 60,000 forints. "And she's pretty," he added.

"You old goat!" Maria Pek laughed. "That's all you ever think about!"

Old man Zentay was amazed.

"Why not? It's a pleasant pastime. We'll spend the old girl's money, and then I'll clear out."

Maria Pek got mad.

"You ought to be ashamed of yourself. They'll be measuring you for a coffin any day now and you'll still be dreaming about women!"

Zentay put down his glass.

"Why mention the end?"

Maria Pek laughed.

"Why not? We can't just wear out like old shoes."

"Anyway, it's not for conversation," he repeated. "One day you just collapse on the street or anywhere. I refuse to allow it into my thoughts . . ."

George Zentay got drunk. Idiotically he sang, *"Hey ho, Fisherman . . ."* Eszter blew up; she called him a drunken beast, an animal. Maria Pek's eyes were bright with wine too. She got mad and chased her daughter out of the room. Old man Zentay followed and stroked her hair.

"I'm sorry Fate threw my son across your path," he said to her. "He'll never be a decent man. He's like his grandfather; he drinks, he whores, he's a spendthrift. My advice is to cheat on him. Then he won't be so sure of himself."

The Seres gave the young couple two changes of sheets and a strawberry-colored eiderdown quilt as a wedding present. Sandor Seres, flushed from the Brügecs wine, rapped on the table and asked for silence. But when he stood up, he was so overcome that tears streamed from his eyes.

"Jani, be very happy!" he said. "Be very happy, Jani, and your wife too! That's all I wish you!"

Then he sat down again. Bela Sapadt kissed him, then Boris, and began to sing lustily: *"The forest is sighing, the reeds are sighing."* They all sang until dawn, pausing often to wish the newlyweds much happiness.

In March Janos Habetler was sent to the cardiac clinic on Lake Balaton. Three months later he came home in excellent shape. On the doctor's recommendation he was pensioned. Zentay took care of the papers; after a lot of running around he managed to get Janos 700 forints a month. The children agreed among themselves that they would add 100 forints each. They gave Maria Pek the money every payday.

In the Nagyfuvaros Street apartment life became intolerable. With nothing to do, Janos Habetler felt as if he were in prison. Maria Pek watched over him so strictly that he could not even step out the door. Newspapers or books didn't interest him, he just paced grumpily up and down the apartment and began to insult his wife with cutting remarks. Then Maria Pek would drink a few glasses of wine and curse her husband hysterically. Sometimes she even punched him in the face. The battle grew more and more brutal from day to day; often they didn't speak for a week, hating each other with bitter, silent intensity.

Hajnalka's divorce went through. The court awarded her 400 forints a month child support. She and Ervin were married in the town hall one early fall morning. They asked two strangers to be witnesses. Ervin bought an Üllöi Avenue co-op on the National Savings Bank plan. He made a down payment of 40,000 forints.

George Zentay was attending evening classes at an economics institute; he was in his last year. He studied with fervent resolve. He wanted to go on to the University after he got his diploma. He was obsessed with the idea and insisted that he would not be satisfied until he was Doctor Zentay.

"Even if the régime changes," he said, "a diploma will not lose its value."

It irritated Eszter to watch him scribbling and erasing in his notebooks. She made fun of him every night.

"Don't get mad, but I can't help laughing when I see a balding man plug away like that. It's not so bad when you're eighteen, but at your age it's very funny."

Zentay blushed.

"I didn't ask for your opinion," he replied drily.

One night Eszter said that she was going to register at the University. Her office would sponsor her—her school record was excellent. She wanted to study law.

"I'll be Doctor Eszter Habetler."

Zentay told her to stop dreaming, because he was not

going to take care of the child every night. Their life became a round of endless bickering. Zentay started to drink again and often came home stoned-drunk. Then Eszter went wild.

"Don't touch me! I despise you! Don't touch the child! Get out! I can't stand the sight of you!"

"Great, that's fine, I'm going!"

But he did not leave.

Tearfully Eszter complained to her family. Maria Pek told her to come home with the child. Gizike saw the situation differently.

"Why should she leave the apartment, the furniture, the washing machine? For Zentay to fritter it all away on drink?"

Jani gnashed his teeth.

"Why do you always have to butt in? You're an idiot! What if some night when he's drunk he hits her over the head and kills her? What will you say then?"

After much crying and arguing, Eszter returned to her home in Kispest. Old man Habetler undressed, crawled into bed, and lit the dragon-headed lamp on the night table. He looked at his wife and said:

"I have to talk to Zentay," he intoned very solemnly. "I won't stand for drunkards in my family. I despise people like that because you can't trust a word they say, not a single word."

Maria Pek paled.

"There you go, shooting your mouth off again!" she screamed. "Are you trying to destroy me? On purpose?"

Jani rushed in from the kitchen.

"Mama, don't start again! Don't start again, in the name of God, or we'll all wind up in the insane asylum!"

Maria spat in his eye.

"You're talking to your mother, you filth!"

"Oh, sure, I know," said Jani. "Mama has three glasses of wine and everybody in the world is filth."

He grabbed the bottle and hurled it to the floor. Then he went back to the kitchen to wash the dishes.

Piroska was pregnant. Jani was like a man obsessed. He hovered over his wife, wouldn't let her do even the simplest things and brought home bananas, oranges, and other delicacies. One night he dreamed of a big ocean again. The next day he told his mother. Maria Pek said not to worry; Piroska was very thin and fragile but the doctors at the Istvan Hospital were very good. She broke into a smile.

"When you wake up in the morning, look right out the window. Then you'll forget your dream."

And she patted his strong hand.

In her eighth month Piroska complained of pains, they came every ten minutes. Maria Pek packed her things, Ervin sent for a taxi, and he and Hajnalka took Piroska to the Istvan Hospital. Jani got there later. The three of them paced up and down the corridor. Finally the doctor came out of the delivery room. He told them he was very sorry, there had been a complication and they would have to do a Caesarean, there was a danger that they would lose either the mother or the child. Jani asked them to take care of his wife. His eyes were full of tears.

Piroska was wheeled into the operating room on a rubber-tired cart. As the doctors were washing up for the operation there was a loud shriek. Unassisted Piroska bore a weak but healthy boy. A month later Hajnalka and Ervin held him up to be baptized in the Nagyvarad Place Calvinist Church. He was named Janos. Maria Pek fried fish and made cheese noodles. Everyone drank wine until morning. There was no happier man than Jani Habetler in the whole world.

The feud between the two old people got worse every day. They hardly exchanged a civil word. Habetler parried coolly and expertly. He could reduce his wife to a fit of hysterical rage with a single remark; his source of inspiration never seemed to dry up. One morning over breakfast he asked her whether Jani's godmother had visited him at the hospital while he was unconscious. Maria Pek put down her cup.

"So that's what's been on your mind! You old fool! Even when you were at death's door that black-haired slut excited your dirty fancy?"

Habetler wagged his head.

"Don't always put Annuska down. She's a respectable woman, a very congenial, nice, friendly and an exceptionally well-mannered creature."

That drove Maria Pek wild.

"You even beat me on account of her! You stomped on me! You pimp! For forty years I worked, I washed other people's laundry while you played around with the cleaning women at the Ludovika. You thought I didn't know? You think I don't know that you slept with Bela Sapadt's wife?"

"Could be," said Habetler. "Why not? If my memory serves me well, she was a strong, healthy, good-looking woman."

Maria Pek howled with pain. Her withered little face convulsed, she pulled at her hair with her clawlike fingers, and her ice-blue eyes filled with tears.

"So you want to get rid of me!" she sobbed. "I'll do you that favor myself! And don't you dare bring me flowers in the cemetery! You're a murderer, a smiling murderer. You skunk! You hypocrite! You no-good scoundrel!"

"For God's sake, be quiet!" said Habetler. "You'll wake up the whole building. For forty years I've begged you to keep that ugly mouth of yours shut, to talk in a decent tone of voice, quietly, the way it's proper. But you only scream at me, at the children, at the neighbors, like a wild pig. You were always as coarse as a horse blanket. Anybody who ever knew us will be my witness. Come on, ask anybody, everybody, our most distant neighbors, my family in Brügecs, or even our own children! Did you ever in your whole life show any respect for anyone? You did not. And did you ever address anybody in the world except rudely? I certainly can't remember a single time. If we were to put it to a vote, nobody in the whole wide world would be on your side."

Maria Pek's ice-blue eyes didn't leave his face.

"May God make you pay for this," she said. "You worm. . . ."

And she left the kitchen and cried.

After such a scene they did not talk to each other for days. Maria Pek prepared his special diet and shoved it wordlessly on the table. The silence would continue until finally Maria Pek dissolved into laughter.

"Eat, old man! To hell with your aristocratic stomach!"

Habetler smiled. Timidly, with a guilty look on his face, he kissed her.

"Thank you very, very much, my darling, my sweet little mama," he said in a choked voice, "thank you for the kind-hearted concern which you have showed toward me since the beginning."

The next day the war started all over again. They dug up dusty memories, they tormented, they sawed away at each other with unappeasable hatred.

Finally Jani asked his sisters to do something to stop the conflict because he and Piroska couldn't get anywhere with their parents. Sunday afternoon the Habetler girls gathered in the apartment. The old couple listened to the admonitions like scolded children, their heads bowed. Hajnalka spoke bitterly with tears in her eyes.

"This is no way to live. Both of you are sick and we don't know which one to worry about more. It's no use for you to promise that you'll behave, the next day you just start quarreling all over again. There's only one solution: Mama should move in with one of us and Papa should stay here, because you two just can't live together."

Maria Pek blushed.

"All right, that's enough!" she said jerkily. "Just you worry about your own problems! You've got more than enough of them. Besides, your father and I got along for forty years, we'll get along now too!" And she laughed with anger and embarrassment.

They seemed to have made peace with each other. Illness ruled Maria Pek's life. Her voice weakened, her strength ebbed day by day, only her eyes were still clear and strict. She had to take lots of medicines. Solvasthmine, Astmamid, Isolanid-Digitalis, Coderil, and tranquilizers. She promised the district physician she would rest, but she was afraid to sleep; whenever she awakened she could hardly breathe and clawed her quilt in agony. She sat up in bed practically all night long, listening to the quiet breathing of the others, and only dozed off a little toward dawn.

Old man Habetler always slept well. He awakened fresh and rested; shaved, shined his shoes, put on his tie, and paced and fretted until nightfall. He insisted that he wanted to work come what may, at least wander around the neighborhood and visit acquaintances. But Maria Pek enforced his doctor's orders and the children's strict admonitions and would not permit him to leave the apartment. In his boredom and impotent anger, he boasted of his health, his strength, his virility. Not even the most hot-blooded woman could complain in his arms, he claimed. Maria Pek cried and called him heartless. And so they jabbed away at each other, perhaps even more cruelly than before.

Early one Sunday morning toward the end of summer, Jani had a talk with his mother. They were in the kitchen and kept their voices low so they would not disturb the others, who were still asleep. Maria Pek sat on the kitchen stool, a bowl in her lap, peeling apples. Jani was shaving.

"Mama, I'm moving out. I'm going to take my wife and my child away from here."

The knife glistened in Maria Pek's hand.

"Where are you going, my son?"

"I don't know. I applied for living quarters. If they don't give me an apartment, I'll transfer to Győr or to some other plant where they will give me one. I can make a living anywhere."

"And the family?"

"I don't want anything to do with them."

"Is that so?"

"Yes. Neither with my lousy father nor with my sluttish sisters. Nor the entire shithouse."

"And your mother? What do you call me?"

Jani washed the soap off his face and dried himself.

"It's impossible to live here. This dirt and confusion can only come to a bad end. I want order in my life, Mother. I'm taking my son away from here."

The old woman sniggered.

"You'll never leave here. If I wanted to, I could poke your eyes out right now. If I wanted to, I could lie down in the doorway and dare you to step over me. I'm your mother. You were conceived for my happiness right here, inside of me, under my heart like the others. I have the right to speak, because I suffered for you and for all the family. Together we lived through good times and bad times and we will stay together as long as I live. And afterwards, too . . . you are my son. Sometimes I laugh when you shout or gnash your teeth or shake your fist . . . but don't hurt your father—he's old, a little crazy. Don't hurt the girls; they're your blood. You have to defend them, I tell you, because you're the man in the family, they have no one but you to lean on."

"Mother," Jani replied, "even if you tied a tractor to my feet, I'd get out of this pig farm. I have a chance to make a man of my boy. It's my right."

With a small smile he slipped into his shirt.

Two days later, on Tuesday, the phone rang in Hajnalka's apartment. It was a frightened Bela Sapadt who said that

Mrs. Habetler was sick, they'd better come right home. Hajnalka was out but Ervin the saxophone player rushed to Nagyfuvaros Street in a taxi. Bela Sapadt was waiting outside the door. Self-importantly he bent close to Ervin and said that in his opinion Mrs. Habetler had tried to commit suicide.

Old man Habetler was wandering around in the kitchen. His eyes darted nervously back and forth. He avoided his son-in-law's face.

"It's very nice of you to come," he said.

Maria Pek lay on the bed in a flannel nightgown. The sun shone on her face, her gray hair was disordered and tangled on the pillow, her tongue, thick and green, protruded from her mouth, her blue eyes stared fixedly at the ceiling. The saxophone player sat down on the edge of the bed, put his arms around her slight body, and laid his face next to her tortured, wrinkled little face.

"Mama, what did you do? Answer me! Mama, do you hear me?"

A tear rolled down Maria Pek's cheek. The saxophone player asked for milk and made her drink some. The old woman burst into sobs.

"You see, I can't even die . . . he said he never loved me . . . that he lived with me out of decency . . . he loathed to kiss my hands because they're so ugly . . ."

The saxophone player rocked her back and forth until she fell asleep. Then he went into the kitchen. He asked Habetler why he had not called a doctor. Janos answered that he hadn't dared oppose her, besides, when it had happened, he was not in the room.

"Then you had better pray," the saxophone player said. "If her body has absorbed it, you'll be going to her funeral soon."

By evening Maria Pek was better. She promised her desperately sobbing children that she would never do such a thing again.

That day was never mentioned again. But Maria Pek summoned her son to her bedside. It was late at night.

"I could not escape," she whispered. "Leave this place. And have a happy life."

Jani Habetler nodded. He kissed her hand.

❖   ❖   ❖   ❖   ❖   ❖

George Zentay came home drunk every night. Eszter lost weight, her hands trembled out of control. Helplessly, with desperate hatred she stared at her husband's fatuous grin.

"You're a beast! Even your own father would stand up in court to testify that you're a rotten, drunken scoundrel. And don't use my soap! Or my toothpaste! You'd better start cutting your beer by a couple of bottles a day, because I'm not going to work for your pleasures! Your father told me to tell you to go to hell. He told me to find myself an honest, decent man instead!"

Zentay pulled off his tie and drank a glass of water. He grinned, but his eyes were dark and sad.

"My God, and to think that I had such an exemplary upbringing!" he said. "I was wakened by actresses every morning. My father would still be hung-over and sleepy. He would hold the phone to my ear and I had to listen to the billing and cooing. Katolin Karady once even sang a song for Chief Inspector Zentay. But let's not be unfair—he did show some concern for me. Once when he was drunk he held a pistol to my head because I didn't want to eat my supper. My mother stood it for three years, then she died . . . yet this fine, upstanding man is my father. On his tombstone I'm going to carve *Here lies nobody*. . . . And you, my girl, are a wretched little hamster. So help me God, you make me sick."

Eszter cried all the time. Finally, on her sisters' advice, she began systematically to poison George Zentay's life. Night after night she goaded him.

"When are you moving? When are you going to get out? When will we be rid of you?"

Zentay kept on repeating wearily:

"I am leaving, I'll go soon."

The family said he would never leave.

Then unexpectedly, at the end of October, he did move out. He took some bedclothes, his camera, and the radio. When Eszter got home from work and saw the empty radio stand, she started to cry.

But next day at Nagyfuvaros Street Gizike stopped her.

"Are you crazy? What if he had taken half of everything! Be glad he only took so little."

In her kitchen Maria Pek wept quietly.

"My God, all three of them, all three . . ."

But the Habetler girls were amused. They tried to console her. No matter where they looked, they explained, they saw only bad marriages. It was just that other women put up with drunken husbands and beatings because they were afraid of what the neighbors might say and, besides, they didn't want to give up half their furniture and other possessions. But they, the Habetler girls, were not like that, thank God, they didn't have a slave mentality, they weren't afraid of being lonely and they could support and raise their children alone.

Jani guffawed.

"That's for sure! One of them will be a pop singer and the other a trombone player! And they can eat cheese noodles every day of the week, as much as their bellies will hold!"

Now both Hajnalka and Eszter started to cry and even Gizike's eyes were wet with tears.

"Is that all you have to say? And if life hurts you? Who do you crawl to then? I took care of you in the Barracks while Mama worked, I took you for walks to the Ringer, I washed you, gave you bread and apples," Gizike countered.

Jani flew into a rage.

"Don't give me that!" he roared. "Don't play high and mighty with me! I know all about you! About your carryings on! Do you think I'm an idiot? I'm going to hang a red light over the door to let everybody know that the Habetler girls are home—come right in—one's better than the other! Jazz, dance, chocolate flips! Just be patient, everybody will get his turn."

Maria Pek screamed.

"It's not true!" She gasped for breath. "Don't listen to him! He's only barking. He always does! He got it from me; he inherited his miserable, nasty temper from me. But he has a warm heart! Your brother will never leave you!"

Jani made a gesture.

"I spit on the whole family! On you too! Don't play the clown for me, it doesn't work, I've had it up to here! I've had enough of you, too, Mama. I've had enough of everybody! Every one of you! Up to my ears. You make me vomit."

Maria Pek just stared at him. Suddenly she threw herself to the floor, tore at her hair until her braids came undone, first above the temples, then at the back of her head. She twitched hysterically. A bump swelled on her forehead. Blood spurted from her nose.

"He doesn't mean it!" she sobbed. "He really has a good heart. He won't let the family fall apart!"

Jani gathered her in his arms. He kissed her tormented, wrinkled face. Tears gushed from his yellowish eyes.

"I'm just yelling! Mama knows me. I'm crazy. Mama, I hope I die if ever in my whole life I desert them even once. A man can't turn his back on his family."

They all kissed each other and cried some more.

Gizike complained that her back hurt. She lay down on the couch in her clothes, and Maria Pek covered her up. A few minutes later she was fast asleep. She slept whenever she had a chance and her back always hurt. But it was no use arguing with her, she refused to see a doctor. She explained that with the monthly payment of 400 forints on the co-op, there wouldn't be enough left over to pay for the electricity, heating, food, transportation, and clothes if she had to go on sick-leave pay.

Agotha was in the seventh grade now. She was a tall, pretty girl—it was not possible to buy her clothes in the Pioneer Store any more. Istvan Hires sent 300 forints to his daughter the first of every month. He worked for an instrument maker in the private enterprise sector; he claimed he earned 10 forints an hour. Sometimes Agotha went to visit him. Hires asked her about her studies and often boasted about how many factories had offered him jobs. His gifted hands were well remembered everywhere. He never asked about Gizike and never spoke about his own life. He bought Agotha a season ticket to the concerts and a bicycle and took her to a performance of *Bank Ban* at the National Theater. Once when Agotha was visiting Juli Csele's daughter came down the steps into the workshop bringing his dinner in a cooking pot. Bobe Csele was a slender, full-breasted girl whose hair was dyed blonde. She wore a violet raincoat. She kissed the balding lathe-operator.

"Hi, handsome!" she greeted him with a hoarse laugh.

Istvan Hires blushed and started to sweep up the shavings under his machine. For the first time in her life Agotha felt sorry for her father.

Jani Habetler's son was sickly, so Piroska stayed home with him for many weeks on sick pay. She was lazy and often slept until ten o'clock or stayed in bed reading; she always piled up the dirty diapers for Jani to wash in the tub when he got home from work. This upset Maria Pek very much. Once, when the two of them were alone in the kitchen, she spoke to her daughter-in-law:

"When a woman has a baby, my child, she cannot stay in bed until ten o'clock. And washing diapers is not a man's job, but a woman's."

The next morning Piroska got up early, polished the brass, did the shopping and cooking, but again she piled the diapers in the tub. In the evening Jani poured water into the washtub.

"I will gladly wash everything for my child. Everything! Not just his diapers, but his shirts and his creepers and his rompers, too. Piroska is weak and I'm strong. I won't let her."

Maria Pek looked at her daughter-in-law:

"Well, my girl, your prayers have been answered. You won't find another husband this crazy in all the world."

Maria Pek probably loved this pale, delicate grandchild best of all. She fed him, played with him, rode him on her knee.

Hopla, Hopla, Hopapa
Here we go with a Hopseessa!

But she was out of breath quickly. Then she would put him down on the bed, sit by him and sing the nursery rhyme over and over again. She had no taste for wine any more. The girls came every day, bringing oranges, flowers, Neapolitan wafers, and chocolates for their father because he liked those best of all. He kissed his daughters and tearfully, emotionally chided them for squandering so much of their valuable money. Then he munched the sweets with his toothless gums. Maria Pek looked on angrily.

"How batty people get in their old age," she said, and cackled tartly.

Every Saturday old man Zentay met with Eszter in the Gaiety Espresso. He had a license to manufacture metal shutters, two men worked for him, all he had to do was travel and take orders. He made a great deal of money and paid his two employees well. He gave his grandchild a fur-trimmed suede coat, a bicycle, and an electric train; every week he stuffed a hundred forints into Eszter's pocketbook. And he tried to console the thin, nervous woman by telling her not to mope over his drunken son—he didn't deserve a second thought. Eszter declared that she wasn't moping, she despised George, she considered him a sewer rat. She had to see him once a month when he gave her the 350 forints for child care, but that was all.

Old man Zentay was beginning to show his age. His movements had become heavy, the wrinkles on his clean-shaven face were rigid, his brown eyes had become a little glassy. Only his hair was unchanged—not a trace of gray and as carefully combed back as always. He didn't chatter about women, love affairs, and doweries any more. He had a couple of beers and reminisced about the distant past. Mostly he talked about his work as a police official, modestly and enthusiastically. The Zentay team had been as well-known in the underworld as in the department, he told Eszter, and that despite the fact that they hardly ever used force when questioning suspects because Inspector Zentay had carefully organized a network of stool-pigeons among the whores, pimps, loan sharks, fences, waiters, and thieves ... he had known every professional burglar of stature personally and often spent evenings in their dives—they respected his expertise. His book about criminal investigation had been translated into many languages and at the Brussels International Police Congress he was the only Hungarian who had been awarded a Master Detective Diploma, of which there were only six in the world. Later he had hidden Jews, the Arrow Cross beat him up, but the Communists did not want his services; first he was pensioned, then deported. He didn't believe in God, jeered at religion and the afterworld, and hated priests because in his opinion they live well without cost or risk.

Jokingly he waved a finger in Eszter's face.

"If in fifty years I happen to die," he said, "don't let any priest near me or I'll climb out of the coffin and kick him in the ass."

At the beginning of November, on a Sunday, Jani's son developed a fever. He cried fretfully. Maria Pek held him on her lap and opened his mouth. She said there was no reason to worry, he was just teething. With her finger she showed Jani the swollen gum.

At nine o'clock in the evening the child got sick. He vomited, then went into convulsions. His whole body jerked and then became rigid. His eyes opened wide and he lost consciousness. Maria Pek shrieked; she flung herself down on the floor and tore her hair.

"My God! Tooth seizure! He's going to die! My Lord, Lord Jesus, why are you taking him away from us?"

Jani shouted at her.

"Shut up, goddammit, Mother! Mother, please be quiet! A doctor, get a doctor, quickly!"

"It's no use!" the old woman screamed. "There's no medicine against death. God never loved me! Why this tiny flower? Why the innocent?"

Sandor Seres rushed to the Emergency Clinic and returned with a loden-coated young woman who examined the child uneasily.

"I'm not a pediatrician," she said. "I'll take him to a specialist."

Piroska wrapped him up and they took him to the White Cross Hospital in a taxi. Jani Habetler put his head down on the kitchen table. His body heaved with sobs.

Monday morning the child was better. When the girls came to inquire Maria Pek assured them that it could be brought home within ten days. Eszter brought fried fish for her mother and chocolates for her father.

Tuesday morning Maria Pek took sick.

"I'm dying," she moaned. "A doctor . . ."

The district physician gave her an injection and left. Half an hour later he was back. By that time Hajnalka was there too. She looked at him with pleading eyes. In reply the doctor made a pitying, helpless, expressive gesture.

"Her heart . . . ," he said and sent for an ambulance.

Maria Pek was sitting on the bed. Hajnalka dressed her in warm panties, black stockings, a nightgown, and her black winter coat. She packed a glass, knife and fork, soap, and a towel in a shopping bag.

The ambulance arrived. Hajnalka asked the doctor to let her ride with her mother. In the ambulance she held Maria close. The wrinkled old face was visibly becoming paler. A horrible fear overcame Hajnalka.

"We'll be right there, Mama!" she kept saying. "We'll be right there . . ."

Maria Pek was taken to the Istvan Hospital. An emergency cot was set up for her. Hajnalka took care of the admission papers, sought out the ward doctor on duty, and gave her 300 forints.

"The heart sounds weak," the physician said. "There isn't much we can do. We'll try oxygen . . . that might help somewhat."

But half an hour later the oxygen still hadn't come. The nurse said the apparatus was out of order, it was being repaired.

Half crazy, Hajnalka rushed to find the doctor. She pleaded to be told where the machine was being repaired—she would speak to the mechanics herself. The doctor was annoyed and uncooperative.

"They can't bring it up before they've finished," she said gruffly. "And when they've finished they'll bring it up anyway."

Not much later the apparatus was set up at Maria Pek's bed. For hours a nurse held the oxygen mask over her mouth a few minutes at a time.

Around noon Sandor Seres appeared with a canister of chicken broth. For a long time he stood silently next to Hajnalka in the corridor. Bewildered, he gripped the handle of the thermos; finally he quietly said good-bye and left.

In the afternoon Gizike, Agotha, Eszter, Jani, Piroska, and the saxophone player arrived. Jani pressed some bills into Hajnalka's hand.

"You take care of everything!" he said. "Give everybody something."

He leaned his huge body against the wall and sobbed. One by one they went into the ward and looked at their choking, unconscious mother. At five o'clock Eszter went to the Kispest kindergarten to pick up her little girl. At six o'clock Janos Habetler appeared in the corridor. He was stooped and bent.

They would not permit him to see his wife. They made him sit on a bench under a blue lamp; she was asleep, they said, she must not be disturbed. At seven o'clock Jani and Piroska took his arm and led him home. Gizike, Agotha, Hajnalka, and Ervin remained at the hospital until ten o'clock when the nurse on duty politely but firmly threw them out. The doctor's room was opposite the stairwell. The saxophone player went in and asked permission for one of the girls to stay with her mother for the night. The doctor shook her head.

"I can't make any exceptions," she said.

"Then perhaps you'll allow me to telephone you here?"

"If I allowed that, the phone would be ringing all night long. There are many seriously ill patients on the floor and their families are just as worried."

"Is there any hope?"

"By morning at the latest edema of the lungs will set in . . ."

The saxophone player bowed his head.

In the morning the sisters did not find Maria Pek in the ward. She had died at four o'clock in the morning.

Janos Habetler sneaked down to the Harp and called the hospital. He got the news over the telephone. When the sisters got back home, he was lying in the janitor's room in a frightening state. His toothless mouth gasped for breath, his thinning hair hung in kinky strands, his mustache was soaked with the tears that poured down his cheeks. He was moaning in ardent pain.

"They wouldn't let me see her! I wasn't with her! I couldn't hold her dear hand! Sweet dear God, you wouldn't let me be with her! How could you, dear God?"

The old man struggled to his feet and rocked from side to side.

"She said she would leave me, she said so! Now her dear, adorable little body will be buried in the ground! She's left me forever! I will follow you soon, dear adorable little Mama. I'll descend into the depths of the grave too!"

The district physician gave the old man two injections. Irritably he said, "Please pull yourself together! This is no way to behave!"

Then he noticed Jani's yellowish eyes. He closed his bag.

"The days ahead will be very hard," he said hastily. "You will all need strength."

They sat Janos in a chair, picked it up by the armrests, and carried the white-faced, moaning old man up the stairs.

Gizike and Hajnalka went to the morgue. The little red-brick building flanked by ancient willow trees stood in a hidden corner of the hospital yard. Behind a yellow door, at the end of the electrically lighted corridor there was another door with a sign, PLEASE RING BELL. An elderly, thick-set man answered. He wore a white cotton suit, an apron, and a cap like a cook's. He had a friendly smile for the visitors.

"You'll have to wait a few minutes," he said. "We're expecting a delivery."

In the waiting room stood a table with worn and faded gray paint and a red bench like those in city parks. The floor was concrete, the walls whitewashed. The only source of light was a casement window, the sky outside was overcast, it was drizzling, so it was dreary and dark inside. After a while the stocky man came back. With the stub of a pencil he wrote the information into a blue-covered notebook. Gizike took the black-silk dress, black slip, black stockings, and high-heeled black shoes out of a bag. The stocky man picked up the shoes.

"These will give us trouble!" he said. "Usually we put black slippers on them because the feet get stiff, you know. Of course, if the relatives wish, I could cut out the heel of these shoes . . . but that's not our job, you know . . ."

Hajnalka gave him 20 forints. The stocky man put all the things in a large kerchief.

"No panties?" he asked.

"No," Gizike answered, taken aback. "We forgot . . ."

"How do you want the hair done?"

The sisters did not answer immediately.

"In a wreath, if possible," Gizike said finally. "Braid it and make a wreath in back."

Then they left.

Gizike and Hajnalka parted at the streetcar stop. On Üllöi Avenue Gizike went into a lingerie shop and bought a pair of light-blue silk panties.

"Something very special, please," she said gently. "It's for my dead mama."

Hajnalka made all the arrangements for a First Class funeral. After a brief consultation with the family in view of their father's alarming condition, she bought two lots in the cemetery—when the time comes, let them lie in eternal peace side by side. But it was very difficult to manage. Two lots, a decorated bier, the glass-enclosed hearse, a hardwood casket, and the uniformed ushers cost almost 5000 forints. And there were additional expenses—wreaths, the carpenters to build the bier, the minister, the gravediggers, and the photographer. The Union's assistance fund helped a great deal. Hajnalka got 300, Eszter 400, Jani 600, Piroska 300, Gizike 600 forints. Gizike's co-workers at the plant took up a collection which came to another 1500 forints. The National Pension Office paid the widower, Janos Habetler, 400 forints. The saxophone player made up the rest.

Hajnalka ordered the black-bordered death notices, too. One was tacked up at the front entrance of the apartment house, the rest were addressed and sent by mail to relatives and acquaintances. Piroska bought a dozen black-bordered handkerchiefs for the members of the family. They did not know what to do about their father. His voice had given out; he just lay on the couch, his chest heaving with loud sighs. His inflamed eyes reflected his violent pain, his tears flowed without pause. Jani hardly left his side.

"Please get hold of yourself, Papa," he begged. "Please, Father, please get hold of yourself."

The old man did not answer. His silent suffering was much harder to watch than his mad frenzies. The saxophone player did not think they should take him to the funeral.

"We can give him a strong sleeping pill," Ervin said. "If he reproaches us later, it's still better than a fatal heart attack at the grave."

The Habetler girls, sobbing desperately, replied that they had no right to deprive their father of his last farewell.

"My mother is expecting him," Gizike said. "The family was always together . . . we must not forget that now."

The district physician thought the saxophone player was right, he was afraid that the excitement of the funeral would be too much; but, seeing Gizike's dismay, he shrugged.

"If you wish," he said, "I'll give him an injection of morphine before you leave. But be careful."

It was decided that Jani should take the old man to the cemetery in a taxi along with the preacher. Maybe the minister would lend him strength and ease the pain during the long ride.

The girls borrowed black coats, kerchiefs, and handbags. Agotha sewed black armbands for everyone. The grandchildren too—they wore them frightened and proud. Jani solved the shoe problem by dying everyone's black.

The Habetler girls lost weight. Their shoulders sagged, their faces aged, their movements became slow. All three of them began to resemble their father. Hajnalka wandered around her beautiful apartment in a daze. The saxophone player took care of the child, washed him, made his bed, and put him to sleep. Hajnalka cowered in an armchair.

"I have no mother any more!" she wailed.

The saxophone player sat down on the floor beside her chair. He took her limp hand and kissed it. They were quiet for a moment. Finally he said:

"Tomorrow, when you say good-bye to her, you will see a stranger's face on the bier . . . I had to tell you . . ."

Hajnalka looked at him. Protest flared in her eyes. Anger. Slowly she withdrew her hand, defiantly pressed her bloodless lips together. Yet she did not dare ask why.

It was not yet half past nine when Ervin and Hajnalka and Eszter entered the cemetery gate. Gizike, Agotha, Eszter, and Piroska were already waiting on the sidewalk in front of Number Nine Chapel. Hajnalka turned to her sister.

"Have you been inside?" she asked.

Eszter nodded. Hajnalka went in and looked at her mother but came right out again. Shaking her head, she buried her face on Ervin's shoulder.

"That's not my mother," she sobbed. "That's not my mother!"

The November drizzle was chilling. Relatives, colleagues, co-workers, acquaintances arrived singly carrying wreaths and flowers.

The Nagyfuvaros street neighbors came in a group. Bela

Sapadt and Sandor Seres staggered under a huge wreath of real flowers, ahead of them the children with a small white wreath, hair and faces soaked. The Zentays—father and son —added such a grand arrangement of roses and cyclamen that the attendants could hardly find room for it on the bier. The Zentays kissed the Habetler girls. George took Eszter's arm. A photographer in a gray raincoat came forward to solicit an order. The saxophone player quietly sent him to hell but Gizike wanted shots of the funeral.

"My father would like to have pictures," she said gently. "He might even want to send some to Brügecs."

The photographer displayed his folding portfolio. There were seven scenes to choose from: the deceased's face on the bier, the removal of the casket, the coffin in the hearse, the funeral procession, the open grave, the lowering of the coffin, the flower-bedecked mound surrounded by the mourning family. The saxophone player ordered ten of each. He gave the photographer 300 forints' deposit and got a receipt.

It was almost ten o'clock. People filled the chapel and lined up to view the deceased; the four-horse-drawn hearse had driven up to the entrance, but Jani, old man Habetler, and the minister had not arrived. The girls wept desperately; they were sure something had happened. The ceremony had to begin exactly according to the timetable in order to avoid congestion and interruptions. Gizike wanted to look at her mother a last time. The saxophone player asked the people to make way for her. Maria Pek's head did not look bigger than a man's fist, her eyes were shut, an expression of complete indifference was on her face.

The taxi arrived at the last moment. Janos Habetler, stooped and bent, walked behind the minister to the door of the dressing room. He was dragging the wooden valise with the minister's black robes, cap, psalm book, Bible, towel and soap.

The Habetler family lined up on one side of the bier. The

minister was a very old man; beneath his hard black headpiece his snow-white hair glowed like a light. He stepped to the head of the bier, Bible in hand, and waited for the buzzing to stop. When there was silence he raised his head and in a surprisingly strong, clear voice spoke the following sermon:

"Company of mourners! We stand here beside the mortal remains of our sister, Maria Pek . . . do not weep, God's love is infinite . . . it is painful that she is no longer among you . . . but you must know and believe that she is with the Lord . . . He called her to Him to end her suffering; now she is serving the heavenly Father among the hosts of His angels . . . we are approaching the celebration of Christ's birth, of Christ who redeems our souls, whose death on the cross opened the gates of the Kingdom of Heaven to us . . . so do not fear, the soul of our departed sister will also be blessed with redemption . . . Lord Jesus, here stands her stricken family, her husband with whom she shared forty years of toil, sorrow, and joy, her four children whom she raised in honor and decency . . . mourn for her, husband, children, sons-in-law, daughter-in-law, grandchildren, relatives and friends, all of you who have come here to pay your final respects, mourn for her and may there remain in your hearts the love which comes from God and is eternal."

Janos Habetler sobbed wildly. He buried his face in his black-bordered, tear-soaked handkerchief and dropped his head between his knees. Jani could hardly hold him.

"My Lord God," he wailed into his handkerchief. "She left me! Sweet, dear, kind Lord, she left me!"

"Father, please!" Jani said, his face white as a sheet. "Father, please don't."

Loud painful sobs shook the girls too. The relatives wept and so did the friends. The aged minister adjusted his scarf; from time to time a gust of biting wintry wind blew through the chapel door. He raised his arm, his hand a bright spot among all the black.

"Brethren, let us sing the Sixtieth Psalm," he said. "Sing it attentively and God's eternal existence will console you."

He began and many sang along. When they had finished the pallbearers started to carry out the flowers, the people moved toward the door too; Jani supported his staggering father, but the minister stopped everybody and said in a high voice:

"Company of mourners! Now let us recite the Credo."

The crowd fell silent. They all looked at the black-robed old man with the Bible in his hand and more and more of them repeated after him: "I believe in One God, the Almighty Father . . ." "Amen," the crowd echoed. The Habetler girls were standing next to the now-empty bier, Juli Csele and Istvan Hires on the far side, Anna Küvecses in front of the silver-hemmed velvet drape. There was a flash of light from the photographer's flash.

While Maria Pek was being carried out to the glassed-in hearse old man Zentay asked the minister to give a shorter sermon beside the grave and to make the prayer brief too because Janos Habetler was in a bad way.

"We will unfortunately have to do without some of your wonderful sermons," he said. "But you will not be blamed since you have always looked after the salvation of our souls with such untiring devotion."

The minister looked, made no reply.

Janos Habetler, who could hardly stand on his feet, followed the hearse leaning on old man Zentay. He walked like a blind man, padding through puddles and horse manure, his shoes and trousers covered with mud. The rain plastered his thinning hair, the water dripped down the lead-colored strands into his collar.

When the procession rounded a bend in the road and the gravediggers, leaning on their shovels, came into sight and behind them the mound of earth which hid the pit, old man Zentay stopped short, left Janos to his own devices, and hurried back toward the cemetery gate.

The minister did keep his sermon brief. Maria Pek was lowered into the earth and the family stood wailing around the flower-bedecked mound. A last flashbulb flared, the saxophone player gave the gravediggers money and sent a child for a cab. Anna Küvecses kissed the Habetler girls. Farther away from the grave at a cement tub where in the summer the gardener stored water for his sprinkling can, the women from Nagyfuvaros Street were criticizing Juli Csele in loud whispers. They called her a shameless whore because she had dared come to disturb the dead. Bela Sapadt pushed her roughly.

"Get out of here!" he said. "Let this family mourn in peace!"

Juli Csele looked around. She was searching for Istvan Hires with her eyes but he was far away smoking a cigarette with George Zentay under a tree and did not see her. Juli looked at the angry faces in terror and began to sob. Jani stepped up to her and turned his yellowish eyes on the others.

"Don't anyone touch her," he said quietly. "She loved my mother."

Finally the taxi drew up. Hajnalka sat next to the driver, the minister in back. Janos Habetler stopped at the car door to throw kisses at the people until Jani told him to finish his leave-taking. The old man looked confused, put his hat on his head, sat next to the minister. They were driven to Hajnalka's. By evening he wanted to be taken home to Nagyfuvaros Street.

One blow brought another, each sorrow was followed by a new one. The worries mounted, the tears, the anguish, and the fear swelled.

The day after the funeral Gizike went out to the Rakos-keresztur Cemetery; from then on she took fresh flowers to her mother's grave after work every blessed day. She wanted to take her father along but Hajnalka and Eszter would not permit that. The old man's health was completely broken. He lost weight, he let himself go, his pale face was always stubbly. His heart acted up again, he felt the squeeze of the invisible hand again, at times he gasped and wheezed. The district physician gave him injections, prescribed medicine, especially Nitromin, which proved very effective for the more violent attacks.

But he could not and did not want to eat, he could not and did not want to master his grief. All day long he stared at the photograph of Maria Pek, threatened suicide, let his feelings run wild, and tormented the family with his heart-rending lamentations.

"I can hear her, she's complaining." He covered his face with his black-bordered handkerchief. "She says the wind is icy, I'm cold, you took me from my warm bed and brought me to this cold cemetery . . . I'll cover you, my adorable, dear, sweet little Mama, I'll lie down beside you, I'll embrace you forever and ever."

Such words made the girls burst into tears. Tears rolled down Jani's cheeks too. He gnashed his teeth.

"Papa, please don't!" he begged. "For God's sake, Papa, please don't!"

They did not leave Janos alone a single moment, took turns watching him night and day. He seemed intimidated by the saxophone player, by his strange, polite smile. If Ervin told him to eat, Janos ate obediently; if the two of them were alone, Janos did not cry, he just chattered along confusedly, told Ervin that once upon a time he was entrusted with rare treasures of a museum but the shiny things had never dazzled him, he had never touched anything that belonged to someone else, never in the whole wide world. He did not want to brag

—he condemned that kind of man and even more so a liar, for lying words hardly ever left his tongue—he had always given his entire pay, down to the last penny, to his poor wife and he only drank wine on special occasions and then only in moderation. He got drunk, as far as he could remember, only twice in his life, once at Jani's christening, once when he had a disagreement with his wife. That time he had gone out and gotten very drunk.

"She was like a wild pig," he said. "Always! Her life long. When she got going, nobody could stand to be near her. My family in Brügecs was very much against my marrying her. I was a corporal then, they had picked a good-looking, well-to-do girl for me, but you know how it was, with Gizike . . . she was very scared . . . I was the only man in her whole life . . ."

The saxophone player loaded the stove. The old man was quiet too. After a while he said softly:

"Jani, Gizike, the girls all think that there was some kind of love relationship between me and Mrs. Küvecses. Because your mother always accused me of it. One couldn't get it out of her head."

The saxophone player shrugged. "I don't think they care."

The old man bowed his head.

"I don't claim that we never kissed because that would not be true . . . but Annuska was a Maria girl, a religious soul, she believed in purgatory and wouldn't do anything but kiss . . . there were other women—I don't say there weren't—but I never spent more than one or two glasses of beer on them, I never took money away from my family, not one single time."

Earnestly the saxophone player reassured his father-in-law, he was absolutely convinced that what Janos said was true, therefore it was unnecessary to waste another word on the matter.

❖ ❖ ❖ ❖ ❖ ❖

Christmas was celebrated at Hajnalka's. In the afternoon, the entire family went to the cemetery in pouring rain. Only the saxophone player and his little boy stayed home to decorate the six-foot spruce tree. It took them almost two hours. When they had hung the last ornament, the tree toppled over. The child laughed but the saxophone player raged. Finally he drove a small hook into the wall and tied the tree to it. They finished just in time.

Gizike, Eszter, and Piroska were already bustling around in the kitchen, helping Hajnalka. Agotha was playing with the children while the old man sat whimpering in an armchair. George Zentay walked in drunk, a sleeping doll for his daughter under his arm. The saxophone player took his green imitation-leather coat and his hat but then asked Jani to entertain his brother-in-law because he had neither the inclination nor the patience for that ill-tempered, wine-sodden man. Zentay was wearing a worn summer suit and a snow-white shirt. He was loud and boastful. He said he had a nice room, he had worked and studied like a Trojan and finished school with honor.

Now came the big task, the University. Nobody could stop him, he was ready to make any sacrifice to get his degree. He would starve, fight, or even risk death for it.

Jani smiled.

"Do you keep away from saloons as well?" he asked.

"None of your business!" George Zentay answered. He paused for a minute. "You think I'm afraid of you . . . but you're wrong, I haven't been for a long time . . . if you were to start hollering at me now with all your might, if you raised your fist at me right now, I wouldn't run away, I'd just laugh. In the future please remember that."

Jani looked at him out of yellowish eyes.

"You're an idiot," he said. He picked up the bronze Buddha that stood on the buffet, then put it back. "If I raised my fists . . . but nobody has to hit you, you do yourself enough harm all by yourself."

A bell tinkled in the other room. Everyone went in. When the last sparkler had burned out, everyone kissed Janos Habetler, handed each other their presents, and then sat down to supper.

Zentay hugged his little girl and hurriedly took his leave.

The next morning the sun shone, the sky was clear and blue. Miklos Szuha's mother came to take her grandson to Rakosfalva. The Habetler family went to church. The old minister gave a good sermon, mentioned Maria Pek and prayed for her soul.

Christmas dinner was at Nagyfuvaros Street. Afterward the girls sat down to add up the funeral expenses . . . who had given how much money, what had been spent for each item. It was not an easy job; there were many small expenditures which nobody remembered.

Hajnalka kept filling up sheets of paper with figures but the total never checked out. After an hour she shoved the pencil in front of Eszter, and said: "You hassle with it."

Eszter didn't get very far either. A hundred forints disappeared, then reappeared again. They argued. Janos Habetler locked the kitchen door so that the neighbors would not walk in and think that his family was fighting over money matters. Jani was not interested, he was playing with his son on the couch. It was getting dark. Piroska told him to help the girls; after all, it concerned him too. But Jani didn't want to, they could tell him if he owed anybody anything, he would pay it and as far as he was concerned the matter would be settled.

Piroska shrugged.

"They've been fussing with those figures since noon."

Eszter looked up.

"Don't worry, we're not going to short-change anyone!" she said. "That's not the way we do things in our family."

"In my family either," Piroska answered and left the kitchen.

Jani looked at his sister but said nothing. Janos Habetler was sitting on the worn old footlocker behind the iron stove. He knit his brow trying to remember who had not attended the funeral to pay final respects to his wife. He was very angry at Miklos Szuha.

"In my opinion he should not have behaved so badly," he complained to the saxophone player, "under any circumstances. When his father passed away, every member of my family went to the funeral, we placed a very expensive wreath of real flowers on his grave."

The saxophone player assured him that it wasn't worth a second thought, a great many people had paid their final respects; there had been so many flowers and wreaths that it was impossible to count them all. The old man wrinkled his brow.

"That's not true," he said. "If ever I see Miklos Szuha again, I'll tell him that in my eyes he is the lowest filthiest man in the whole wide world. And if he says anything I consider insulting, I won't be responsible for my actions. Because you see, my boy, I can be very good, or I can be very bad. Let whoever riles me beware because when that happens I can't have any consideration for anybody, but anybody in the whole wide world."

His face was serious, threatening. Motionless he stared down at his folded hands.

Finally the Habetler girls figured out that Jani owed Hajnalka 12 forints, Eszter owed Jani 80 and Gizike 140 forints, which she paid immediately. Then it occurred to Gizike that they ought to pay Hajnalka for Christmas dinner because that must have cost a pretty penny. The saxophone player rejected the idea, said something very ugly, then helped his wife put on her beige sheepskin coat.

"Let's go," he said. "I have to play tomorrow night and I'd like to get a little sleep for a change."

But he didn't get to sleep that night either.

The sky was overcast and threatened to snow as they hurried along Berkocsis Street. They caught a taxi at the corner of Jozsef Boulevard. In the elevator the operator rubbed his hands together and said he would bet anything that the city would be white by morning. The saxophone player suggested they postpone the bet until August.

At home they first had hot baths, and afterward ate supper in pajamas. The saxophone player talked about the future. He was seeking to collect a group of compositions which were appealing and modern in sounds and which he could play at foreign music festivals as well. Hajnalka remembered a poem they used to sing at school. She hummed it. Ervin nodded sleepily.

"Sounds good," he said. "Festive. But it's for organ or harmonica. Piano and guitar maybe. It couldn't be orchestrated for wind instruments."

The doorbell rang. Annoyed, the saxophone player reached for his terrycloth robe and went to open the door. George Zentay was standing in the cold hall in his green imitation-leather coat and gray hat. His smile was frightened and apologetic.

"My father is dead," he said. "I've been wandering around the city for hours. I thought you wouldn't mind if I came and warmed up a little here with you."

A tear rolled down Hajnalka's cheek.

"My Lord, how you punish us."

She put on her blue silk robe embroidered with dragons the color of orange peels, kicked off her black-and-gold knit slippers and curled up in an armchair. She was shivering. The saxophone player got out a bottle of cognac but couldn't open it. Zentay pulled the cork, poured drinks, and lit a cigarette. After a brief silence he said:

"I had a feeling something was wrong this morning. I phoned him twice, first at nine, then at eleven, but there was no answer. At twelve I went over to his apartment. I rang the bell but nobody answered. I smelled gas. I sensed he wasn't alive any more but I didn't dare go in alone. I shouted for the superintendent. He called a policeman who broke down the door. My old man was sitting on the toilet with his head propped against the wall. That's how he died. The policeman opened the windows because the gas was unbearable."

"Suicide?" the saxophone player asked. Zentay looked at him.

"No," he answered. "Definitely not. No, he was drunk. He had put some meat in the oven, he must have turned on the gas and forgot to light it. That's what the police think too."

Nobody said anything.

Zentay took a small mirror out of his pocket, adjusted his tie, and wound his gray wool scarf around his neck.

"Well, I'd better be going—I've got an hour's ride to get home, way to hell and back. A man pays 200 forints a month for a hole-in-the-wall and for it has to walk miles in the rain and mud. It's a miracle I haven't sprained my ankle in some stupid pothole."

"Why don't you sleep here?" the saxophone player said.

Zentay didn't want to stay, he said his camera was in Pestlorincz, he was going to take it to a used-instrument store in the morning, maybe he could get three thousand forints for it to pay for the funeral.

Hajnalka stepped to the window and parted the yellow drapes. The snow was falling heavily.

"Don't go," she said. "The snow is falling so hard you can barely see the street. Stay, if only out of superstition; don't leave here tonight . . . you'll slip on the ice with that bad foot of yours. I'll give you some broth, some good hot chicken broth like Mama always made. And some stuffed cabbage. You can have some head cheese too. With tea and rum."

"No, I've got to go home. I'll be careful. Once I'm home there's nothing to worry about . . . I can't drink because I've only got five forints in my pocket and if I can't fall asleep, there's my little girl's photograph on the wall opposite my bed."

He kissed Hajnalka, shook hands with the saxophone player, and left. Barely twenty minutes later he was back.

"I'm scared," he laughed. His laugh was too loud, it frightened him, he fell silent. He wiped his wet face with his handkerchief. "You can laugh at me, kids, and so help me God, it is laughable, but that's how it is."

Hajnalka gave him some broth and stuffed cabbage. After he had eaten he asked them to excuse the ridiculous state of his nerves, quietly said good night, and went into the other room. He did not lie down, but paced up and down.

Hajnalka and Ervin listened for a long time. Finally Hajnalka sat up in bed and switched on the light.

"If we don't do something he'll keep that up all night," she said. "Give him some cognac, he gets high pretty fast—it might make him sleepy."

The saxophone player didn't like the idea, said that to fill Zentay with liquor was a risky business. Drunk he was belligerent and rowdy, he either cried or fought, but one thing was for sure, he would be unmanageable. But Ervin called him anyway.

Zentay drank calmly, deliberately. Half a liter of cognac was gone already but neither his eyes nor his speech showed any effects. Nor was he angry because the saxophone player wouldn't drink along; on the contrary he declared that it was quite unnecessary, he would drink the entire bottle all by himself. He sat at the table in his white shirt and talked quietly, slowly, practically without pause, smoking one cigarette after the other. Occasionally he glanced at Hajnalka and with a sad smile asked her to forgive this crazy night. Hajnalka lay in bed, the down quilt pulled up to her chin. She told him not to be silly and showed her healthy white teeth in the dull light.

Zentay continued to talk about some designer to whom he owed 150 forints, about cybernetics, and expounded on the dizzying results of space exploration.

"I'll still be able to take a trip to the stars," he smiled self-mockingly. "There won't be any security checks, passports, visas; I'll just pay my fare and fly away to some distant planet."

Then he spoke about an excellent cookbook he read every evening. He was learning to cook and he explained in detail the preparation of several dishes. The weary saxophone player poured more cognac. Woodenly Ervin kept saying, "Drink, fellow, drink!" Zentay reached for the glass eagerly, giggling as though to say, "You see, it doesn't matter how late it is, how much I've had to drink, I still don't feel anything, I'm still not dizzy." Yet after a while his speech became halting, he lost the thread of his thoughts, he knit his brow in concentration, shook his head. He complained bitterly about the head of the personnel department because he would not let him attend the University. It was absurd, he said, he had been with the enterprise for twelve years, he had repeatedly received awards for excellence and in '56 he hadn't done anything because he was on crutches. That man had said to one of his colleagues—and Zentay apologized in advance for the exact quotation—"Zentay ought to be glad that he has a hole in his ass and not try to usurp a decent worker's or peasant's place at the University."

By this time Zentay's eyes were flaming. He explained passionately, with excited gestures, that if they said that he ought not deprive a decent person of a chance to study, that obviously meant that he was not decent. And that was slander. Let them prove he wasn't, it was a legal matter, it belonged in the courtroom, he wouldn't stand for it, come what might, he was going to work for a degree.

It was well past midnight when the saxophone player poured out the last drop of cognac. Annoyed and reproachful, he looked at his wife. Hajnalka was sleepy and exhausted too; she could hardly keep her eyes open. Slowly, heavily, Zentay got to his feet. He stared at them morosely.

"I smell gas."

It was no use telling him that there was no gas smell, he looked around the room restlessly and finally went out into the hall to make sure the gas valve was turned off. He came back, sat down at the table and fiddled with the empty bottle. Then he buried his forehead in his hands.

"He always combed his hair so carefully. Who would have thought he had so little left? So help me God, I saw it today."

Tears welled in Hajnalka's eyes. The saxophone player took a pair of dark blue pajamas out of a chest of drawers and handed them to Zentay.

"Lots of my hair is missing too," George said sadly to Hajnalka. "Your sister pulled out a whole fistful. Just the other day he said I ought to go back to her, to kiss her hand because I would never find a more decent woman. But I'm not going back. I've had enough. I'd rather learn to cook and wash my shirts myself—as long as I don't have to see her."

"She doesn't miss you either," Hajnalka said. "Let's go to sleep. I can't keep my eyes open any longer."

Zentay tried to pull himself together. He grimaced and jabbed at his forehead with his index finger. Stuttering, faltering, he explained that he had not meant to speak of his wife disrespectfully. There could be no doubt that she had been faithful to him; at the bottom of her heart she was superstitiously afraid of God, of His punishment, he was afraid that perhaps her second child would get sick and die like the first. Of course she was passionate like her father. She had his hot blood. Once she started, she wouldn't stop, she would go to bed with everybody. But that was nobody's business except her own, although he could say without any hesitation that if he wanted to, peace could be restored any time, all it would take was a bouquet of roses and an Australian wool sweater. Then he asked the saxophone player to accompany him to the toilet, but at the door he stopped short. Ervin had to push him. Afterward he begged Hajnalka's forgiveness again. He started to cry and demand that all the lights be turned on immediately or he would throw himself out the window.

Hajnalka got mad. She rebuked him roughly, demanded that he behave properly, and show some consideration for them, he should go straight into the other room and sleep.

Zentay raised his fist.

"Shut up!" he shouted. "You didn't see the crate they carried him out in! That wasn't a coffin!"

Waving his arms in the air he shouted that the police official was a brute, the bastard had called him to the telephone just as they were carrying the old man out—he had to step over him.

He was silent. A look of fear came over his face, he glanced around uneasily.

"It wasn't suicide," he burst out. "He said we'd spend New Year's Eve together, he'd buy a bottle of cognac and we'd pick up a couple of cute kittens on the Boulevard, we'd play around with them all night long. Of course if I had been at his place Christmas Eve, I would have noticed the gas fumes . . . he was waiting for me, he was cooking a roast for me . . ."

He lifted a tearful face to the saxophone player. Perhaps he wanted to say something else but he only grimaced. He picked up the pajamas lying on the floor and went into the other room. They heard him switch the light on, mutter something to himself, and then start to hum. He plumped the pillow and whistled:

"Hey, fisherman, hey . . ."

At dawn they went into his room. They found him leaning on his elbows at the open window, still whistling. His bare torso was silver with snow.

The winter passed quickly. In February it was still bitter cold, then suddenly it turned mild, there were a few days of rain and without further transition it was spring. The windows at the Metal Finishing Plant were propped open. Jani Habetler took over his machine at six o'clock in the morning, oiled it, changed the power belt, and switched on the motor. He was working a piece of aluminum. Around nine the redhead, Grof, came over to him. He blinked rapidly, idiotically. Jani turned him around to face the light, pulled his upper eyelid down over the lower, tore off a piece of paper, licked it, and took the sliver out of Grof's eye. The redhead made a trial wink and nodded that everything was okay.

"Are you going to take that school job?" he asked.

"Yes," Jani said. "I plan to start painting the first thing Sunday and finish by dawn Monday morning."

The redhead pondered a moment.

"It's not a good idea to get mixed up in public business. They always ask for a bill."

Jani shrugged and said that he wasn't worried. The Parents' Committee had asked him to do the job; they were going to pay the 600 forints out of their own treasury. He would do a good job. A little moonlighting wouldn't make them hang anyone or even lock him up.

"Or do you think they would?" He moved his yellowish eyes.

"Well," the redhead answered, "they might do you a favor and fine you a few hundred forints."

He spat on the concrete floor and walked away.

Jani put the work he had finished in front of the radiator, wiped the wet metal shavings off his work shoes, and went out into the yard. Bela Klein was hollering in the doorway of the warehouse. There was a bunch of red and blue slips of paper in his hand. His gold tooth flashing, he called everybody by their first name. But the men didn't mind. Good-humoredly they addressed him as Mr. Klein and laughingly asked him how his grocery store was doing, how much was he getting for a dozen eggs.

"A pengö twenty," he answered. And he cursed the cruiser *Aurora* for not firing on New York in 1917 instead of St. Petersburg. The leaders laughed loudly. George Zentay smiled, too. He was standing with them, in brand-new overalls, leaning against the side of the truck. His face was dirty and shiny with sweat, his hair was full of gray strands; when Jani Habetler touched his arm he shuddered. He looked frostily at his brother-in-law and was quiet for a moment. Then he grinned with that drunken grin which drove Eszter to the brink of madness.

"Hail to the proletarian!" he said sarcastically, and made a deep bow.

The Cemetery of Rust is a yard enclosed by a stone wall behind the warehouse of the Metal Finishing Plant. A railroad comes in through a high iron gate and ends at the loading platform. On either side of the spur, discarded machines, huge boilers, unidentifiable monsters haphazardly push into the black mud and cinders; rusty arms point to the sky, waiting for a fiery reincarnation.

George Zentay was sitting in the shade on a discarded girder. His legs were crossed, his denim pants slid up, revealing poison-green nylon socks. He was leaning comfortably against the stone wall. Awarded his own unreasonable mood, he concluded it would be smarter for him to keep quiet, for he might stray onto dangerous ground and get beaten up, like not long ago when some streetcar conductors in a wineshop on Calvary Place had. He knew you couldn't play around with Jani. Jani kept watching him. But Zentay was beyond caring.

With a wide grin he said that his brother-in-law could dispense with the usual sermons, he admitted that he was lit up again, he had had a half-dozen glasses of wine, he felt fine on this lovely spring morning, after all he was in an interesting environment in the company of his beloved relative. The only thing he was afraid of was that as soon as his delightful euphoria wore off his good mood would vanish with it. And that was bad because then he got idiotic ideas, stomach cramps, and headaches and he turned nasty and quarrelsome, so nasty that he would even pick a fight with a tree on the street.

"According to medical science, after drinking the blood sugar falls to a low level," he said didactically, holding an index finger up in the air. "That's why you drink beer the morning after, it kills the hangover. But I don't give a damn about that. I drink for the sake of peace, to spare my fellow man another surly bully."

"You're just as unpleasant drunk as sober," Jani said. He picked up a rusty chain next to his boot, turned it around in his hands, and threw it over his shoulder among the junk. "That's how you screwed up your whole life. You drank, you whored, you quarreled with everybody. You couldn't get along in my family either."

"I'm not the only one," Zentay answered. "Even the saxophone player got out and he didn't drink or whore. Yet he walked out with only the shirt on his back and a hole in his shoe. He left everything behind."

Zentay glared provocatively at his brother-in-law, waiting, but Jani did not react. He just sat on the turned-up crate and stared fixedly at his boots. Zentay suddenly felt pity, discarded his cigarette, took a sheaf of typewritten papers out of his pocket, slapped it with the back of his hand, and started to talk about something else. In a quiet voice he told how the personnel manager at the Milling Machine Enterprise had fired him after twelve years of good honest work under Point C of the Labor Law. It was illegal, so he had gone to the editor of *Nepszabadsag* and asked for help, citing the resolution of the Twenty-second Congress. The editor had looked into his case very conscientiously and very thoroughly, with positive results, but in view of the journalist's friendly advice he did not intend to press his case and return to the Milling Machine Enterprise because the management would just cut his throat again, this time more cleverly. So he had started to watch the newspaper ads to see where an expert with a great deal of experience was needed and finally he had found a new, excellent heavy industry where, so help him God, his name was already known and they said they would gladly employ him as a chief labor analyst.

He lit another cigarette and in a self-assured, conceited tone and with a disagreeable smile he explained that they had promised him 2800 forints a month. After a thorough discussion he had accepted the offer. The job would include him in the enterprise's 1962 five-year plan, he would be responsible for checking of time sheets against the over-all fulfillment plan, the productivity proportion of hours compensated the examination of the serial use of power sources, the establishment of proper cycle values, the reduction of paid time, the preparation of the necessary norm receipts, the assigned quantities in comparison with the house bills, the monthly distribution and examination and control of the staff groups.

"It's all here at my fingertips. As soon as this place returns my workbook and declares that it no longer lays claim to my services as a loader—it's only a matter of a few more days—I'll go to work. Class origins aren't important any more, only your ability. By August, by God, I'll swing myself up and with bonuses I'll be good for 4000 forints a month."

Jani Habetler knitted his brows.

"Amen," he nodded. "And then some night you'll get drunk in an espresso—you'll be asked for your identification and they'll see that you're on sick leave. The new enterprise will be notified and you can go right back to the newspaper editor and try your luck all over again."

Zentay shifted his gaze from Jani's yellow eyes and examined his own cracked, dirty fingernails. A crooked smile on his face, he told how he had bought a bottle of champagne on New Year's Eve which he intended to take out to the cemetery. But even though he offered a cab driver a hundred forints the fellow refused, explaining that the gate was locked and it wasn't right to disturb the dead at that hour of the night. Then he had gone to the Adam Buffet, asked a cheap little dame to have a drink with him. Later he smashed the glasses and the bottle on the floor and someone had called the police. He had to tell that he was on sick pay status, and was being treated at the Neurological Clinic in Lorinc. His arm was still numb, he couldn't sleep, he tossed and turned and worried. Mornings he felt as if someone had just slugged him.

Jani stood up and dusted off his pants.

"Don't drink. You've had a few now and you're already as yellow as a lemon."

Zentay grinned.

"That's because I live on bread and lard, dear brother-in-law."

Suddenly he was filled with fury. He paled, locked his arms around his knees, and with a harsh laugh looked up at the other's face. He could not and didn't want to control himself. Thoughts roiled in his head. He gesticulated wildly, sometimes choking with sobs, ran his fingers through his hair, held his fist in front of his mouth, and coughed painfully. Hatred gave his incontinent sentences strength; whether he raised or lowered his voice it flashed like his eyes. Once and for all rejecting any moralizing he acknowledged that he was a depraved character, a sewer rat. All he wanted was to be left alone; he had said good-bye to the honorable family, he had left the apartment, the furniture, the washing machine, and if they wanted he would return the radio and his one suit of clothes and walk around naked; all he asked was that he not be preached at about decency and that his little girl not be told that her father was a bastard and a good-for-nothing. He handed over 350 forints every month, they had accepted it from him up to now, nobody cared whether the unskilled laborer had enough to eat—no, no one was interested in that. It was always the same thing, all three husbands paid while the poor martyred women remained in their nice apartments, went to expensive hairdressers, and felt terribly sorry for themselves because nothing they ever undertook succeeded.

"Shut up!" Jani said. He rested his yellowish eyes on the wildly gesticulating man and quietly warned him once more: "Shut up!"

But Zentay just smiled. His face was white. Sweat beaded on his forehead, his eyes moved restlessly. Irritably he declared that now he, the sewer rat, was going to have his say for once. He had his own opinion of the honorable Habetler family, of the grieving old man who, after twenty years without, had just decided to get false teeth and now goes to his wife's grave every afternoon, freshly shaved, his shoes polished, and his pants pressed.

"Fantastic, isn't it? Instead of tea dances he hangs around the cemetery to make acquaintances and court widows."

He climbed off the traverse and stepped over to Jani.

"Why don't you say something?" he demanded. "Why don't you call me a liar?"

"You're filth," Jani said quietly. "Ten years you lived with us . . . our mother emptied the bedpan from under you . . ."

Zentay was silent for a minute. Then he said, "That's

—210—

right, cling to your mother . . ." He smiled sadly. *"Hopla, hopla, hopappa . . .* now she's gone too . . ."

A man appeared at the far end of the yard, turned on the water faucet, bent down, stuck his head under it and took a drink, shook the water off his face, and hurried away. Zentay made an ugly face.

"So I'm filth? And what about all of you? Hajnalka ditched her second husband too, but she still collects 400 forints a month from her first. And Gizike is crazy, she stares into space for hours, has nightmares, and moans that her poor little mama is dead, but she has two lovers, men with families who console her with shoes, stockings, dresses . . . decency . . . morals . . . it might interest you to know that she cheated on her husband too! Only Istvan Hires was vainer than Miklos Szuha—he kept his mouth shut."

"Shut up!"

"Why should I?" He laughed. "Why don't you preach at me now? At the sewer rat? I drink! You bet! I still do. The whole world walks all over me, the lowest skunks spit in my eye, lousy bureaucrats cut my throat if they don't like my face and you and your kind dare preach at me! You whom I surpass despite this system. I live a hundred times better than you do. I have become a Chief Labor Relations Manager and I'll get even farther, I'll get my degree even if I have to fight every lousy bureaucrat single-handed. You dare to preach at me? By what right? The system kisses your feet and begs you to take the trouble to attend the University, to become doctors, judges, officers, technicians, chiefs of police, chief engineers, chiefs this and chiefs that. And what do you do? You crawled out of your Barracks slums but you still live the same way you did before! Jazz, dancing, and hip, hip, hooray! You stuff yourself full of cheese noodles and fried fish, belch, and then you crawl into bed, dear Comrade Habetler!"

Zentay lit another cigarette.

"Don't look at me like that!" He laughed sardonically. "Take you, for example. You earn more than 2000 forints a month, you moonlight as a housepainter, you wash, you cook, you keep house, you play with your son. Have you ever seen the inside of a theater? Have you ever read a book? And it's people like you who hold the power, lathe-operator aristocrat and war victim! Why, the woman you loved and your little girl were gassed at Auschwitz because of a slight lapse of memory."

Jani threw a fist. In the face.

Zentay fell backward onto a heap of rusty machinery. He fractured his skull and died instantly. For minutes the lathe-operator couldn't tear his yellowish eyes away from the horrible sight. Then he raised his powerful hands to his face and groaned like a wounded animal until some men led him away.

❖   ❖   ❖   ❖   ❖   ❖

It was hot that July. Agotha was on vacation at a student camp in Siofok, Hajnalka's little boy was in the country with Miklos Szuha. Hajnalka and Eszter were getting ready to go to the small six-room rest house of Eszter's enterprise in Miskolc–Tapolca. It was more than forty-five minutes until train time. Gizike boiled eggs for the trip, made salami sandwiches and washed fruit. She stuffed the food into a nylon bag and put it in Hajnalka's fashionable red-and-blue-striped beach-bag. Old man Habetler was childish. He wanted to talk to a lawyer, insisting doggedly that his lovely little wife's cousin, one Jozsi Stadinger, a stonecutter, was beaten to death during the White Terror—that fact should be put on record somehow, as well as the fact that he, Janos, had served in the Red Army.

"That's the absolute truth," he said. "In all my life I never told a lie. And if this statement is put on record, my

pension will be raised by at least 200 forints . . . if not more
. . ."

Hajnalka phoned for a taxi. Tearfully they kissed their father good-bye. Gizike helped carry the heavy suitcases downstairs. For a while the old man puttered around the apartment, looked at the bronze Buddha standing on the buffet, wiped the dust off the fat belly. Then he went into the kitchen, filled a milk bottle, and began to water the flowers.

ABOUT THE AUTHOR

Generation of Rust was published in Hungary when Endre Fejes was in his middle thirties. Mr. Fejes, of working-class origins, was employed in a large factory in Budapest until he began to give himself seriously to writing. Orphaned by the war, Mr. Fejes lived in various parts of Europe, working in mines and factories. After the war he returned to Budapest, where he still lives with his family. He is the author of numerous short stories and this is his first novel.